THE SECOND CHANCE HOLIDAY CLUB

Kate Galley

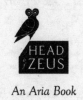

An Aria Book

First published in the UK in 2022 by Head of Zeus Ltd,
part of Bloomsbury Publishing Plc

975312468

A CIP catalogue record for this book is available from the British Library.

ISBN (PB): 9781804542231
ISBN (E): 9781804542217

Typeset by Siliconchips Services Ltd UK

Printed and bound in Great Britain by
CPI Group (UK) Ltd, Croydon CRO 4YY

MIX
Paper | Supporting
responsible forestry
FSC® C171272

Head of Zeus
First Floor East
5–8 Hardwick Street
London EC1R 4RG

WWW.HEADOFZEUS.COM

For three incredible Septuagenarians

Sue
Valerie
Andrea

Chapter One

Fledgling

I'm kneeling on the floor in my husband's study. My ancient knees are arguing with each other in the deep pile carpet while my fingers tap their way along the underside of his desk, as if I'm playing a soundless piano.

I knew the day would end like this, in here, although I'm not sure what I'm going to find. Certainly a lot of paperwork, which I'd expect from Tony, but perhaps, if I'm lucky, some cash, or a secret savings book, some long-forgotten Premium Bonds. Or maybe a stack of those men's magazines; I shudder at the thought, but really, my husband wasn't that kind of man. I can hear my sister's voice immediately, *Tony was a man, it's all men*, in that self-satisfied way she has, the voice of unfounded authority, despite her having only sixty-eight years to my own seventy-six. Our mother had cut her parenting teeth on me. She had eight years to get used to motherhood, duty, care, but the true flood of maternal love didn't seem to materialise until Carol popped into the world. But then, she'd been a beautiful baby; easy to love, to spoil.

Bingo! My fingers find a lump of Blu-Tack with a key stuck in its grip. I pull hard and the whole lot comes away, a sliver of lacquer with it. The key is almost identical to the one for my jewellery box, which I do keep locked even though Tony says it's pointless. It's not heavy – someone could just walk off with the whole thing if they felt so inclined, he said. Even so, every night before I go to bed, I remove my gold locket and lay it carefully inside the velvet-lined box, lock it up and pop the key into my bedside drawer, because you can never be too careful. Tony said it would be better if I slept with it around my neck, because a burglar would be hard pushed to walk off with me. He could be a little cruel like that sometimes.

Of course, Tony's desk is a different matter altogether. There are three drawers, but it's only the bottom one that's locked. I think, perhaps, I always knew this, but hadn't had the inclination to understand what that might mean; until now, that is.

The key slips easily into the lock and with one quick turn, I have it open. I rock back onto my heels to relieve the pressure on my knees, but this just causes more pain in my hip; I'm not made for crawling around on the floor any more. Ignoring the discomfort, I take a glance inside. My first thought is that it's almost empty, and with it comes a sense of disappointment. In reality, there are only a few things: a couple of folded newspapers, an Airfix model of a Spitfire with pots of paints and glue, and a lilac-coloured envelope; the name on the front isn't my husband's. Suddenly, though, the significance of so few items elevates them to a greater importance.

My eyes return to the envelope and the colour of it. Tony wasn't a man who was into pastel tones; he was a lover of stags' heads and horse brasses, paperweights and paintings of battle scenes and brooding skies. He certainly wasn't interested in pretty things. Just the thought of him using lilac stationery is ludicrous. It wasn't even well hidden. Yes, it was locked, but I could have asked him what was in it any time I liked, of course I could. But instead, he chose to hide the key and I chose not to be interested. It occurs to me that these are exactly the sort of things I was expecting to find and my throat tightens. All of a sudden, I'm undecided – maybe today isn't the day to be looking, after all.

I close the drawer with a bang that disturbs the air around me, and the scent of the lilies, orchids and roses that have been arriving all week invade from the hallway and living room. Carol sent most of them. She said it added a certain drama to the occasion, but despite me suggesting I had quite enough of that going on, the flowers kept arriving.

I stand now against protesting hips and pause to allow the pins and needles to stop and for a moment of dizziness to pass. My head is still a little fuzzy from the sherry I had at the wake and I wait with one hand on the wall, taking in the deep lines and liver spots, how dry my skin is. I make my way slowly to the kitchen, my hand brushing the wallpaper as I go, the flock soft under my fingertips, the sturdy wall only a whisker away in case of a fall. I contemplate another drink – I quite like the haze – but that really won't do. Instead I fill the kettle, then pour some away, take two cups from the cupboard and put one back; *silly old Evelyn Pringle*.

Taking my tea into the living room, I sit on the settee, change my mind and settle in the armchair – Tony's armchair. I'd like to feel the weight of a cat on my lap, or perhaps it could be curled up on the rug in front of the gas fire. I had wanted a real fire in a stove with a proper crackle and an occasional roar, but Tony wouldn't have it. He wouldn't have a cat, either – he was allergic to their fur; although I glimpsed him once, through the kitchen window, stroking next door's tabby as it rolled around in a patch of sun on our driveway. I'd watched him when he came back in for signs of a rash or a sneezing fit, but there had been none. Perhaps his allergy came and went as often as he did himself.

As soon as I woke this morning, I imagined myself going through Tony's things. I thought about it at the hairdresser's, while the girl tried to curl my straight white hair, and when I made up my face and wrestled myself into my black wool dress, and again when Carol arrived with her husband to take control of the day. I was still thinking about it when Tony's coffin disappeared behind the curtain. While I should have been focused on the enormity of never seeing him again, never sharing another meal, a conversation, a bed with the man I'd been married to for fifty-eight years, I'd actually been imagining myself coming home, kicking off my shoes and walking straight into his study to rifle through his possessions. With good reason, it would seem.

The crematorium had been stuffed to the rafters. All of Tony's golf chaps had been there, the Rotary Club lot and the self-named *Book Busters*; ridiculous title. Tony had led the campaign to save the local library from closing a few years ago; an odd undertaking for a man who barely picked up a novel. He liked a cause, though. Well, he liked a cause outside of this house. All those people and their husbands and wives was too much for me. I kept to the shadows, my heart keeping up a relentless thrumming, my breath hot and fast in my throat. I'd let Carol meet and greet, make sure there were enough sandwiches at the wake. It was impossible to miss the tributes murmured from group to group, though. Tony was well liked, he was a super golfer, the best person to find for a pint on the nineteenth hole, had done so much for the community, a wonderful problem-solver. I should have felt so proud but, to be honest, I'd lost touch with who they were talking about.

I sip my tea still thinking about sherry and what would it matter if I did have another drink, who would know? I can imagine my sister, though, thinking of me as a lonely widow, a bit drunk most of the time. She once said that Tony was my anchor, my rock, that I'd be lost without him. We were watching a documentary at the time about birds nesting high up in cliffs and the fledgling had just hurled itself from the top. I was the chick and Tony was the nest, according to Carol, who'd had a fair amount of gin. I told her the fledgling looked liberated, but then it hit the rocks below before being snatched up in the jaws of a predator. *Stay in the nest, Evelyn*, she'd said, but where she thought I might contemplate going was anyone's guess.

Abandoning my teacup to the side table, I make my way to Tony's drinks cabinet, the idea of more dry sherry already warm on my tongue, when the shrill ring of the telephone stops me. I consider ignoring it, but then lift the handset from the hook anyway, regretting it the moment my sister's voice comes at me from down the line.

'Evelyn, I'm just phoning to check you haven't hit the sherry again. It was a big day today and you did so well.'

Carol starts the sentence like a competent human being, but by the time she reaches the last three words, her voice descends to a pitch usually kept aside for children and small furry animals.

'I'm just having a cup of tea, actually,' I say, moving back towards my cup and away from temptation.

'I really wish you'd let me stay tonight, so you're not on your own. I could be in the car and with you in half an hour.'

In just thirty minutes, Carol could be here, in this house. We could go through the contents of the drawer together, ruminate about what it means, consider next steps. But it wouldn't be like that. Carol would take the matter entirely out of my hands and besides, I haven't examined the contents of the drawer properly yet, haven't found all there is in there waiting for me. And it's not just about what's in the drawer – there's the ring to consider, too.

'I'm fine,' I tell her. 'I'm going to have a nice bath and an early night.'

I'm actually going to finish that bottle of sherry and watch some rubbish on the television. I usually like a bit of notice when Carol's coming, to dot about a few thank-you cards from her grandchildren, bring out that ghastly vase my niece bought me for my birthday.

'You know, you could come and stay with me and John. I could look after you, we could talk. Maybe being in the house without Tony is too much for you. He was a big part of your life, you know.'

I stifle a sigh.

'Yes, he was a big part of my life, he was…' I find myself trailing off before I can finish.

'Oh, Eve, it breaks my heart to think of you being alone. Is there anything I can say to persuade you to come?'

'Carol, I've spent most of my married life alone. You know how often Tony was away – I think I can cope.'

I wonder for a moment what would happen if I accepted the invitation, though. Carol doesn't really want me to stay. It's her birthday in a couple of days and she's probably got her daughters and grandchildren visiting – I'd be in their way. I can picture my sister trying to enjoy her special day with her perfect family: cake, presents, balloons – they always go over the top – and then offering lonely, childless old me, sad and pathetic looks. It's tempting to call her bluff, though, just to hear her try to squirm out of it, but I let her off the hook; I really haven't got the energy for games.

'I'm honestly OK. I've got to get used to being on my own. Thanks, though; it means a lot,' I say, although really it means next to nothing.

'Well, make sure you eat one of the meals I left in your freezer. You need to keep your strength up, take your mind off the pain.'

Am I in pain? I'd certainly been in shock when I first heard Tony had died, but that's to be expected when the police turn up on your doorstep and tell you your husband's been found dead in his car on the hard shoulder of the M3. A heart attack; nice and quick, they'd said, he wouldn't have suffered. In fact, he was halfway through cleaning his reading glasses, his outdated 2013 road atlas open in his lap, a neat diamond ring in the top pocket of his best suit. He was supposed to be at an antiques fair in Sevenoaks, Kent.

By the time I saw the ring, it was in a sealed plastic bag

along with his own wedding band. They clinked together like something to celebrate, teasing me. The policewoman handed it over and smiled sympathetically, said what a lovely surprise it would have been and what a shame he'd never got to give it to me himself. I'd agreed, a smile fixed to my face, and then spent the whole of the bus journey home trying to pull it from my ring finger where it was wedged, having never made it much past the end of my fingernail.

'I'll speak to you tomorrow, then. Perhaps I'll pop over in the afternoon,' she says, but I don't answer, hoping my silence is enough on the matter. 'Sleep well, Eve.' And then she's gone.

For a moment I want to phone her back, tell her I do need her, that maybe it would be best if she did come and stay. I could pretend to play the part of the grieving widow, and it wouldn't even have to be a part – I could try to do it for real. There would be no ring, no letter, just the memory of a dear dead husband and Carol's sympathy. I could forget about the drawer, ask my sister to tip the contents into bin liners and leave them for the dustmen. They're due in the morning – it could all be gone, nothing to sort through, nothing to find. But there is something hiding in the third drawer down – a siren call I know I'll be unable to resist much longer. Tony has been dead for ten days and I've been restraining myself all that time. 'Your husband is resting with us,' the funeral director had advised me. It was hard to think of him there, cold, still; neither word I'd usually associate with my husband. It was as if he hadn't really gone. But he has now, and he's safely in the ground so he won't be popping up behind me while I'm rummaging.

With a large glass of sherry in my hand, I walk back towards Tony's study, but deviate at the last minute into the dining room. I feel a burning need to see something. Opening the door of the teak sideboard, I pull the wedding album out from underneath Aunt Sylvia's best linen tablecloth. The lace one has disappeared – to Carol's, probably.

I can't remember the last time I looked at our wedding photographs. So many of the assembled guests have long since died, so the moment to reminisce has ceased and instead has become an awakening to my own mortality. I quickly flip over the paper leaf and straight to me and Tony on the steps of St Mary's Church. My wedding dress had been my mother's and probably the only thing I'd managed to procure before Carol. A fact that had kept a small smug smile on my face until Carol had said she wouldn't be seen dead in that hideous old thing, anyway. Looking at it now, I have to wonder if she'd had a point. It had to have a panel added to allow a little more give in the stomach area, and my mother, the seamstress and myself had all played a game where we'd agreed it was just because I was a bit fat. How could it possibly have been fifty-eight years ago? I pick up my drink and swallow half in one go.

I'd always told myself that Tony was a strong man, but if I'm honest, he looks terrified in this photo. Flicking through the album to check his expression in each one, I can see his fear give way to something a little more relaxed, something closer to resignation. I've never looked so closely before. Usually I'm focused on myself: was the set of my hair old-fashioned, even for 1964; should I have worn more make-up for the camera; was it obvious I was pregnant? The trouble with photographs is they tell stories that are probably best left in the past.

I close the book with a thump and put it back in the box, back in the sideboard. A sob begins in the base of my throat, but I swallow it down until it sits as an angry lump in my stomach. After turning out the light behind me, I refill my glass and take it into the study.

I lift the items from the drawer and lay them on top, but it's the envelope I'm most interested in. My hand closes around it and I pull it gingerly towards me as if it's either precious or flammable, perhaps both. On it is the name Margaret, written in my husband's clumsy hand. That's it, nothing else, no address and no surname.

'Margaret,' I say out loud, rolling the name around my tongue, checking it for familiarity. 'Margaret Pringle,' I try again, with less conviction, but then the other woman never got to be Mrs Pringle. I imagine myself saying: *Have him, he's yours – he snores and leaves the toilet seat up. He's eighty, you know.* But that's the sort of thing Carol would say, not me. Besides, Tony is dead – there won't be another Mrs Pringle now.

My eyes are drawn to the ring still in the plastic bag on the desk where I left it when I got home from the police station. A circle of gold, set with numerous diamonds nestled into the band itself, somewhere between an engagement and a wedding ring. I'm sure there's a name for that style of ring, but I can't seem to grasp the word.

I pick up the envelope again and slide Tony's letter opener through the top, pull the paper out, smooth it with my hand, then take a breath.

My dearest darling Maggie,

I have something I want to tell you, something I need to tell you, but it's going to be as hard for you to hear it as it is for me to write it.

I stop reading, quickly folding the paper shut against my chest. A chill shoots through me like a frozen fist and for a mad moment I wonder if it's Tony's, but I don't believe in ghosts. With the letter still clutched in my hand, I leave the room and hover for a moment outside in the hallway, listening for… what? There's nobody here. Then walking back into the study, I close the door behind me anyway, just to be sure.

Lowering myself into his chair, I unfold the letter and begin to read.

Chapter Two

The Meadow

The number 300 bus trundles its way through the woods and down the hill towards town. I'm sitting on the lower deck with my handbag clutched tightly in my lap and my umbrella pushed neatly through the handles. Outside the sky is heavy, threatening, waiting for the right moment to let go of the torrent that surely must come. It's been ten days since the funeral – ten angry days since it became clear I won't be able to grieve like a normal widowed 76-year-old, because Tony hasn't left me with that luxury.

I shuffle across the seat to press the button and a buzzer alerts the driver. As I pull myself up to standing, the bus lurches before coming to a stop and I'm propelled forwards, my body hitting the seat in front, my handbag falling to the floor.

'The Avenue,' calls the driver as I bend to retrieve my things, embarrassment coursing through me.

A young girl glances up from under the anonymity of her headphones and immediately looks away before we make eye contact, before I can humiliate myself further by asking her for help.

I've started getting off the bus two stops early so I can walk the last stretch into town. *Use it or lose it*, is something Carol enjoys chirping at me, but that's not the reason I do it. I like to see how the development is coming on: forty-eight deluxe retirement apartments that each cost more than a substantial family home. It's on the site of my father's old furniture factory and the last asset Tony sold after running it into the ground. Luckily, the land was worth considerably more than the failing business.

The apartments look appealing, certainly from the artist impressions on the large billboard. It displays the idea of a lifestyle more than it shows the accommodation, though. That's what people will buy into – they'll want to be the sunny, smiling couple, holding the hands of a much-beloved grandchild; although the models they've used hardly look old enough for retirement, let alone warden-controlled living. Clinging to the railing, I lean closer and imagine buying an apartment myself, condensing my life into something that's easier to look after, now that it's just me. It's the communal living that doesn't appeal, though; I'm not that sociable.

I never really forgave Tony for letting the factory go, even when the proceeds of the sale arrived in my bank account and I had to look twice to believe it, and that was after Carol's cut had been transferred. I remember how proud my father was in its heyday and how little it meant to my husband. And now, it seems, I have something else to add to the list of things for which I won't forgive Tony.

The first spots of rain begin to fall and there's a wintery

edge to them, like icy needles on my face, so I don't linger but step away from the fence, push up my brolly and begin the walk to the high street. It's two weeks until Christmas and it occurred to me only yesterday that I should have bought Carol and John a gift, also my nieces and their offspring. I had the perfect excuse for not having to go through the rigmarole of sending Christmas cards – who knew a dead husband could come in handy – but I'm not sure the excuse really extends this far past the funeral, especially not with my sister. Hopefully, it's not too late to buy them some book tokens.

By the time the clouds burst open, I'm just outside the library. My eyes lift to the plaque on the wall above the door, recently hung by the Book Busters. A tribute to Tony and all his hard work in saving the library. I sniff loudly – they have absolutely no idea. I step inside and stand for a moment to shake out my coat and watch the progress of the sleet as it works its way down the window. I leave my umbrella propped by the door, next to the Christmas tree decorated with hard-baked biscuits in the shape of windows. Boiled sweets have been used to imitate stained glass. They catch the light perfectly as they swing from the draught coming in through the gap in the door. The children at the local primary school are invited to make them and then to help to decorate the tree each year. It's a tradition that stretches all the way back to when I last worked at the school. The sight of it makes my heart expand and then fall sharply back. I move away – it really is draughty by the door.

'Morning,' chirps a librarian from the children's section.

She's on her hands and knees tidying the books in the low boxes, straightening the rug where they sit for story time on Monday afternoons. She plumps the colourful beanbags ready for them. By three thirty, the children will file in, pick up the books and drop them on the floor, kick up the rug and squash the beanbags. She's rather wasting her time.

'If you're looking for anything in particular, then let me know if you can't find it. We've got some great new releases on the front display if you're interested.' She pushes herself up to standing and brushes her hands down the length of her skirt.

'I'm not here for books. I want to buy some book tokens.'

'We don't sell things like that in here, I'm afraid. You'll have to go to the newsagents or maybe the supermarket – they definitely sell them.'

'You don't sell book tokens in a library?'

'No, I'm sorry, we don't.'

'For goodness' sake.'

I do mean to say this under my breath, but the S's seem to rattle out of me as if I'm a snake. The woman narrows her eyes, but I ignore her.

This isn't going to be the quick trip I anticipated. I'm now going to have to walk all the way to the other end of town. Glancing out of the window, I see the weather hasn't improved. In fact, I'd say it was a little worse.

'Oh, I hadn't realised it was so grim out there,' she says, her voice less jolly now. 'Well, have a browse while you're here, wait for it to clear.'

It sounds like more of an order than a suggestion, but it doesn't seem as if I have much choice anyway.

I wander over to the non-fiction section and glance across the spines of cookery books, childcare and crafts. There's one on quilting and for no other reason than its colourful spine, I pull it from the shelf and begin to flick through.

'Evelyn?'

I don't have time to duck or hide. I merely glance at my watch before looking up, hoping whoever is there will see I'm in a terrific hurry. It's Rosamund Pearson, the old school secretary. I try to shove the book back on the shelf, but the whole lot have slipped down into the gap, and I grapple with them as she prattles on about how nice it is to see me and how long it's been. And then comes the inevitable.

'I was so very sorry to hear about Tony. The funeral was beautifully done, but I'm afraid I didn't quite get a chance to speak to you. You seemed so… busy. Tony's death must have been quite a shock for you. Not that death isn't always a shock, of course, but it was very sudden in your case.' She clamps her lips together with an audible smack and a pink tint spreads across her cheeks.

I finally find a gap for the book and push it in so fast, it hits the back of the shelf with more force than I intend. She lowers her voice, which I feel is a little late, and touches my arm with gentle fingers. I have to fight the urge to shake them off.

'How are you doing? Are you coping?'

'I'm very well, thank you,' I say curtly.

'Well, you've always been a trooper, that's what I say.'

I wonder who she might say that to, who might want to discuss what a trooper I may or may not be.

'It must give you immense comfort being here, under the roof your wonderful husband saved from the scrapheap. He really was the instigator of our Book Busters group. What a star Tony was, such a great loss.'

I have a sudden urge to tell her, tell her exactly what Tony was – that might shut her up. I pinch the back of my hand underneath my sleeve to stop myself, but she's already moving on.

'So, now that you perhaps have more time on your hands, will you consider joining our little sewing group? You can't tell me you're not tempted,' she teases, pointing at the book I was looking at.

This is the second time she's asked me and I'm beginning to wonder at her motivation. My thoughts turn briefly to my sister. Of course. Carol's husband used to work with Rosamund's husband and I know their paths have crossed, because she told me. An image of them talking about me appears unbidden – the two women with their heads together discussing sad old Evelyn, talking about my private business, what an absolute trooper I am. I experience a wave of shame that sweeps through me, leaving a prickle of anger in its wake.

'You'll have to excuse me – I have things to do,' I say, walking abruptly away, leaving Rosamund with something else to discuss with my sister.

Outside, the sleet has turned to heavy fat drops of rain that make a splash as they hit the pavement and I hurry down the street with my umbrella open above me once again, my handbag tucked tightly under my arm. It's only when I'm halfway home on the bus that I realise I forgot to buy the book tokens.

There's a silver car on my driveway and as I walk up level with it, the door opens and my sister steps out. She has a silk scarf over her hair, even though the rain has now stopped. The dark bank of cloud has finally moved away, leaving a hopeful slip of something paler behind it.

'I just tried to phone you, but of course you don't have your mobile with you,' she says, cutting through any need for pleasantries.

Carol is a little taller than me, slimmer, and has the same chestnut-coloured hair that our mother managed for years before she eventually went gracefully grey. My sister seems determined to hang on a little longer. She's wearing a trouser suit as if she's stepped out of the office, even though she's never had a job outside of the home. Her shoes are always beautiful; little heels and dainty points. I glance down at my own – sturdy, sensible, navy – but then I could never squeeze my bunions into a shoe like that.

'I didn't take my mobile out with me,' I tell her while rummaging in my bag for the front door key, all the while trying to remember what sort of state I left the house in this morning. Carol won't need much to assume I'm not coping. 'I just popped into town to go to the butcher's, that's all.'

I want to seem as if I have purpose, perhaps that's why I lie, and I can hardly admit to forgetting her Christmas present, but it's too late anyway – Carol is staring at my empty hands.

'I put in an order; they're going to deliver at the weekend,' I say quickly.

'Oh, I didn't know they delivered.'

'And I popped into the library,' I say, ignoring her question, because I know for a fact that they don't. 'I saw Rosamund.'

That prickle of anger appears again and I'm prepared for an argument, but then the passenger door opens and Oscar, my niece's boy, steps out. The anger is immediately replaced with something else, something I don't acknowledge.

'We were passing after a trip to the dentist and thought we'd pop in to say hello, didn't we, Oscar? Say hello to Great-Auntie Evelyn.'

'Can I use your toilet?' he asks me, his eight-year-old body already halfway to my front door.

I raise a hand towards him, although I'm not sure why, and then let it fall limply by my side. I catch my breath and avoid Carol's eye.

'Yes, of course,' I say, stepping forwards and unlocking the door. 'You know where it is, don't you?'

But he's gone, flying down the hallway at speed, his flame-red hair – just like his father's – disappearing into the cloakroom.

'So, I saw Rosamund,' I try again after shutting the door behind my sister.

'Oh, how is she?' she asks, innocently enough, but her sideways glance tells of something more.

'She asked me to join her sewing group, again.'

'You should; it would do you good.'

'I don't sew; I'm not interested.'

'Rosamund is a lovely woman. Easy to talk to if you make the effort.'

'I'm not interested, Carol.'

'Think about it.'

I'm about to respond, when the flushing of the toilet interrupts my thoughts. A second or two of silence follows and then the sound of Oscar washing his hands. We steal a glance at each other and share a small smile.

'He's a good lad,' she says.

Carol hovers in the doorway of Tony's study, surveying the room – I forgot to shut the door. There's nothing incriminating to see, though, because I tucked it all back in the drawer ten days ago, but I feel the presence of the letter as if it's a heart beating to get out. It's not the only presence in the room.

'Have you decided where you're going to scatter his ashes?' she asks, glancing at the urn on his desk.

'No,' I reply, although I do have my eye on the compost heap.

When you're ready,' she says. 'I can help you to—'

'Thanks,' I interrupt. 'Cup of tea?'

They don't stay long. Oscar is bored and my biscuits aren't exciting enough. I have nothing that I'd be happy for him to play with, either. I stand on the driveway waving them off, half glad of the solitude again but half sorry to shut the door. Carol will be taking Oscar home now, looking after him until his mother gets back from work – his prep school closes for Christmas earlier than the school in town. Then she'll drive home to John and enjoy a meal he's lovingly prepared for her. Just another day in her wonderfully perfect life.

My scalp prickles and my arms begin to itch, and I turn to Tony's study, my fingers finding the door handle. I snatch the letter back out of the drawer and tuck it into the pocket of my cardigan. Letting myself out of the kitchen door, I then march across the lawn to the meadow behind the house. Tony talked me into us buying this piece of land, so it wouldn't be built on, so we could enjoy more solitude, and even though I wasn't sure at the time, it did turn out to be one of his better decisions.

I pace and I read, my mood darkening further and my feet becoming increasingly wet through my shoes. The grass is long and nothing much flowers now until the snowdrops appear next month, in January, but it's still a beautiful place. The wild clematis clings in the hedging, its beards blowing in the breeze, and the seed pods of the teasels are ready for when the goldfinches come. It's become a sanctuary to me, regardless of the time of year. I come here to think. In the summer I walk round it, looking out for red clover and cornflowers once the flush of spring bluebells has gone. I sit among the cow parsley, unseen from the house, to ponder all the things I find it impossible to think about indoors.

'What have you done, Tony?' I say, staring down at the letter and then back at the house. I take in a breath from the freezing air, chilling my lungs, and this time I shout it. 'What have you done, Anthony Pringle?'

My hands are shaking now with the cold and I stuff them into my pockets, the letter with them. I march back through the meadow, the garden, and into the house, where I take the key for the garage from the hook.

His car is inside from when John drove it back from the police station. Unlocking the door, I expect a hint of Tony – a whiff of his aftershave, perhaps, or something worse – but all I can smell is the upholstery shampoo from when he last had it cleaned. I stare at the driver's seat for a moment, where he took his last breath, and wait for some deep emotion to overwhelm me, but all I have is anger.

There's nothing on the seats or in the footwells, but then Tony was a meticulous and tidy person. I think I'm only just discovering how precise he actually was. I duck my head back out of the car and walk round to the boot. His golf clubs dominate the space, but there's also a large fishing umbrella, its pleats folded to perfection. I pull at the side pockets, but they're empty save for a couple of carrier bags. Where is it? Slamming the boot shut, I duck back into the car and pull the glovebox open – and there it is: the road atlas.

Page 22 has the exact place where he died on the M3. I half expect an X marks the spot, but of course there's nothing. I got my information from the police; the M3 heading south. I turn the page and follow the road until it ends at Southampton. Was this where he was going? Is this where Margaret lives? I turn the page again: Bournemouth and Poole, and then back: Fareham and Portsmouth. I flick through the rest of the pages, hoping for enlightenment and nothing at the same time, and then I find it, stuck in the back, and I know exactly where he was going.

Chapter Three

Turkey and Tinsel

When people say they haven't slept a wink, I generally don't believe them. I'm sure the truth is, they drop off occasionally, but don't acknowledge those moments. I, on the other hand, see every second, minute and hour throughout the entire night. Images of Tony in his car swirl through my thoughts; where he was going, what he was doing, what he'd already done. Do I wish I hadn't opened that drawer, looked in that atlas? Yes, I'd like to go back to being blissfully unaware – I've managed well enough until now. By morning, both my mind and body are exhausted, but it's still a relief to get up.

I pick up the phone to call Carol when I'm out of bed, when I give up the pretence of rest, but replace the receiver before the call connects. Is it pride or shame that stops me? Do I imagine her discussing everything with Joan, or is it something else, something that runs a little deeper?

Last night's dishes sit in the sink and the washing machine still blinks at me with a long-finished cycle that I'm going to have to wash again. There's my bowl of uneaten cereal on the draining board; I've given up the pretence of hunger, too. Not even my regular morning cup of tea can tempt me today, but I do force down a small glass of cold milk – I can't leave the house without anything passing my lips. It sits heavy in my stomach like a chilly mistake.

In the bathroom, I slide a shower cap over my hair, carefully tucking in each strand. I have an appointment with Doctor Graham this morning and I do like to look my best when I go to see him. I take my pills from the cabinet and swallow them with a splash of lukewarm water from the tap. And it's this act that decides it, this small moment of control, and perhaps the sight of Tony's toothbrush that I pull from the shelf and drop into the bin. I need to get a hurry on. My appointment is at eleven thirty, but there's something I have to do first.

I'm surrounded by glossy pictures of faraway golden beaches and glittering cities, huge cruise liners and ancient ruins. All places I've never been to and I'm hardly likely to, either – it's all quite overwhelming. The travel agents has been in the high street for fifteen years and I've never set foot inside. There's a strong aroma of coffee from a machine at the back of the room that competes with the plasticky smell coming from the brochures. On my near empty stomach, it's making me feel nauseous. I rather hope to get this business sorted fairly quickly.

The trainee – a young man called Gavin, according to the plastic badge pinned to his lapel – is obviously bored and desperate to try out his repertoire. He offers me a cup of coffee, which I decline, and takes me through the Great Wall of China experience on his computer screen with an eagerness that I'd usually find irritating. But recent events seem to have changed my focus and to be honest, it does look rather wonderful. I don't want to curb his enthusiasm, but I'm worried he's going to be very disappointed when he finds out where I actually want to go.

'So, what do you think?' he asks with a look that suggests he has a first-class, round-the-world cruise in the bag.

This is going to be awkward.

'I have an address,' I say, pulling a slip of paper from my handbag.

This is what I'd found stuck inside the back cover of Tony's outdated road atlas. Also stuck there was a ticket for the Wightlink Ferry. One of the many things I've learned about my husband since his death is that he seemed to have a penchant for Blu-Tack.

I watch Gavin's face drop. He probably thinks I'm just a silly old woman asking for directions. I hand it to him anyway and he takes it reluctantly.

'I need to get there. What would you suggest is the easiest way?' I ask.

'The Isle of Wight? A car, I suppose, and a ferry, obviously.' He turns to his computer screen and with a quick and determined flick of the mouse, China has disappeared.

'I don't drive, though,' I say, picturing Tony's beloved Jag in the garage and a fleeting thought of renewing my driving licence.

'Well, I dunno, a train?'

His colleague, a plain girl with a determined air and plastic fingernails, ends the call she's been on and taps at a calculator on her desk, probably working out her commission, before turning to offer Gavin a tight look that lets him know she thinks he's an idiot.

'So, what we'd do now, Gavin, is ask the lady how long she plans to stay, what sort of accommodation she's looking for, that kind of thing, and then we can put a package together. OK?'

With more reluctance, Gavin brings his computer back to life and starts clicking on options, the Far East clearly still on his mind.

'Do you see this as a day trip or are you likely to require accommodation for an extended stay?' he asks, boredom dripping from his voice.

I can't even picture myself travelling to the Isle of Wight, let alone having a holiday there, but it's unlikely I can manage what I need to do in a day.

'I suppose a couple of nights would be a good idea.'

I imagine Carol's reaction when I tell her I'm going away. It brings a small smile to my lips followed by a twisting in my guts.

He looks at the address again and clicks around his screen at lightning speed.

'There's a coach trip leaving on the 23rd for four nights. It's a Christmas break – you know, one of those turkey-and-tinsel things. How does that grab you?'

'Oh, no, that's no good. I expect I shall be at my sister's for Christmas itself,' I tell him, although the very idea of Christmas at Carol's with her smug family doesn't bear thinking about.

'Not if you're on the Isle of Wight,' Gavin says, a hopeful look suddenly brightening his face. He's forgiven me for China.

'Good point,' I say, contemplating the possibility. 'That's actually a very good point indeed.'

I walk down the high street towards the doctors' surgery, pulling the hood of my raincoat tighter around my face. A chill wind has picked up, making my umbrella redundant, and if I hadn't seen the weather forecast already, I'd be convinced that snow was on its way.

The waiting room is surprisingly quiet for a Tuesday morning. Usually, it's brimming with people who weren't quick enough to get a Monday appointment but who have spent their weekends inventing illnesses, talking themselves in and out of high blood pressure, heart attacks, strokes, no doubt ready to waste the doctor's time with nothing much more than overindulgence and trapped wind. It's Wednesday that's usually quiet; they've given up and gone back to work.

I wait ten minutes for my appointment, my eyes on the flashing wall display, which pings with the name of the patient and the doctor they're due to see. A flagrant flouting of patient–doctor confidentiality, but no matter how many times I've complained to the reception staff, it remains in use and, of course, I wouldn't dream of wasting Doctor Graham's time by complaining directly to him.

I'm on the edge of my seat, ready to spring up and away from the waiting area as soon as I'm called. I'm determined that others won't be able to put my face to the name and see which treatment room I'm going to, probably trying to guess what ails me. People are so nosey. The display lights up – Evelyn Pringle Room 4 – and I'm off as fast as my arthritic hips will allow, with a momentary pause outside the door to tidy my hair.

'Mrs Pringle. Please, come in. Do take a seat.'

Doctor Graham is a man of about fifty with a few flecks of grey in otherwise perfectly dark chocolate-coloured hair. He's one of those men who manages to radiate a calm authority combined with an ability to get you to open up. Sitting in the chair he offers me, I wipe a finger across my upper lip, suddenly feeling a little warm.

'What can I do for you? How have you been?'

He taps on his keyboard as he talks, one eye on me and one on the screen. Of anyone else, I'd think this rude, but Oliver Graham is a very busy man and an excellent doctor, and besides, I find the tapping reassuring. Suddenly, he stops and turns to give me his full attention. His gaze makes me feel as if I'm in some sort of confessional.

'I think my husband was about to commit bigamy,' I say, straightening up in the chair and taking control of my emotions.

Doctor Graham doesn't flinch; he's highly trained not to be shocked by whatever a patient tells him and only the merest lift of one perfectly shaped eyebrow now gives him away. He doesn't say anything, though; he always gives me plenty of time to get things off my chest. I can often talk to him for ages without receiving any response, he's so polite like that, not hurrying me along with unnecessary questions.

'That is unexpected,' he says. 'And how can I help? Perhaps your prescription...'

'As you know, Tony died nearly four weeks ago,' I say as the doctor presses his fingertips together just under his chin, which only goes to accentuate the strength of his jawline. I hurry along, not wishing to waste his precious time. 'When he died, he had a diamond ring in his pocket and I have reason to believe he was on his way to propose to another woman. I know what you're going to say – it was what the policewoman suggested – that it was a present for me, but look,' I say picking up my handbag from the floor and beginning to rummage through the contents.

My fingers brush a used handkerchief, a rarely opened pocket diary and half a packet of Polo mints until they make contact with the ring. I pull it out and proceed to pop it on my finger, more carefully this time, where it sparkles in the bright artificial light of the room. It clearly doesn't fit me.

'I've always had fat fingers,' I say with an odd, misguided pride, but the words are out before I have the chance to change them. 'He'd never have bought this for me.'

'Do I remember correctly you saying your husband was a bit of an antiques man, Mrs Pringle? Perhaps it was an investment.'

I'm thrilled he's remembered that detail about Tony. Again, demonstrating what a conscientious doctor he really is.

'Yes, he is.' I swallow. 'Sorry, was. But not for jewellery – never that.' I slip the ring back into the bag. 'I found a letter, too; intimate, confessional.'

I lick my lips. The realisation this isn't just a flimsy story from a weekly women's magazine but my own husband's life hits me like a sharp and unexpected jab to the ribs. Said out loud, the words make the situation incredibly real. If the doctor recognises my distress, he doesn't say, but then I've become adept at covering up these sorts of moments.

'I can see it's been a very difficult time for you, Mrs Pringle. We have people you can talk to. There's a group, too – very welcoming. I think they meet on Thursday mornings at the village hall.' He begins pushing a pile of untidy papers around his desk. 'Here we are. They're called The Ark – a church group, I think.'

He hands me a colourful leaflet and I baulk at the elderly faces beaming up at me from the front. The thought of Thursday mornings in the village hall talking about grief leaves me cold. How can I possibly unpick the layers of how I feel about Tony's death? Could I sit there and say that some days I'm actually glad that he's gone? And that on others I experience a physical ache for the man who everyone else knew? I glance back to the doctor, but his attention is on his computer; our time is nearly up. I can't really blame him – I'm already several steps ahead of him – and besides, Tony always said I was never very good at telling a story, so I'm probably not making much sense. A wave of desolation catches me out and I grip at the arms of my chair, suddenly frightened I'll be pulled away with it.

'Look, Doctor Graham,' I say, desperate for him to grasp the matter. 'I just want to make sense of it all, to really understand.'

But this, of course, isn't entirely true, because I've had most of the ugly facts laid out for me in Tony's letter. I do understand, but I don't want to put a name to the true motivation for what I'm going to do next, because it isn't very nice.

He nods sagely, for long enough for me to think he might have all the answers, but then abruptly stops.

'Grief is like that. I really think the group could help you to understand, to make sense.' Then after a pause, 'I see that you need a prescription for your anxiety medication. I can help you with that today.'

He turns to matters easier to follow and I loosen my grip on the chair.

'That was the main reason I came, actually. And now I'm going away, so I'll need to make sure I have enough.'

'Away for Christmas? That's nice – probably good to take your mind off things,' he says as the printer trundles out the prescription. 'Off to your sister's?'

Another detail remembered, another thrill at his thoughtfulness.

'I'm convinced that surrounding yourself with your family at this obviously troubling time will be the best thing. Let them look after you.'

I can't imagine anything worse.

'I'm going on a coach trip, actually,' I say with a confidence I don't feel.

In fact, I have a sneaking suspicion that I've lost my tiny mind. I begin to imagine the conversation I'll have to have with my sister. Carol will probably agree that I've lost my mind, but I don't want to share those details with the doctor.

He turns to offer me his full attention again, not with the understanding look I'm so accustomed to, but with a shock that he doesn't take the time to check.

'On a coach trip? On your own?' he asks, and I can't help but be a little hurt at his obvious assumption it's unlikely that a, I'd be going anywhere, and b, I wouldn't have a friend to accompany me. Of course, he's correct on both counts. 'I think that's wonderful, Mrs Pringle,' he says with such affection that I nearly expire on the spot.

Immediately, I decide to omit the real reason for my trip while I have him in such raptures. I look up at his delighted face. If I tell him why I'm actually going away, I have a feeling that I might lose his regard for my new-found intrepidity.

Maybe, for now, it's best if I keep it to myself.

Chapter Four

Isle of Wight or Bust!

When I was sixteen and Carol was eight, our father, Ron, won the football pools. It came as a huge shock to our mother, Elizabeth – or Liz, for anyone with a death wish – who didn't even realise he played them. Who did she think the man was who popped round every Thursday evening rattling a bag of coins? I'd asked her. Church business, she'd snapped before going back to fuss over Carol. She'd grumbled on about why it had to be associated with football and why couldn't it be cricket or tennis, indeed any sport less associated with thuggery.

My mother was an enigma to me. She considered herself to be a class above everyone else and was proper to the point of crippling; however, this didn't fit in with the life she'd carved out for herself. A former shop assistant and married to a man who worked in the local furniture factory was hardly living the dream. She'd put our father forwards for the role of church warden, unbeknown to him, which was a step in the right direction, but it wasn't enough to get her into the clique she'd been trying to infiltrate for years. But, when Dad started an impromptu dance around the living room carpet of our compact semi-detached, shouting, 'I've only gone and won the bloody pools,' things started to turn around for us all.

When my father told my mother how much he'd won, for the first time in living memory she was speechless. We bought a detached house closer to the better part of town and my mother began a campaign to penetrate a far more select coterie. Staving off my father's attempts merely to continue working at the factory, my mother persuaded him to buy the business – a decision for which he'd later be very grateful. She turned it into a family enterprise overnight by putting me to work in the office, even though all I'd ever wanted to be was a primary school teacher. My mother had nothing but deaf ears by that point – she was finally in her element.

I didn't have too much to complain about, though. Having largely moved unnoticed through my life to date, I suddenly found myself a figure of interest. I was soon on the receiving end of some admiring glances from a few of the young men working at the factory, but it was only one man in particular who I wished was admiring me: Anthony Pringle. It seems odd now, how much time I'd spent trying to catch his attention, when perversely, he always seemed to be looking the other way. 'Careful what you wish for,' my mother had once said to me. Quite possibly the only useful piece of advice she'd ever imparted on her eldest daughter, but one that I'd chosen to ignore.

Perched on the edge of a kitchen chair, I bend to lace my shoes. My movements are purposefully slow, allowing time for an intervention – for the telephone to ring or someone to come to the front door with an emergency – but of course this doesn't happen and so there's a crushing inevitability with each twist and tie, each loop and tuck.

I've spent the last fortnight talking myself in and out of this trip, even going so far as to write a list of pros and cons, and then a subheading: Honest Reasons. But there was only one word that came as I moved my pencil across the page: spite. And no matter how hard I'd rubbed at it after, you could still see the faint trace of the letters on the paper.

Carol told me I was mad and demanded to know what on earth had possessed me to book a holiday at a time like this when I should really be in the bosom of my family, but, if I did change my mind would I be OK with a camp bed in the snug. My relief was palpable when I replaced the receiver, but once I'd started to pack my suitcase, the reservations returned.

I stand and take my coat from the back of the chair, push my arms into the sleeves and begin to fasten the buttons, all the while listening to the hollow tock of my mother's grandfather clock in the hallway. It's been a comforting sound, grounding me in this house, reminding me that I'm still here, even though Tony isn't, but now it seems to be hurrying me along, propelling me forwards at a pace that leaves me with little chance to change my mind.

I make sure the windows are locked and remember they haven't been open for weeks but check for a second time to be certain. I close the curtains at the front of the house, because those windows face onto the road, and then begin to fret it'll be obvious I'm away. What if someone has been prowling around? They'll already know I'm a woman on my own, now I'm a woman not even at home. Who would leave their curtains closed all day? But then who would leave them open all night?

I've always been a little jumpy about being on my own. When Tony went away on his fishing trips, golfing weekends or an excursion to an antiques fair, I'd try to make the house look as inhabited as possible. I have a ritual of drawing the curtains in all the rooms, upstairs and down, before reversing the process first thing in the morning. Even the rooms that are never used any more; the two guest bedrooms and the room at the back of the house with a view out to the meadow: Stephen's room.

I'm beginning to remember why I never stay away overnight – there's too much to think about, too much to do. It would be good if a neighbour could pop in for me, make the place look inhabited, but there are only three other properties on this quiet stretch of road and I don't talk to the owners. They all seem to have such busy and important lives, families; I have nothing in common with them. I haven't really talked to anyone since Tony went and barely did before that, either. I'm not much of a one for meaningless small talk; Tony was always the conversationalist.

There's a picture of him on the radiator shelf in the hallway – not a particularly good one; he hasn't combed his hair properly. I run a finger across the top of the frame and grimace at the dust, pull a handkerchief from my pocket to wipe it. I want to say something to him, but I'd feel silly talking to a photograph and anyway, I'm not sure I can control my tongue, so instead I give a curt nod as I swallow a tickle at the back of my throat.

Eventually, I decide to pull the curtains until they're

almost closed. That way, I could be in or I could be out, but I'm not happy about it. I rummage in the drawer for the phone number of the insurance company, ready for when I get home and find the place turned over.

I open the front door onto a damp December day. Mist hangs in the air with the promise of more rain and I get flustered about my hair, pull a hat from my handbag and lower it carefully onto my head. There's a moment as I stand on the doorstep when the house echoes with emptiness behind me and I almost allow it to draw me back into its safety, but with an effort, I close it and lock it, and check it is locked by leaning my full weight onto it. I rattle the doorknob several times before I pull the handle up on my wheelie case and trundle off down the road in the direction of the bus stop.

The coach is waiting in a lay-by next to the community centre, the side emblazoned with The Get Go logo, and I've been sitting in the bus shelter for ten minutes plucking up the courage to walk across the road and get on board. Just the thought of it's making me nauseous. The other passengers queue to put their suitcases in the space under the coach. None of them seem to be talking to each other and I'm not sure if this is a good thing or not. One of my many concerns is being pinned to my seat by an annoying chatterbox, but I also recognise that if there's no conversation at all, the journey will drag. Then I remember that I'm on my own, I don't have my husband to do the talking. I watch the driver packing the luggage efficiently. He seems competent, cheerful, like he knows what he's doing, and unlikely to cause a multiple pile-up on the motorway en route to the ferry.

Spots of proper rain now begin to pepper the air around me and I notice there's no longer anyone left standing on the pavement – they've all boarded. I can see their heads bobbing around behind the glass, lifting small bags into overhead lockers and finding their seats. My stomach twists and churns as I wonder how long the coach will wait and how I'd feel to see it pull away without me.

Standing up, I hoist my handbag back onto my shoulder. What was it Doctor Graham once told me? 'It's not good to watch life from the sidelines.' It's this thought that propels me across the road. I can't go back next week and tell the doctor I gave up; it would be humiliating. It's only when the driver catches my eye and waves a hand that I realise I could have just lied, invented a holiday story for the doctor, but it's too late now.

'Mrs Pringle?' he says, looking at his clipboard and also at his watch.

I bristle on the pavement beside him. I'm never late for anything.

'About bloody time,' comes from someone on the coach, and I look up into the face of a balding man, who glances away when he sees I'm glaring at him through the glass.

He probably didn't expect his voice to carry down the aisle and through the door. A fact that he perhaps should have given a little thought to before opening his mouth.

'I'm never late,' I say pointedly to the driver, and even though I can hear how sharp my words are, he just smiles. It's well-practised, almost charming.

He takes my suitcase from me and pushes it inside the

guts of the coach. It's instantly lost among the others. I have to resist the urge to climb in to retrieve it, make a speedy exit before he ticks my name on his list. I shove my hands deep inside my pockets.

'And you're not late now, Mrs Pringle. In fact, you are perfectly on time,' he says, tapping his watch. 'I'm Alan, your driver and guide. Shall I call you…' He looks back at that clipboard again. 'Evelyn?'

'No, thank you,' I say, pushing past him.

Every second I spend outside talking to him are precious minutes I could be inside, not being late. Besides, I've made my decision now and would rather just get on with it. I step onto the coach, aware all eyes are on me. I bitterly regret those wasted moments in the bus shelter. Now, I have to contend with making an entrance – not something I'm used to.

Suddenly, I remember that when I booked the trip at the travel agents, Gavin talked me into paying an extra ten pounds to have a seat at the front, and I'm grateful to myself now for that moment of extravagance and forward-thinking. The very idea of having to walk past all the others to get to my place would be excruciating. I look at the faces of those I'll be spending the next four nights with and don't encounter a single smile. My own lips are pursed, my teeth clenched.

'I'm never late,' I tell them all, quietly this time, and turn away to take my seat by the window.

The driver closes up down below and the moment to tell him, discreetly, that I've made a mistake has gone. Watching the rain drops slide down the window, I try to breathe through the fluttering in my throat. My legs urge me to get up, to take flight – I've put myself into an impossible situation. And then Doctor Graham's mantra starts in my head: five things you can see, four things you can touch, three things you can hear, two things you can smell, one thing that makes you happy.

I'm about to start counting the flecks in the pattern on my skirt, when my attention is caught by a woman across the aisle getting out of her seat. It's the heels of her shoes that I notice first; like long, thin pins, completely inappropriate for a coach trip, surely. I let my gaze travel further up while the woman pushes a bag into the locker. She has the tiniest waist I've ever seen. Her top rides up out of her trousers as she stretches and I have to look away, but not before I see the bones of her spine, the pale white of her skin, and the line of dark purple bruises on the top edge of her hip. The woman quickly tucks herself back in and sits down in her seat. A flush of embarrassment touches my cheeks and I pull a book from my handbag and pretend to read.

A volley of pinging noises are suddenly emitted and I turn my head to see the woman across the aisle from me grappling with her phone. Her expression is fearful as she reads whatever is there. Then she swipes her finger across the screen and it goes black. I do think it's terribly bad manners to have your phone going off like that in a public place.

The driver is in his seat now and he turns to look down the coach at us all. He pinches the fleshy part of his nose and I assume he's suppressing a sneeze.

'This is your driver speaking. Cabin doors for departure,' he says in a nasally voice as the door hisses closed. 'Tray tables and seats in their upright positions.' He pulls his fingers away, grinning at us all, and I turn my head to see the reaction of the others. Nothing – not a smirk or even an eye-roll. Everyone looks bemused. He's completely missed the mark.

'Righto, let's get going. Next stop Winchester Services. Should only take about an hour and a half. We have one other person to pick up.'

He turns back to face front, starts the engine and with a sigh he should have tried harder to suppress, he pulls out of the lay-by.

By the time we turn into the car park of the service station, I've settled back into my seat and my anxiety has retreated – found a little hiding place to hover in, primed and ready for its next assault. The paperback I borrowed from Carol is closed in my lap. Doctor Graham suggested the trip away would relax me, help me to rediscover the joy of reading. I can't get past the first page.

The driver informs us that we have half an hour for a comfort break and I've never heard such a ridiculous phrase for popping to the loo. He also reminds us about the other passenger who's joining us and I glance at the empty seat next to me. It would be just my luck. I get up quickly before the lot at the back try to get off and block the aisle. The driver has stepped out and is standing on a grass verge smoking a cigarette. He's suddenly gone down a little in my estimation.

'May I have my suitcase from the coach, please?' I ask him as he emits a cloud of noxious fumes into the air above my head. Instinctively, I duck.

'Mrs Pringle, the coach will be locked at any time that I'm not with it, so you have nothing to worry about.'

He smiles at me again and somehow, because he has that cigarette in his fingers now, I don't find it quite so charming.

'Well, I'd like to have it all the same. I've heard stories about luggage going missing, people without clothes for their holidays. I don't want to spend my break away shopping for essentials because you've lost my case.'

'I think you'll find that lost luggage generally happens at airports. I can assure you, I've never lost a bag and I've been driving for many years. In fact, if I can let you into a little secret...' He drops his cigarette to the ground and I have to step back. I don't like people sharing their secrets, offloading their grubby affairs and intimate business. 'This is my last trip with The Get Go. After this, I'll be retiring. New year, new start. I'll have time to do the things I always wanted.'

He looks a little wistful for a moment, almost sad, and I give him a minute to compose himself.

'Well, my suitcase, if you could?'

'Right,' he says. 'I'll just see if I can dig it out.'

I hear that sigh again as he turns away. He really should learn to control himself.

After washing my hands thoroughly, I join the queue for the dryers – only two in good working order for twenty cubicles, no less than four more with stickers on them apologising for inconvenience. I wait for the woman in front to finish while drops of water fall to the floor from my fingers. Significant inconvenience indeed.

When I finally get my turn, my distorted face looms at me from the reflection in the dome metal attachment. My hair is so white now. I think the salon I attend must have enhanced mood lighting, because even though the girl who does my hair often suggests I think about a colour to brighten me up, I never feel the need. I do now, though; in the harsh lavatory lighting, I look positively ancient.

I'm disorientated when I leave, because I turn the wrong way and end up next to a pop-up shop selling vulgar mobile phone cases. I manage to avoid the enthusiastic eye of the shop owner, but my attention is drawn to the woman who has tucked herself behind the racks, a mobile phone clamped to her ear. She's wiggling her hips in a tight-fitting dress as if she needs to use the toilet and clearly doesn't care who overhears her conversation.

'I'm sorry, darling, you know I am, but I can't help it.'

She has the phone between her shoulder and her ear, and her considerable bosom is pushed up under her chin. I'm not quite sure where to look.

'The doctor told me I'm hugely infectious and shouldn't be near anyone.'

The woman lets go of a theatrical cough and then moves round to fiddle with one of the cases; a pink one covered in glitter, surely designed for a little girl, not an ageing woman. I pick up a case myself and listen in.

'I know you're sorry I won't be there to prepare the Christmas dinner, but honestly, I'm not. I've cooked sixty-two of the damn things.'

She has a whiff of the North in her accent, which I can't quite place but seems to come and go as she talks. Watching out of the corner of my eye, she moves the phone away from her ear and winces.

'Yes, of course I know that's not the only reason you

want me there, and obviously I'll miss seeing Lotty and Ed, but I'll come up in the New Year. And anyway, I'm sure they won't care if I'm not there for Christmas – they'll be up to their armpits in chocolate. Look, darling, I've got to go. I can feel another coughing fit coming on.'

She turns away from the stand and closes a hand around the phone, but I can't help but hear every word.

'Helen?' she says. 'I really am sorry.'

Taking the phone from her ear, she looks at the screen then puts it back.

'Helen?' she says again.

But from the look on her face, it's obvious that Helen has already hung up.

'You want that?' a voice asks me. 'It's good quality, only fifteen pounds.'

I realise I still have the case in my hand; a drab brown one that, I assume, is supposed to look like leather but fails in the most spectacular way. I shove it towards the man and turn away quickly. I'll leave these two fraudsters to it.

Chapter Five

It's a Folly!

Dragging my case behind me, I scurry back across the car park, irrationally annoyed by my almost encounter with the woman outside the loos. Someone else being deceived, somebody else being lied to.

'Doesn't anybody tell the truth any more?' I mutter.

'Steady on there, Mrs Pringle. Plenty of time to get to the ferry. Glad to see you so keen, though.'

Alan, the driver, and his grin greet me as I arrive at the coach. He stamps on yet another cigarette with the toe of his boot before reaching into his pocket and popping a piece of chewing gum into his mouth, as if that somehow reverses the effects of his vice. He's managed to swap one for another. I decline his offer as he holds up the packet to me.

'You're going to be the first person back on board,' he says.

Silently, I hand over my case before stepping up and sinking into my seat. A melancholic wave engulfs me and a ridiculous tear begins to prickle in the corner of my eye. I quickly blink it away.

'What are you doing, Evelyn Pringle?' I whisper to my reflection in the glass. 'No good can come of this.' But I know it's a bit late for thoughts like that.

I sniff briefly as I catch sight of the rest of the group and watch as they move like a pack across the car park. Some of them are talking now; at last, they're beginning to make a bit of an effort. I count them all onto the coach, including the woman across the aisle from me in the other window seat. She wasn't talking to anyone and now looks as if she's trying not to be noticed. Her hair is cut into a sleek ash-blonde bob, quite a young style for a woman of her years, the back, point perfect against the bones of her spine that protrude from the collar of her sweater. I notice the thin line of pure white regrowth gleaming at her crown, though and can't help but be surprised by that tiny flaw, because otherwise, the woman is immaculately turned out.

Her forehead is resting against the glass, her arms tucked tightly around her body. It reminds me of when I finally realised my dream and taught music and movement at Springfield Primary School. Pretend you're a tree or a flower. Use your body to show us how you feel. The woman looks like an apology. I have a sudden urge to speak to her, but as I shuffle forwards in my seat and open my mouth, someone steps into view in the aisle, making me jump.

It's a tall woman with a lot of make-up and a helmet of dark blonde waves. She seems to have a taste for cheap-looking jewellery, which clatters around her neck and on her wrists as she moves. Her dress is too tight for her and she appears to be pulling in her stomach, perhaps to make her bust look bigger. She's the woman from outside the bathroom, the remaining passenger, the liar.

'Hello to you all,' she announces as if she's onstage, her accent now firmly in the South. 'I'm Cynthia.'

She's even caught the attention of the window woman, who looks up and tries on a smile that doesn't suit her. A murmur of response ripples around, but I don't join in. The woman waits for complete silence and then slides into place next to me. Of all the empty seats she could sit on, she chooses this one. I lift my head to face her and am met with a garish grin, far too much lipstick.

'Cynthia,' she parrots unnecessarily.

'So I gather,' I reply before turning my body away, seething into the pages of my unread paperback.

At Portsmouth, I'm keen to get off the coach and as far away from Cynthia as possible. The woman has been sucking boiled sweets for the entire journey, twisted round in her seat to talk to the woman behind her in such an awkward way that one of her legs has been grazing mine in a manner far too intimate for my liking. My body is wound so tightly I feel as if I could easily spring off the ferry and into the Solent. It isn't to be, though. When Cynthia turns back, ready to disembark, she clutches at her knee and grimaces in pain. Why the woman insists on behaving as if she's in a West End production most of the time is beyond me.

'It's my knee!' she says again, this time directly at me, as if there's something I should be doing about it. 'I'm waiting for a replacement…'

The rest of the passengers file off the coach and I can only watch them go. I'm trapped in my seat. It seems we're both waiting for Cynthia's knee replacement.

The driver comes to her aid, which I assume was the plan all along, the way she simpers at him. She clings on to his arm as he helps her down the steps of the coach and laughs, an absurd sing-song trill, when he asks her if she has a walking stick.

'Silly me,' she replies. 'Can you believe I managed to leave it at home? To be honest, it wasn't really the look I was going for.'

I want to take my suitcase with me, but there's no chance now that Cynthia's monopolised the driver, so I tuck my handbag into the crook of my arm and bustle past them both and up the stairs to the ferry's lounge area.

This is only the third time I've been on board a ship. Many years ago there was a day trip to France with the school, but I spent most of that dealing with a lot of seasick children. There was also a quick hop between Weymouth and Guernsey with Tony just after we got married. It was never referred to as a honeymoon. I can distinctly remember how ill I felt. Seasickness, morning sickness or nerves, I'm not sure which, but I can conjure that feeling as if it happened yesterday rather than all those years ago. Tony had told me I was neurotic and disappeared to the bar, leaving me to *get on with it*. I'd made my way up on deck and watched St Peter Port come into view on my own, my hand gripped tight to the railing. I remember how blue the sky was, a cerulean blue that you'd expect in the Mediterranean, and I felt as if I'd arrived in a foreign country rather than the Channel Islands.

I glance out of the window now as we begin to move out of the harbour. The sky is leaden and the rain beats a steady tattoo against the glass.

'Sit here, if you'd like.'

Looking round, I see the immaculate woman from the coach sitting on a long settee, a low plastic table in front of her. She has her mobile phone clutched in her hand again even though the screen is black. I wonder why she doesn't just put it back in her bag.

'Thank you,' I say, not wanting to be rude but having to shrug off my wish to be alone as I slide onto the seat next to her.

I have a cup of tea that I've bought in the café; overpriced and served in a cardboard cup that's proving difficult to hold. It's beginning to burn my fingers, so I put it down on the table and sit back, my handbag clasped tightly in my lap.

There's always been a sturdiness to me – I'm used to carrying a little extra weight. Big-boned, my mother called it, and told me I could never be *really* thin, even if I starved myself, which I considered a ridiculous statement for lots of different reasons. I've never thought of myself as particularly fat, but right now I feel frumpy next to this elegant woman.

There's a loaded silence as I try to think of something to say, but before I can find any suitable words, Cynthia hobbles over, still clinging on to the coach driver's arm.

'Do you mind if I join you, ladies?' she says, lowering herself onto the opposite settee without waiting for a response.

I have to fight the urge to get up and find somewhere else to be. The woman has no shame. The driver places a large glass of wine down in front of her, his eyes not on Cynthia or me, but on the other woman. His smile mirrors hers – hesitant. There seems to be something sparkling between them. I have to look away.

'Alan, you're a star. Thank you so much. I'd have been really stuck back there without you,' Cynthia says, tucking her purse back into her handbag and breaking any connection that Alan might have been trying to make.

'No problem at all,' he says. 'Get that down you and you'll be fine. I'm going to grab myself a coffee – see you on the other side.' He beams at us all before moving away.

Not for the first time, I have serious doubts about this Christmas Coach trip. It's given me the perfect excuse to avoid festivities at Carol's, but what with sparky Cynthia, and Alan, the perpetually cheery driver, I'm beginning to wonder if my sister's would have been that bad. There's obviously the particular reason for my trip, which I'm trying not to think about until I absolutely have to, but perhaps I could have managed a train journey and crossed as a foot passenger, maybe a simple guest house for a night. Gavin didn't suggest any of those as options. What possessed me to join a group? It's too late now, though – I'm committed. Just that thought brings a looseness to my limbs and I reach for my tea to give my fingers something to do. Cynthia beats me to it, scooping her wine glass off the table.

'Here's to a great few days, ladies,' she says. 'What a jolly three we shall be. I'm Cynthia, as you know, and you are…?'

She looks pointedly at me, her eyes bright with amusement, and I have no choice but to disclose my name.

'Evelyn,' I mumble.

I don't want to become a three with these women just because we all sit in the front row of the coach together. I don't want to become a three with anyone else, either. I also don't feel the need to join in with the toast – a cup of tea in a disposable cup doesn't have the same celebratory quality – but the other woman does, with her glass of sparkling water. Perhaps it's gin, but it can't be – nobody with a waist that small drinks alcohol, surely.

'I'm Joy,' she says. 'Nice to meet you both.'

'Joy – what a lovely name,' Cynthia says, and not to be outdone, I smile and nod along in agreement.

'I hope the crossing won't be too rough,' Joy says as the ferry begins to pick up speed.

We've cleared Portsmouth Harbour now and hit bigger waves out on the Solent, our drinks starting to sway along with the ship.

'Don't you worry about that, Joy,' Cynthia pipes up. 'I was talking to a lovely woman behind me – Sheila I think she said her name was. She was telling me she was nervous about the crossing too, but I assured her that the ferry would have ample life jackets in an emergency, probably a raft or two, and I'm pretty sure the Solent isn't that cold, not even in December.'

'How very reassuring,' I say and then, when I hear my scathing tone, I attempt to soften the words with a lift to my lips, almost a smile.

Opposite me, Cynthia raises her eyebrows, but if she thought she was being subtle, she wasn't. I'm a very perceptive woman.

I catch sight of a child standing alone, her thumb in her mouth and a finger in her hair. She twirls the strands into a spiral, letting it fall from her fingers before finding another piece. Her eyes are darting about. Is she looking for her mother? I'm half out of my seat, when a man catches hold of her hand and she reaches her arms to be picked up. She calls him Daddy and I begin to lower myself back down.

'Are you all right, Evelyn?' Cynthia asks, her beady eyes following mine.

'A child,' I say. 'I thought she was lost, but...'

I reach for my tea again, willing my fingers to stop trembling. I keep my eyes down into my cup, but I can feel Cynthia's gaze on me. And then it's gone and I look up to see she's talking to Joy.

'Have you done a coach trip before, Joy?' Cynthia asks after taking a long swig of her wine.

I want to tell her she has some red staining on the corners of her mouth but can't quite seem to find the words.

'No, I haven't. Actually, this was a bit of a last-minute decision,' Joy says and then begins to bite nervously at one of her fingernails.

I notice all of her nails are bitten. Another flaw I hadn't seen before. Joy isn't as immaculate as I first thought.

'It was for me, too,' Cynthia says, and I don't disbelieve her.

'You felt well enough to travel, then?' I ask, and enjoy the way that her head snaps round to look at me.

'Sorry?'

'Oh, it's just that I think it's always important to be on top form when going away...' I trail off, wondering if I only imagine Cynthia squirming.

The crossing is only forty-five minutes from Portsmouth to Fishbourne and we're ushered back to the coach almost before we've finished our drinks. The driver returns to help Cynthia, but she waves him away. Apparently, a large glass of wine and whatever tablet she threw down her throat are ample to have her up and walking again.

She sways and giggles her way back down the stairs, and I don't have any more tuts and audible sighs left in me by the time we're back in our seats. The sweet-sucking starts again as the coach begins to roll down the ramp and off the ferry. Rhubarb and custard fills the air and when Cynthia leans forwards to put the packet back in her handbag, I take the opportunity to steal a sideways glance at Joy, who's staring at her phone again.

The screen is still black and no sound is coming from it. I wonder if she's waiting for a call or a message, or perhaps she's just one of those people who are wedded to their devices. My nieces and their children are like that, always jabbing away, never quite giving you their full attention – rude, really. Even Carol, to some extent. I can never understand why people are so wrapped up in technology, why they can't learn to live in the moment. I have brought a mobile phone, but sensibly, it's switched off and buried in my suitcase.

All of a sudden, Joy pushes her phone down, deep into the gap between the seats, and looks up, catches my surprised eye. But then Cynthia sits back, her unnecessarily large chest bridging the gap, spoiling the view.

The rain seems to have lifted and there's a slip of sunlight escaping through the clouds. The coach is alive with chatter as we make our way to the hotel. I can't believe I'm actually here on the Isle of Wight. It's the most reckless thing I've ever done, but then I have to remind myself, I haven't actually done anything yet.

Joy has moved to the empty seat and has started another

conversation with Cynthia across the aisle. They're talking about what the hotel might be like and I begin to imagine how it'll feel to sleep in a strange bed. Trying to push the thought of home from my mind, I tune in to the conversation beside me.

'The pictures looked quite nice in the brochure,' Joy says. 'There weren't many photos of the inside, but the garden looked really pretty.'

'My neighbour booked it for me on her laptop. Perhaps I should have paid a bit more attention,' says Cynthia, pulling a sheet of paper from her bag. 'She printed this off for me.'

She peers closely, through her pink-framed glasses, at the tiny picture of the hotel and I glance down at it, too. It's the same photo as the one I saw on Gavin's computer screen and I suddenly realise that I hadn't been paying much attention when he booked it, either.

'Well, folks, we're here!' Alan pipes up from the front of the coach.

He swings off the main road onto a gravel driveway, just as the sky darkens again, the ray of sunshine disappearing instantly, which some might say is apt. The sign above the doorway says The Welcome Rest in faded lettering, but the 'R' has fallen backwards, pushing the 'e' against the 'm', making it difficult to read.

'This isn't right, Alan,' I say. 'It's the wrong hotel. We're supposed to be staying at The Cedar Lodge.' I pull the sheet of paper out of Cynthia's hands and check the name at the top. 'See,' I say, waving it in his direction. 'The Cedar Lodge.'

Alan pulls some of his own papers from a folder tucked beside his seat and glances through them.

'I've got The Welcome Rest here,' he says, turning the sheet round so we can see.

I take in the building and the surrounding gardens, but I'm struggling to find anything remotely welcoming or restful about it. It may once have been spectacular – the façade could have been fairly grand with its Victorian turrets, twisty chimney pots and large sash windows, but there are so many later editions that the charm has been swamped with unsympathetic, practical extensions. Plastic windows dominate most of the single-storey add-ons and there are more flat roofs than are aesthetically pleasing. The garden is unkempt with weeds growing through the paving slabs right outside the double front doors. Surely it wouldn't take much to pull those up, at least. I'm not holding out a lot of hope for the interior. The place is a dump.

'This can't possibly be right,' I say to nobody in particular, and my comment is met with a ripple of agreement that works its way from the back of the coach to the front in some sort of unenthusiastic Mexican wave.

'People get murdered in hotels that look like this,' comes from someone behind me, and one brave person laughs.

I turn to look at Cynthia and find her paused, mid suck, her face contorted into a grimace. She'll probably rally though; people like her always do. The 'let's make the best of it' attitude really grates on me. Sure enough, Cynthia manages to unpick her frown and after taking an audible breath, she smiles.

'I expect it looks prettier in the summer when the borders are full,' she says.

'They're full now,' I reply, 'with litter.'

Cynthia doesn't respond. Her eyes are off, looking for something else to prove me wrong.

'Look, there's a lovely little folly, down by the edge of the lawn. I'll bet there's a spectacular view of the sea from there.'

'That's not a folly,' I say. 'Are you blind? It's a shed.'

The coach driver stands at the front ready to address us all and I'm just glad that we have someone to take control of the situation. He'll have us out of here in no time and along to The Cedar Lodge Hotel.

'Well,' he begins, and there's a pause as he stares out of the window, his back to us, his expression hidden. He turns around with a tentative smile that seems at odds with the rest of his face. 'Let's get inside and see what's what, shall we?'

'Yes, let's,' says Joy.

This surprises me, because she doesn't look like the kind of woman who stays in places like this. Obviously, another person with a tendency to rally. Alan doesn't seem to be able to keep his eyes off her and I see Joy's true motivation suggested in the fluttery glances she sends his way.

'I'm going to get the hold open and start unloading cases, if you'd all like to follow me,' he says, and I realise I might actually have to do a little rallying myself.

Chapter Six

The Welcome Rest

The hotel doesn't improve on closer inspection and without the rain drops on the windows of the coach to soften the impression, it stands an ugly monster against the grey sky. The weather looked to be improving as we left Fishbourne, but now it's descended again; either that or perhaps the hotel has a dark cloud all of its own. We don't linger outside; it's so cold that everyone is happy to file in to the foyer, hoping for a miracle.

The word that's on my lips when I take in the interior of the hotel is *drab*. I don't even realise I've said it out loud until the man standing next to me agrees with a grim nod, his wife's head bobbing up and down also. The walls are covered in an unpleasant purple flocked wallpaper and the carpet is best described as busy. I don't even want to think about the stains that it covers up, the bacteria colonising it. Admittedly, I haven't spent a lot of my life in hotels, but even I can recognise that this is substandard. No one seems impressed and apart from Cynthia's rallying cry of 'We can make the best of it' – no surprise there – the rest of the coach party are having loud, disgruntled conversations.

Alan is talking to the woman behind the reception desk, hopefully telling her that we're going elsewhere, but I'm not particularly hopeful, what with the amount of time she's spent shaking her head at whatever he's saying. He turns and slowly walks back towards us, his face set in resignation.

'Right, folks, the manager has laid on some complimentary drinks and snacks in the bar for you while the staff allocate the rooms. I suggest, for now, to keep your bags and suitcases with you.'

I clutch the handle of my case a little tighter, worried that somebody might take off with it.

'But we're not honestly staying here?' I say, surprised that no one else has.

'Just get yourselves a drink and I'll join you shortly,' Alan says.

'Do we have any choice?' I look behind me for moral support, but the party has moved into the bar, no doubt seduced by the offer of free drinks.

I stand for a moment, undecided. I'm not just going to be fobbed off. But everyone has disappeared and I'm left under the watchful eye of the receptionist, who is repeatedly clicking her pen, I think rather menacingly. I follow the others.

One by one, we sit down in the Draylon upholstered seats. I can detect a faint trace of stale cigarettes but can't decide if it's just a nasty reminder of days gone by when smokers could do as they pleased, or whether Alan has moved in this direction. I wrinkle my nose in disgust. Cynthia heads over to the bar and finding nobody serving, comes straight back.

'I expect the complimentary drinks will be tea and coffee,' I say, my tone clear in its disapproval.

'I wouldn't mind a Tia Maria,' Joy pipes up, sitting down next to me. 'It's not very warm in here, is it?'

I watch as Joy rubs her hands together, her rings clinking against each other on her bony fingers, the large diamond in her engagement ring catching my eye. So, she's married, or was married. Cynthia wears a lot of rings, I've noticed – three on one finger alone – but no wedding band. I glance down at my own modest ring with its tiny sapphire chips and try not to think about the pretty diamond-and-gold band in my handbag. Although now it's in my mind, I feel the presence of the offending article acutely. My eyes flick down, expecting to see the ring working its way out of the zip pocket to deposit itself on the tabletop for all to see. My face feels hot and I clamp a hand over the bag, push it under my chair.

Through the door behind the bar, two teenagers – a boy and a girl – scurry in with trays of cups and saucers and begin to lay them out on a table by the French windows.

'No cloth on that table,' I observe with a tut.

'No booze, either,' muses Cynthia as the staff set up a steaming urn and a percolator of coffee and begin to rummage in a Tupperware box for teabags. 'Brings back painful memories of Sundays in the church hall.'

'It's only two thirty in the afternoon,' I say, glancing at my watch.

'We are on holiday, Evelyn! I'd say I have some catching up to do,' she says, and Joy giggles nervously.

I purse my lips. I feel like the party pooper, when really, afternoon drinking is a no-no in any civilised person's book. And anyway, we both know Cynthia had a large glass of wine on the ferry, so why would she keep up such a pretence? Perhaps she has a problem with alcohol – that would explain her being a liar.

The young man appears at our table, his appearance a little scruffy, his shirt not ironed properly and his black hair wild, as if it hasn't seen a comb recently. Quite fitting, I think as I take another look around the tired interior of the bar. A prickle of shame nips at my unkind thoughts, though, because actually, it turns out he's affable, and the tea is nice and strong, the cakes and biscuits he offers, appetising.

'I think Alan is going to sort this, take us to the correct hotel. This place just isn't acceptable, is it?' I look at the two women for approval, but Joy looks vacant and Cynthia, sceptical.

'I don't think we'll be going anywhere. It's the day before Christmas Eve – where do you think we're going, Evelyn?'

'I expect we're going to The Cedar Lodge, the hotel we're supposed to be booked into.'

'I imagine there's been some sort of mix up,' Cynthia says. 'But, this isn't that bad. It was quite a cheap holiday to be fair. Not the worst place to spend Christmas.'

I stare at her, weighing up my need to know more about her but, at the same time, not wanting to get into a conversation. I also feel an unpleasant longing to *out* her for the conversation on the phone in the service station and the words spill out before I can stop myself.

'Do you not have any family to be with at Christmas? Are you on your own?' I ask her, but find these last words almost get stuck in my throat.

'On my own, yes,' is her quick reply.

She almost sounds happy about it – maybe she is – but then I notice the tremble in her fingers as she reaches for a chocolate digestive.

'What about you, Evelyn?'

Too late, I remember that questions follow questions and a hot flush creeps up my neck. I take longer than usual sipping my tea. Rather too long, it turns out, because Cynthia's next question is rather like a poke in the eye.

'Do you have any children?'

'I'm on my own, too,' I reply, at lightning speed this time, and really hope it's only me who can hear the tremor in my voice.

Cynthia's gaze lingers. It's assessing – knowing, somehow – as if she can see right into my mind and my darkest thoughts.

Joy gets up abruptly, slightly wild-eyed. 'I need to use the bathroom,' she says and disappears out of the room towards reception.

We watch as she scurries away on her high heels, her arms tight across her bony chest, her hands tucked into the folds of her sweater.

'Coffee goes straight through me, too,' Cynthia says, and I'm immensely thankful to Joy for her timing.

Cynthia goes back to stuffing biscuits and that horrible moment passes.

We assemble back in the foyer and I'm expecting to be ushered back onto the coach. Then, Alan appears and my hopes are dashed with his first few words.

'Welcome to The Welcome Rest,' he says, and a groan goes up from the group. 'I'm sorry to say that The Cedar Lodge Hotel can no longer accommodate us, and my manager has arranged this hotel as an alternative. It seems I'm always the last to know,' he adds under his breath, but I can hear him clearly. 'The staff have come in to work for us and we should be grateful for that.'

I glance across at the receptionist who looks at us as if she hopes we will all expire immediately.

'Shall we stay the night and see how we feel tomorrow?' he asks, and his question is met with grudging agreement. I can't believe they've all given up so easily. I'm about to voice my misgivings, but Alan disappears and the receptionist is now handing out keys and issuing instructions of where to find rooms. A group move off with a porter towards a lift in the corner of the foyer, Cynthia and Joy among them.

'Is that it, then? We're just going to accept this place?' I call after them.

'It'll be fine. I think we've probably got what we paid for,' Cynthia calls back, and Joy just shrugs.

Before I have an opportunity to offer up any further sort of complaint, I've had my own room key whipped away from me by the scruffy teenager, who the receptionist calls Liam. I struggle to keep up with him as he leads a few of us off to another lift, where we all squeeze in together, far too close for comfort, and I lower my gaze to stare at my shoes. We shuffle out onto the first floor in silence and Liam deposits each person at their room as we go, muttering something that I can't quite hear, but it's clear he's not happy. I begin to lose all sense of direction as we work our way through the maze of corridors.

'Do you mind slowing down? I can't possibly keep up with you at this pace,' I say when it's just the two of us.

As we move further away from the main part of the hotel,

the atmosphere becomes damp, chilly, as if someone has left a door or a window open, but I have a nasty feeling it's just because the heating isn't on.

'Sorry,' he says, coming to a halt beside me, giving me a moment to catch my breath. 'We're really short on staff. It's a bit of a nightmare, to be honest.' As soon as the words are out of his mouth, he looks a little relieved; as if he's finally glad to be sharing that information.

'I'd have thought there would be more staff for Christmas, not less. How many guests are staying?'

'Just you lot off the coach, that's all – thirty-eight. It's because of the double booking at The Cedar Lodge, you know, otherwise we wouldn't be open.' He scuffs the toe of his shoe into the carpet. 'It's why Mr Jackson's got the hump; he couldn't care less about this place any more. I mean, I was pleased to be asked to work – I get time and a half and that – but some of the staff haven't turned up, so it's all been dumped on us. Oh, look, it's snowing!'

I follow Liam's gaze out of the window while trying to process everything he's just said. Huge flakes are falling, possibly the biggest I've ever seen. For a moment we both just watch it, mesmerised as they twist and turn in the air like pieces of frozen cotton wool. There really is something lovely about the first snow of the winter, before it settles and becomes an inconvenience to everybody. The roof of the shed is already white, down on the edge of the lawn. A folly, indeed. Ridiculous woman!

'I don't really know what you're talking about,' I say, bringing my thoughts back inside this chilly corridor. 'Who's Mr Jackson?'

He begins to walk again, taking my suitcase, and it bumps along behind him over the lumpy carpet. I follow.

'I don't know too much, just what I overheard Mr Jackson saying on the phone. He's the manager.'

'And what was he saying?' I ask as we come to a stop outside room forty-eight and Liam pushes the key into the lock.

'That he wasn't happy about the balls-up, err, sorry.'

He winces at his choice of words, but I brush it to one side with a quick flick of my hand. I'm far more interested in what he has to say about the hotel.

'So, Alan's right and we should have been staying at The Cedar Lodge and it was overbooked? I assume that it's a much nicer hotel?'

'God, yeah, it's really nice.'

He pushes the door open and an even chillier blast of air hits us. I shiver.

'And they probably put their heating on,' he adds with a wry smile.

'So, we're an afterthought? Those who booked late get dumped here?'

He walks into the room and I step in behind him, immediately dismayed at the décor. The furniture seems cheap but not cheerful and even from here, the bed looks as lumpy as the hallway carpet. The wardrobe appears to be leaning against the wall in disgust and the curtains are cowering either side of the window as if they'd be embarrassed to be seen covering it. It's all so shabby and made worse by the room temperature.

Liam puts a hand onto the radiator before pulling it back sharply. He crouches and begins to twist the thermostat until unpleasant gurgling and rattling sounds begin to work their way into the system. Then he gets back to his feet, clearly unimpressed.

'It's bloody freezing,' he says with no apology for his language this time, but I couldn't agree more. 'This just isn't good enough, not for any of you. Leave it with me. I'll see why the other rooms aren't available, or at the very least I'll get you some thick blankets. I wouldn't want my gran staying in a room like this,' he says with such feeling that I experience a moment of pride in the young man.

That thought disappears, though, as he walks out of the door; I doubt very much that a teenage boy is going to be able to improve this situation.

I find Cynthia in the bar playing cards with Sheila, the fearful sailor, a bottle of red between them on the table. She's changed into a loose-fitting blouse the unfortunate colour of bile. They look as if they're passing the time, waiting for something to happen, but I have a strong suspicion that they're courting disappointment. I hesitate now, unsure what to do. There's hardly anyone around, no one on reception, no one behind the bar, and I wouldn't put it past Cynthia to have liberated that bottle of wine.

There's an odd empty feeling about the place, a distant lack of atmosphere. Suddenly, I remember Gavin's words at the travel agents: turkey and tinsel. There are no Christmas decorations anywhere. Not usually one to worry about such things, I can't help but think it would have been an easy way to make us feel more welcome. But then I remember Liam saying that we were last-minute, unexpected. All the same, a Christmas tree would have been nice.

My fingers are beginning to ache from the firm grip I have

on my handbag. Tony's letter is inside, nestled at the bottom like a dirty secret, which of course is exactly what it is. It's as if I'm carrying round an unexploded bomb and when I imagine handing it to this Margaret woman, it'll probably go off like one. I want to get rid of it as soon as possible.

'Care to join us, Evelyn?' Cynthia's voice drifts into my thoughts.

'I'm not much of a card player, really,' I say.

'Join us for a glass, then.' She tries again.

'I can't believe they haven't decorated the place,' Sheila says. 'Not even a tree!'

'I was just thinking the same,' I reply.

'It is a bit bloody cheerless in here, I agree.' Cynthia lays down her hand of cards with a flourish and Sheila groans. 'I did ask at reception if they were going to organise some decorations and was told that there were some in the store and if I was that bothered, I could do it myself.'

I turn to her, indignation bubbling on her behalf. 'They actually said that to you? How rude!' I say, but that tiny moment of potential camaraderie between us is lost the moment Cynthia's mock outrage becomes laughter.

'I know, what a cheek,' she replies, still laughing. 'I'm thinking about doing it, though, what do you think?'

'I think you've lost your mind!'

I've had enough of this infuriating woman and her odd ways. I'm absolutely sure I wouldn't be spoken to in that manner – I really don't understand Cynthia. Maybe she's touched in the head.

'Are you OK, Evelyn?' she asks, her glass paused midway to her lips, or possibly the table. The speed it goes up and down, it's impossible to tell which.

I turn away, ignoring her, and catch sight of Alan and Liam dragging in a huge Christmas tree through the front doors. Well, I assume it's a tree, but when they drop it on the floor in reception, it mostly looks like a pile of wet green plastic. Cynthia jumps up and begins clapping her hands together like a demented puppet.

'Oh, marvellous,' she crows. 'We can really get the party started now!'

I glance back at the bottle on the table, which is empty, and the way Cynthia sways as she walks.

'Now? I thought you'd already started,' I say, but I'm not sure she hears me.

She's pulling at the tree, one limb outstretched and looking very much as if it's about to part company with the rest. Joy arrives quietly beside me, announced only by her floral perfume.

'What's going on?' she asks as we're joined by other guests.

It's a couple of degrees warmer down here and the lure of that heat is obviously too much for us all.

'A Christmas tree,' I say. 'They've found one and Cynthia's trying to dismember it.'

Joy laughs and it lights up her whole face. A sparkle brightens her eyes and she looks different for a moment, but then she seems to change her mind and snuffs it out, crosses her arms over her body and tucks herself up again.

The ping of the lift announces others and I turn to see the rude, bald man from the coach and his wife walking out. Neither look happy. He strides across the carpet, his face a shade of crimson that tells of trouble. The man's wife hurries to catch up with him.

'Alan! I want a word,' he bellows across the room, and everyone stops what they're doing to look at him. 'This place is abysmal. We've stayed in some low-star hotels before now, but this one really takes the biscuit. I demand to see the manager.'

Alan lowers the part of the tree he was holding and makes his way towards the furious guest, his hands raised in a gesture of surrender, but the man hasn't finished. I get the impression he's barely started.

'The manager isn't here at the moment, Barry. I'm sorry, but there's not much I can do about that.'

'No manager? At Christmas, too? It's an outrage! Do you know, the shower in our room is so pathetic, I had to keep moving around the cubicle to get wet and then it cut out completely. I had to rinse my Wash & Go under the tap in the sink!'

I can see Sheila's shoulders moving up and down in silent laughter and she's not the only one. I don't particularly like Barry, but he does have a point. I do have to wonder, though, why he's having a shower at two thirty in the afternoon.

'Tell him about the toilet, Barry,' says his wife, jabbing repeatedly at his arm. 'A weak flush,' she continues, without giving her husband time to respond. 'That won't be able to cope with Barry's morning constitutional.'

Full-on laughter now from the Christmas tree, Cynthia can't contain herself and she tries to take a step towards us, but I can see what's coming; the base of the tree is right at her feet and she trips. There's a moment while her limbs seem to decide where they're going to end up and then she lands on top of the piles of branches in an unladylike heap.

Nobody speaks or moves for a second and then Cynthia raises her hand in the air.

'I'm all right,' she says as Liam attempts to get her into an upright position.

Alan rushes over to help him; after all, there's quite a lot of Cynthia.

'The fairy goes on after the lights,' Alan says as they get her to her feet and between them help her back to her seat.

'So, what's to be done, Alan?' Barry starts up again. 'You're not just the driver; you said you were our guide, too.' He has his hands on his hips, an exact mirror of his wife, albeit a larger, lumpier version.

'Oh, pipe down, Barry.' Cynthia drains the contents of her glass and bangs it down on the table. 'Look around you – no one else is moaning.'

I'd like to interject – I certainly have some grievances to get off my chest – but Alan is suggesting drinks. More drinks – as if that'll make everything better. He ushers the seething couple towards the bar, Barry's retorts, aimed at Cynthia, disappearing with him. Liam follows.

A sense of purpose settles over me then. This lacklustre backdrop for Christmas is probably a blessing. I can do what I came to do without interference. With everyone preoccupied in the bar, I can slip out without being noticed, keep my head down, stay under the radar and leave the others to make what they will of their Christmas break.

Chapter Seven

East Street

Upstairs, I pull on my coat and scarf, take my gloves from the pockets. The thought of an arctic hike is suddenly very unappealing, but I'm on some sort of automatic pilot and don't seem to be able to stop. It's only when I'm back in reception that I realise I have no idea where I'm going. Alan is now standing near the door with his mobile phone clamped to his ear, but he finishes his call as I approach him.

'Mrs Pringle, how are you settling in?' he asks with a look that suggests he's braced for a negative response, which is very observant of him.

'I'm glad you ask, Alan. The hotel is substandard, the staff, few and far between. I don't hold out a lot of hope for the meal tonight and that,' I say, pointing out of the window and across the lawn to the so-called folly, 'is a shed.' I fold my arms across my chest, aware that the action accentuates my displeasure, so I purse my lips to go with it. 'Is there somewhere else we can go? Like The Cedar Lodge?'

'I can understand your concerns, Mrs Pringle. Believe

me, I share them. Can I be honest with you?' he says, and again I feel myself being drawn into his confidence.

This time, though, I don't take a step back but actually unfold my arms and try to relax my face, suddenly remembering why I approached him in the first place.

'Go ahead.'

'I've been on the phone back at base, but The Get Go aren't being terribly helpful. I'll level with you – it's the day before Christmas Eve. No hotel is going to take a coach load of guests.'

He almost parrots what Cynthia said earlier. I wonder if the two of them are in cahoots.

'So, we're going to be here for the duration?'

'Yes.'

'Well, the very least they can do is put up that Christmas tree,' I say.

Alan laughs. 'I'm sure we can manage that.'

'Can I ask you something?' I rummage in my bag, keeping the letter tight to the side and out of sight. My fingers find the slip of paper with the address and I pull it out and hand it to him. 'Would you be able to tell me where this is?'

He gives it a quick glance before tapping the screen of his phone. Within seconds, he's turning it round for me to see.

'So, this is us here, the flashing blue dot, and this is your address, just where the pin is.'

My eyes follow the line that appears, guiding the way. A couple of roads separate the hotel and the house where my husband's lover lives: East Street. It's close. It's very close. It's too close.

'Thank you,' I say, and see he's looking at me enquiringly. The instinct to walk away and not offer any sort of explanation is overwhelming, but then I remember my plan to stay under the radar. 'A friend lives there. I thought I might pop a last-minute Christmas card through their door.' I'm surprised at how easily the lie slips from my tongue.

'That's a lovely idea, but take care. That snow is getting heavier and it'll be dark soon.'

I turn to look out of the large front window and he's right. Those few flakes that were coming down earlier have doubled in their efforts. The window ledge has a layer an inch thick stacked up and the lawn is white now.

'Alan?' Liam appears, looking flustered. 'Barry's kicking off again in there. I don't think the whisky was a good idea.'

'Righto, on my way,' Alan says, and the two men turn and walk away.

I push my fingers into my gloves and the address back inside my bag, then I pull the door open and slip out into the chill afternoon air.

The going is harder than I thought it would be and despite the temperature out here, I have a prickle of sweat on the back of my neck from my efforts. What looked like two short roads on Alan's phone have turned out to be surprisingly lengthy. Every step I've taken, each crunch of my boot in the snow, I've had a mantra running in a loop in my head; telling me I can turn round any time I like, that I don't have to do this. But still my legs keep propelling me forwards and the light is disappearing fast.

The house is almost at the end of the street and the road is intersected by a lane that looks as if it might lead down to the sea. In fact, the closer I get, I hear the rolling waves as they hit the beach, the sound of shingle being pulled away underneath, and again, and again. When I was a child, I thought I'd like to live by the sea. I imagined a little cottage on the cliffs with a craggy path down to the beach. I think we must have stayed in something similar when I was very young, as it stuck so acutely in my mind. Instead, I've spent my entire adult life almost as far away from the sea as is possible.

The house I'm looking for is number forty-eight and the irony of the fact it shares its number with my room at the hotel isn't lost on me. It's almost as if my husband is dictating to me from beyond the grave, perhaps having another little laugh at my expense. My body gives an involuntary shudder, but I push away any thoughts about Tony. Since I left the hotel, the temperature has plummeted. I can no longer feel the end of my nose, and I pull my collar closer and my hood lower.

All of the houses are modest terrace properties and most of them have been decorated for Christmas. Lights twinkle in windows, becoming ever brighter as the daylight fades. Inflatable snowmen wave from doorsteps and signs inviting Santa to stop by poke out of tiny squares of front lawn. Some have forfeited their gardens for a single parking space, but there are still cars nose to tail on both sides of the road. It's a busy street, full of families, no doubt. It's not what I was expecting.

Standing outside the gate at number forty-eight, I can't help but try to make a comparison to my own home, but there really isn't one to make. My father's money ensured that we had the opportunity to buy somewhere large and comfortable when we first got married. We were very lucky to begin in the sort of property that retired people aim to hang on to, long after their children have left home. The sort of house where Sunday lunches are plentiful, grandchildren come to stay in the holidays, Christmas dinner is always served for all. And then many years later, the garden becomes too much, or the stairs are troublesome, so there is, at last, a move to a luxury apartment or a small bungalow. This house here is exactly what we'd managed to avoid.

Was Tony leaving me to come and live in a starter home by the sea? Was he so much in love with this woman that he was prepared to give up all of his luxuries, or was he planning to take all of my money with him? My thoughts swing like a pendulum between anger and grief until they settle somewhere dangerously close to encompassing both.

My dearest darling Maggie. Oh, she's in for a big shock.

I open the iron gate that squeaks in protest and walk up the path towards the house. There are lights strung along the low fence that separates the garden with next door; plastic lanterns that dangle from each post before continuing underneath the bay window and finishing at the door. My heart is beating furiously, my breath coming in short, sharp bursts. I'm on the step, with my hand reaching out to rattle the brass knocker, and then I stop. I look down at my clumpy boots, my sensible winter coat with its extra padded hood, and think how I must look with my face poking out from underneath it, wet from the snow, the front of my hair stuck limply to my forehead. I can't see my husband's lover looking like this.

All of a sudden, I have absolutely no desire to see her. I step back, look up and down the road, conscious of how I'm drawing attention to myself, but there isn't anyone around. All sensible people are indoors, out of this weather. Street lights are beginning to come on. It's only ten to four, but the day is over. I picture Cynthia and Sheila with their wine, and laughing, despite the awful hotel, determined to enjoy themselves. I suddenly feel rather foolish and very much alone. It occurs to me that I'm delivering bad news, and at Christmas. What sort of person would do that?

Reaching into my bag, I pull out the letter and stare at the woman's name for a moment, following the loop of Tony's handwriting, allowing the anger to surface again. I trace my gloved fingertips over the tape that I've used to secure it at the back and then in one quick motion, I step forwards and push it through the letter box.

'Can I help you?'

The voice comes from my left, from next door, and I'm so startled, I slip backwards off the doorstep, my hand shooting out to grab hold of the fence. An unladylike '*Ooff*' escapes as my hip jars, but I do manage not to fall on my backside.

'I'm so sorry. I didn't mean to shock you. Are you OK?'

I look up to see an old man in a huge duffel coat holding an umbrella in one gloved hand and a shopping bag in the other, which he quickly puts down before placing his hand on my arm. I know it's meant to be a gesture of reassurance, but I don't appreciate how forward he's being.

'I'm fine, thank you,' I reply brusquely, pulling away from his grasp. 'I just slipped; no harm done.'

'She's not in,' he says, rather loudly for my liking, and I wish he'd lower his voice.

He could be wrong and I don't want to be discovered on her doorstep now. In fact, I really just want to leave.

'Fine, thank you. I'll come back another time,' I say,

with no intention of doing that at all, before turning and beginning to walk back down the path.

I've done what I came to do. When this Margaret woman, *Maggie*, gets back, she'll understand what it is to have the blinkers pulled off, to see what her life really consists of. I don't need to see her; it'll have to be enough just to have delivered the letter.

'Are you a relative of Sarah's?' the man asks, and my head snaps back round to face him.

'Sorry?'

'Or perhaps you're a friend.'

A flush rises on my cheeks despite the cold. 'I understood it was a Margaret who lived here. Is that not the case?'

He walks a couple of steps to join me and lifts the umbrella over both of us, but his moment of chivalry is lost on me, because a horrible gnawing sensation has begun in my stomach.

'Sarah lives here. Perhaps you have the wrong house,' he says, and I pull the address from my pocket and show it to him.

'You've got the correct address all right, but the wrong person, I'm afraid.'

'Well, I know I have the correct address, I can read,' I snap, pointing at the number hanging to the left of the front door. 'But how have I got the wrong person?'

'That I can't help you with,' he says, looking a little taken aback.

And as well he should, because this really has nothing whatsoever to do with him.

I stare back at the piece of paper, as if by some Christmas

miracle it'll all suddenly become clear, but there it is – I have the right house and the wrong person. The implications of this are not good. In one way, the relief of getting rid of the letter is immense, but the satisfaction of Margaret finding out Tony's dirty secret has gone. She'll never know what the man she was involved with was capable of. Perhaps it's for the best, though. Would I ever have been truly happy about someone else's misfortune? Tony duped us both, but still, I'm not generous enough to allow this woman into my league of grievances. I sigh deeply.

'Well, it looks like I put the Christmas card through the wrong letter box. I don't suppose you have a key? Perhaps you could open the door and let me have it back?'

'I'm sorry, I don't, but I know Sarah will be home tomorrow afternoon, if that's any help. She's visiting a friend,' he tells me, and I have to wonder if Sarah knows her neighbour is a blabbermouth.

I could come back. I'm not entirely happy with leaving the letter with a stranger, but then what does it matter – even if it was opened, it wouldn't mean anything to whoever read it. There's no address or surname on it. A feeling of disappointment settles over me; what an utter wasted journey.

'Thank you,' I say, and walk back through the gate and out into the street.

The snow has eased up a little, but what's fallen has settled, dense in places, and the temperature is still falling. I contemplate my walk back up to the hotel. It was hard enough walking downhill; the return will be so much more difficult. All this snow will probably ice up overnight. I wonder about the trip out to Godshill and the Needles tomorrow, too, and whether or not it'll go ahead, but I'm really not interested in an outing with a coach load of strangers. I didn't realise I'd signed up to some sort of holiday club. What I'd like to do is go home. Suddenly, I feel incredibly tired. Trust Tony to have the wrong address. And then it hits me – maybe it's just the wrong number. Maybe Margaret does live in this street and Sarah knows her, will pass the letter on to her. But I won't get to see her. The thought that has been pricking at me appears again. Because, of course, I've been wondering what Margaret looks like, how old she is, how pretty, how thin. Who is this woman who's captured my husband's heart?

'Excuse me.' It's the neighbour again. He's walked out to join me on the pavement. 'I've just thought of something. I have an uncanny knack for remembering people's names. An odd one, I know, bearing in mind I'm eighty-one.'

He laughs at this, although I don't join in.

'Sarah's mother… I could be wrong, but I'm pretty sure I remember her being a Margaret,' he says, and I nearly lose the use of my legs.

I reach out my hand and grab hold of him, my gloved fingers gripping at the toggles on his coat.

'Are you OK?' he asks. 'Are you having a funny turn?'

Oh, God! There's a daughter. My need to leave the house, the street, the island is suddenly acute. My head is full of flashes of possibilities, and none of them good. I loosen my grip, turn and, as fast as I can, walk away. The neighbour is calling after me, but I put my head down and allow the whooshing sound of blood in my ears to drown him out.

There's an atmosphere at the hotel by the time I get back. It's not the sad, oppressive one I left behind, but an upbeat, almost jolly mood fills the air in reception. Alan is holding on to the artificial Christmas tree, which is now in an upright position, and Cynthia, Joy and Sheila are giving instructions as to where it should go. They're so wrapped up in their task that they don't see me come in through the door behind them and I quietly skirt the edge of the area unnoticed.

Through in the bar, a couple sit quietly together, discussing something intently, their heads so close they're touching. Perhaps they're planning an escape. I wonder if they'd take me with them. I'm soaked through and exhausted from the march back up to the hotel. My hip is aching, I feel a little dizzy and my heart hurts.

The young lad, Liam, is walking out of the lift as I approach and I know I must look a fright, because he offers to take my arm and calls me Mrs P.

'Thank you, I'm fine,' I say quietly, but he ignores me and slides his arm though mine.

I'm taken by surprise, but before I know it, he's walking me through the open doors of the lift.

'I'm on the case for sorting out the rooms for you and the others. The ones in the main part of the hotel are bigger and more comfortable, warmer. I don't really see why you can't use them, regardless of what you paid, but I'm getting a bit of gyp off Eleanor. She's not working tomorrow, though, and not back until the day after Boxing Day, so leave it with me.'

I hear him talking but don't take in what he's saying as we ascend to the first floor. Instead, I look at our reflection in the mirrored interior of the lift. I'm a dripping wet old woman with ruddy cheeks from the cold, and damp, limp curls frame my face where my hood has failed in its job. Liam, on the other hand, is fizzing with enthusiasm and youth, his skin the picture of health. You can almost see the sparks flying from him. And as is always the way, and without really wishing to, I begin to think about my own son, wondering what Stephen would look like now, what he'd be doing. But I need to stop that direction of thought before it gets out of hand. That's a path I can't traverse.

Liam makes sure I'm safely in my room and that the radiator is working before he leaves. He tells me he's been roped into kitchen duty tonight as they're so short-staffed. He's excited about it – he loves cooking, apparently – but thinks he'll mostly be washing-up. I am listening to him, but again, his words seem to wash over me, his sentences coming at me in waves. I manage to smile and it must be enough, because he leaves, closing the door behind him.

I shrug off my coat and it hits the floor with a soggy thump. When I bend to retrieve it, my bones creak with the effort. The hangers in the wardrobe are all free as I haven't taken the time to unpack my suitcase and I pull one out, slide my wet coat onto its arms and look around for somewhere suitable to hang it. The radiator under the window is throwing out some heat now; I can smell the dust coming from it as it warms. Pulling the dressing table stool over to it and levering myself up, I reach with trembling arms to hook the hanger over the curtain pole. My legs feel like jelly and for a moment I wonder if I'm going to be able to get down, but I do manage, by holding on to the edge of the curtain as I do, very nearly pulling the whole lot off the wall.

Sitting on the edge of the bed, I contemplate a warm

bath but I haven't the energy to run one. It's 5:43 p.m., according to the clock on the cabinet, and a fleeting image of me getting dressed, tidying the front of my hair and going down for dinner passes somewhere in the back of my brain. Instead, I lie down and then curl up on my side on top of the covers, drawing my knees in as far as I can, and reach out to turn off the bedside light.

Chapter Eight

Confession

I'm in the meadow behind my house. The sun has bleached the grasses to gold and the poppy seeds I scattered have now grown, their tissue-paper petals catching the breeze. It's my 'one thing that makes you happy' on Doctor Graham's list. I should probably be grateful to Tony for his insistence on buying the land, how it's increased the value of our home, set us apart from the sparse properties along our isolated road, but I don't like to think about my husband in relation to that special place. It belongs to me and Stephen.

I'm transported, weightless. The meadow is endless and the house seems so very far away. We're walking hand in hand through the grasses to our picnic rug, Stephen's toy cars and trains lined up along the checked fabric. We're preparing to play a game: roads and rails and sky. And then he lets go of my hand.

There's an irritating tapping noise in my ear. I'd like it to be a woodpecker in the poplar tree on the edge of the meadow and I try to focus on that possibility, but I know it isn't, I know I'm dreaming. The old springs from the bed poke into my side and I can smell the damp from my coat warming above the radiator.

'Evelyn?'

Now I have a voice to go with the tapping; a sing-song trill with a note from the North. I wait – the voice might go away.

'I can get a key from reception, you know. Liam said you weren't feeling very well and asked me to check you're OK.'

Reaching out, my hand finds the flex and I click the lamp on, roll onto my back and blink as my eyes adjust to the light. There's a huge crack in the ceiling, running from the light fitting to the coving. Perhaps the hotel might fall down and we can all go home. Somehow, though, I just don't feel that lucky.

'I'll get the key then, shall I?'

Cynthia is sounding more convincing through the door now and with a long sigh, I swing my legs round and find the floor. I'm still a bit unsteady and glancing at my watch, I see how long I've been lying down. It seems like forever, but really, it's only been an hour.

'I'm coming,' I say, irritated, and push myself up from the bed, trying one leg in front of the other.

I reach the door and pull it open, to see Cynthia standing there with Joy hovering just behind her.

'Alan said you'd been out in the snow delivering Christmas cards,' Cynthia says sharply. 'It's really not the weather to be out, especially not on your own.'

She has her hands on her hips and she's looking me up and down, assessing me for what, I don't know.

'We're going down for dinner. Are you coming?'

I look past Cynthia at Joy, who's changed into a peacock blue, wool dress that skims her thin frame, her tiny hip bones poking into the fabric. She has a peach cardigan around her shoulders, too, and the colour shouldn't work with the tone of her dress, but, of course, on Joy it does; perfectly. And yet she hangs back, unsure, still with the apologetic air of earlier. I want to reach out my arms and hug her, a very unusual feeling for me, but instead my fingers find the limp piece of my hair at the front where it didn't survive the outing and Joy's gaze follows.

'I'll go and get my hot brush,' she says simply.

Cynthia uses the moment to gain entry to my room and taking a quick look around, even she doesn't bother to rally on its shabby behalf.

'What a dump! I thought my room was bad, but this is worse. Right, what are you planning to wear?' She gives my unopened case a wry look, then lifts it onto the bed and flings the lid open.

'Cynthia?' I say, and she turns to look at me.

'I know, I'm being bossy, I can't seem to help myself. But you know, Evelyn, when I first saw you on the coach this morning, I felt an instant warmth emanating from you,' she says, and then throws her head back, a rumble of laughter erupting from her. Her chunky wooden necklaces clatter together. 'Well, perhaps a kindred spirit, then.' This last she delivers with another of her knowing and frankly unsettling looks.

'Cynthia?' I try again, and decide I'm going to ask her to leave, but that isn't what slips from my lips. 'I've done something terrible. Something truly awful, and I have no idea how to undo it.'

She opens her mouth to say something, the smile disappearing from her lips, but Joy suddenly appears in the doorway with the hot brush in her hand.

'It's still warm,' she says, and I look down as Cynthia takes hold of my arm and guides me to the dressing table stool.

'Right, then, you work your magic, Joy, and I'll get the wardrobe sorted.'

I wonder if I'm having an out-of-body experience. I can feel Joy gently brushing the front of my hair and the warmth from the hot brush as she skilfully twirls it. I can hear Cynthia rattling the hangers in the wardrobe, but it's as if I'm detached from the experience, and I wonder if I'm in shock.

'Done,' Joy says, stepping back, and I look at the three of us reflected in the mirror.

Cynthia, dressed in a long colourful kaftan, is holding up my grey skirt and navy floral blouse. It's the only thing I possess with any sparkle in it, but goodness, it looks dreary next to the other women's clothing.

'This, with your lovely locket, is perfect,' she says, holding them out as tentatively as you would a hand to a frightened dog.

My fingers reach to the locket on the gold chain that now hangs permanently around my neck. Tony was right – it's safer there.

'You pop them on and we'll wait downstairs for you.' As she hands over the clothes, she gently squeezes my arm. 'Let's get a drink and we can talk,' she whispers.

I can feel myself being drawn into her confidence and I don't like it.

There are a long row of drinks lined up on the bar: red and white wine, and what looks to be overly concentrated orange juice, which Liam is pouring. It took everything I had to get dressed and come down, and now I'm here, I wonder why I've allowed a stranger to take control of me.

'I recommend the red wine, Mrs P. I'm not old enough to drink it, but I am old enough to know it's the only drink here at the correct temperature.'

'Thank you for earlier, Liam,' I say quietly, trying to draw as little attention to my embarrassing display as possible. 'I think I was just cold after my walk.'

'There was a lot of snow and it's baltic out there. I've got to walk home in it later,' he says. 'Maybe I should borrow a tray from the kitchen and slide down the hill – it'd be quicker.'

His eyes sparkle with amusement, but his expression suggests he'd like to do it.

I smile back at him. 'That sounds like fun,' I say, although of course there's nothing I'd like to do less.

I remember standing on a hill in the snow many years ago with Carol, watching her girls slide down in the sledge that Tony had made for Stephen. I also remember asking them to get off it.

Liam disappears into the kitchen and I pick up a glass of red wine. It's not actually that nice and doesn't warrant a discussion of its bouquet, because it doesn't have one. I knock back half the glass anyway.

Looking around, I see that most of the guests seem to have grouped up, found their counterparts, and there's a pleasant buzz in the air. Even Barry and his wife aren't scowling, but they sit alone. I sip at my wine, hoping it'll improve the more of it I drink, as I work out where to head. I have a sudden yearning for Tony's comfortable chair, a nice mug of hot chocolate, the *Radio Times* and a plan for my Christmas viewing. And then Cynthia appears by my side and I won't tell her, but I'm grateful.

'Evelyn, you're looking lovely,' she says. 'I've got a table for us *three front-row ladies.*'

She manages to make it sound sleazy, as if we're on a table of ill repute. I lift my glass to my lips again and find that it's empty. It's not just the room that has a pleasant buzz now.

'Let's grab a couple more of these while they're still free, shall we?' Cynthia says, picking up two glasses and motioning for me to do the same.

I imagine she must want me to take one for Joy, so I follow her lead, but when we get to the table Cynthia's saved for us, I can see that there are already two full glasses in front of Joy and two bright spots of pink dominate her cheeks.

'Hi, Evelyn,' she says. 'Are you feeling better?'

Alcohol appears to agree with her; she already seems more relaxed.

I sit down next to her and pop the glasses on the table. There are six lined up in front of us now and I'm so embarrassed what people will think. Looking around the room, though, I can see that most tables are the same. The group has livened up, but I still have a nagging in my gut and my limbs are like lead. It's going to take more than one glass of wine for it to go away.

'Thank you for doing my hair,' I reply.

'It was a pleasure. I'm not good at many things, but I'm OK with a hot brush.' She leans closer. 'Do you want to see what we've been up to this afternoon?' she asks me, and I have to stop myself from saying no. It almost erupts out of me and I put my glass to my lips to squash it.

'Joy has worked so hard. She's been really creative,' Cynthia says, giving me a sideways glance.

It's a reprimand. I should have said yes, I realise a little late, but I'm not a naughty girl who needs to be told what to do. I take another sip and stare back at her. Joy beams at the praise as if she's unused to such approval. She seems almost childish, or like an animal desperate for a shred of affection. It gives me an uneasy feeling, but I'm not sure why. Perhaps the wine is affecting me.

Reluctantly, I follow them through to reception, which has been transformed into a glittering spectacle. The wet green plastic from earlier has been turned into a sort of tree. It's been strung with lights that are probably responsible for keeping it upright and baubles dangle from most of the limbs. There's a star on the top that doesn't look like it'll stay there long; it's already at a peculiar angle. A collection of large paper snowflakes hang from the ceiling all covered in glitter, a string of twinkling lights have been strung across the archway that leads to the dining room and two large glass bowls filled with silver baubles, lit from underneath, sit on either end of the desk.

Both women look at me expectantly. I need to say something nice, I realise, but the only word that comes to mind is tacky.

'I obviously had to work with what was available,' Joy says, her face already starting to fall.

My mind produces an image of the Christmas tree in the library, with those lovely stained-glass biscuits.

'You have been very busy,' I say. What is wrong with me? Why can't I just say it looks nice? 'It looks nice.'

'Don't bust a gut there, Evelyn,' Cynthia chirps.

'There's more in the store, so we're going to do the dining room tomorrow morning. Staff seem to have left us to our own devices, so we're taking full advantage.'

Joy seems happy enough with my comment, but Cynthia performs one of her well-practised eye-rolls.

'Personally, I think it's a bit of a cheek to expect guests to decorate the place themselves.'

'Evelyn, of course you have a point,' Cynthia says. 'But who's going to do it if we don't? And think how much nicer our Christmas meal will be if we can get the place done up.'

She's right about the dining room; it does need decorating. If there was a Christmas tree or indeed any hint of Christmas at all, we might be able to look past the fact that tonight's meal, although satisfactory in content, was cold. I now realise the clever use of free wine earlier; no one's complaining because everyone is just a little drunk, myself included.

When I pop to the loo, I find that I'm swaying in front of the mirror. I lean in to take a closer look at the old woman reflected in the glass. My hazel eyes stare back at me, but despite the carefree feeling the wine has given me, I can see the guilt and regret shining starkly out of them. Suddenly, I'm back on the door step with the letter in my hand deliberating over whether to post it or not. But I no longer have the luxury of that decision, because it's already done. Pulling back from my reflection, I smooth my skirt and brush a non-existent thread from my blouse.

I'm going to have to do something about the letter, but what?

'Ladies, what can I get you?'

Liam finds the three of us at a table back in the bar. This time, Cynthia has chosen a spot in the corner tucked away from everyone else. If I wasn't so drunk I wouldn't have followed them. I need to detach myself from this situation, because I think she has an ulterior motive.

'I'm going to call it a night, but thank you anyway,' I say.

'Nonsense! Two large brandies for us and for you, Joy?' Cynthia ignores me with flick of her hand.

'Oh, Tia Maria, please,' she says. 'I've been looking forward to this.'

'I'm not that fond of brandy, actually.'

I'm trying to think if I've ever had one. I remember Tony drinking it and I'm pretty sure I sniffed some once. I seem to remember it affecting my eyes.

'Just the one nightcap.'

Cynthia is very persuasive, like Carol. I have to be very careful around my sister when my defences are low; Carol can have me agreeing to things I don't want to do. Carol and Cynthia would get on well – or kill each other, perhaps. Liam returns with our drinks and I lift mine tentatively to my lips, sniffing at the amber liquid. There it is again, before I've even taken a sip, I can feel it burning my eyeballs.

'You're supposed to be drinking it, not huffing in it, Evelyn!' Cynthia says when I begin to complain. 'Get it down you.'

After a moment's hesitation, I knock some back and

allow the warmth to penetrate the length of my throat and into my stomach. I place the glass back on the table; it's frighteningly strong stuff, nothing like the house wine we've been drinking all evening.

'So, Evelyn, do you want to tell us what you've been up to this afternoon, sneaking around in the snow?'

Cynthia's direct question throws me for a moment. I wasn't expecting her to get straight to the point, but my thoughts are becoming fuzzy and I can't think of a good enough reason not to tell her.

'I had a letter to deliver and I went out to post it.' I'm 90 per cent sure I'm slurring some of the words together; in fact, I'm 80 per cent sure it's ninety.

'A letter? Alan told us it was a Christmas card,' says Cynthia, narrowing her eyes.

'Well, Alan had no business in telling you my business.'

'I'm sure he didn't mean any harm. He's such a lovely man,' Joy says.

We both turn to look at her and watch a flush of deep red creep up the pale skin of her neck. She picks up her drink and buries herself in it.

'He is,' agrees Cynthia.

'Is he?' I say.

'I'm sorry, Evelyn,' Cynthia says. 'You're right, it's none of my business. I'm just a nosey old bag, always have been. But we were worried about you earlier. You looked like you were in shock, but maybe it was just the cold.'

Joy's eyes dart from one of us to the other and I swirl my drink around, watching the liquid coat the sides as I turn it. It's odd to be huddled in the corner with these two, near strangers, both wanting to hear what I have to say. People tend to talk *at* me these days; they don't often listen. I take a breath and before I can change my mind, I allow the words to tumble from my mouth.

'I found a letter that my husband had written. It was addressed to a woman called Margaret and he was in love with her.' I pause to check their reactions and watch as eyes grow wider, as they lean forwards, eager for more, and there's something compelling about having their full attention, so I oblige. 'It wasn't just a love letter; it was a confession, too.'

'He confessed to being married to you?' Joy asks.

'No, there's no mention of me at all. It was worse than that.'

'Worse than writing a love letter to another woman!' Cynthia scoffs. 'I have no time for that nonsense and neither should you.'

'It was confessing to something he'd done. Something he'd done that had resulted in another man's death. He knocked down a cyclist with his car.'

I watch their reaction over the rim of my glass as I take another sip. They're dumbfounded.

'But what's that got to do with the woman? Why's he telling *her*?'

'Because…' I pause. There's no escaping it – I pause for effect. 'Because it was the woman's husband who he killed.'

They both gasp, hands finding their mouths.

'So, you think he murdered the man?' Cynthia says, and Joy gasps again.

'No, I'm pretty sure it was an accident.'

'You should ask him,' Joy says from behind her hand.

'I can't – he's dead.'

That shuts them both up.

'He was found dead in his car when, I believe, he was on his way here to see this woman. Not to confess – I think that letter was just for his own benefit, to assuage his guilt. I don't think he had any intention of sending it. I think he was on his way to propose to her, but he died never having made it.'

I stop now, resting my hands in my lap, feeling the full weight of Tony's confession as if it were my own.

'God, Evelyn! What a letter to find. So, you decided to deliver it yourself,' Cynthia says. 'I don't blame you; I'd have done the same. This woman has the right to know who was responsible for the death of her husband, even if it was an accident.'

'I believe he felt guilty – I'd like to think he had the ability for that, at least. And I believe he wanted to be with her to make amends. He was on his way to propose, to commit bigamy, I suppose.'

'Why are you so sure about a proposal?' Cynthia asks. 'It's quite the leap.'

'When he was found, he had a diamond ring in his pocket and he was wearing his best suit.'

'Ahh!'

There's a loaded silence around the table as we digest the contents of our conversation.

'So, what happened? Did you find the house, the woman?' Cynthia asks. 'I'm imagining quite the tête-à-tête.' She's pushed her drink to one side and is leaning her elbows on the table. Joy is sitting back with her arms folded.

'I found the house, but no one was there. So I pushed it through the letter box.'

'Oh, shame. Well, the most important thing is you've delivered the letter now. You can draw a line under it. The woman can do whatever she wants with the information. She never received the proposal and is no longer any concern of yours,' says Cynthia.

'It's a bit spiteful, though,' Joy says quietly.

'It's worse than that,' I say, ignoring her words, the fact that she's picked up on my true motivation. 'Once I put the letter through the door, the neighbour told me that a woman called Sarah lives there and that it's her mother who's called Margaret. I've delivered it to the wrong family member – one who probably shouldn't read it.'

I let that sink in for a moment, watching as they struggle to know what to say. Cynthia opens and closes her mouth like a deranged fish, but it's Joy who finally speaks.

'Evelyn,' she says, suddenly gripping my arm. 'You need to get that letter back.'

Chapter Nine

Back in Time for Breakfast?

It's Christmas Eve and the snow has stopped falling when I pull back the curtain to peep outside. Everything is white. The hotel lights flood the lawn and stretch just far enough to draw the eye to the edge where the moon illuminates the sea. I slide the catch open on the window to hear the waves crashing against the shore. I wonder what it would be like to stay here in the summer months; it would be warmer for a start. I shiver and snap the window shut against the chill morning air, my face cold where I've pressed it too near to the opening.

Despite the water I drank when I came back to my room last night, my head is heavy and there's a flicking sort of ache behind my eyes. The brandy had been a mistake, and perhaps also my confession. My thoughts return to our tight huddle at the corner table in the bar. My bold words, the alcohol loosening my tongue as I shared my darkest secrets with the other women. Actually, not *my* secrets – Tony's; I managed to keep most of mine to myself.

I feel as if I should regret it and in the cold darkness of this early morning, I do. In just a few hours of barely knowing these women, I've divulged information that I should most certainly have kept to myself. I blame Cynthia entirely. Her insistence on plying me with alcohol and her nosiness has left me in an awkward position. Joy has hatched a plan to get the letter back and for some unknown reason, I've agreed to go along with it.

It's five o'clock and I'm sitting on the bed, fully dressed with my coat, hat and gloves on. I must still be drunk, because I'm at a loss as to why I've allowed myself to be talked into this caper. No, I won't be going. I'm not one for impulsive decisions and this one is surely the most ridiculous. I'm beginning to remove my gloves determinedly, when there's a soft tapping at the door, and my stomach drops.

We make our way slowly away from the hotel, kicking up the snow on the gravel drive as we go, silent to start with, all lost in our thoughts. Mine are wrestling with my wish to turn round, but my need to have the letter back in my hand is overwhelming. When we're out of sight of The Welcome Rest, we begin to talk and Joy blurts out that she doesn't really have a plan at all, and my nausea swells.

'That's it, then. I think we should turn back,' I say. 'There's no link to me personally; perhaps this is getting out of hand.'

'No link to you personally?' Cynthia rounds on me. 'I'm sorry to point out the obvious, Evelyn, but who else is going to be putting a confessional letter through the door? I think there are too many unanswered questions.'

'I think we should just concentrate on the matter in hand,' I say, not wishing to think about unanswered questions.

'Let's keep going; I have a good feeling about this,' Joy says.

Thank goodness one of us does, because it feels foolhardy and reckless to me.

'What if we're seen?' I ask.

'Don't worry about that. We're just three old women, probably a bit demented and definitely lost,' Cynthia says, and Joy looks up at me.

We silently agree that Cynthia is delusional if she thinks we can get away with that.

'Carol singers?' I suggest. 'You two sing and I'll grab the letter.' I'm not sure where that comes from. Both women turn to look at me, incredulity on their faces. 'It was a joke,' I mumble.

'Oh, sorry, Evelyn, didn't know you did jokes. That's a turn-up,' Cynthia says, and Joy giggles.

I ignore them both.

'Right, I have a story,' Joy says. 'If we're seen, we just say that one of us has lost our cat and we're looking for it. It's a bit flimsy, I know, but it does seem a touch more likely story than three carol-singing pensioners breaking into a house.'

They both laugh at that, but I don't join in and it dies away fairly quickly when the reality of what we're doing settles back over us. It's the first time the words 'breaking in' have been uttered, but how else did I really think I was going to get the letter back?

'And Sarah's not due back until this afternoon?' Joy asks.

I'd forgotten I'd told them that, too.

'That's what he said.'

'There is another option, of course. Just ring the bloody bell this afternoon and ask for it. Make up some story of putting a friend's card through the wrong door. Of course, you'll have to act surprised when the woman mentions the coincidence of your friend sharing the name with her own mother,' Cynthia says.

'Tony always said I was never very good at acting.'

'Perhaps we shouldn't put too much faith into what your husband said. It sounds to me as if he wasn't the best judge of right and wrong,' Joy says sharply, and Cynthia's stomach suddenly rumbles.

'Oh, I hope we're back in time for breakfast,' she says.

We're in the street now. It's deserted – unsurprisingly, as it's so early. I notice that some of the Christmas lights have been left on overnight. They look pretty, twinkling away in the dark, making the snow sparkle. It's not a scruffy street – even in the middle of winter, you can see that the front gardens are looked after, tidy, especially number forty-eight.

'Keep walking,' hisses Joy as I put a hand out to open the gate. 'We're going to have a look round the back.'

I'm not sure when Joy decided to take control and I glance at Cynthia assuming I've missed something, but she just shrugs. We both troop along behind Joy to the end of the street, where the narrow lane intersects. We follow it round and I can see I was correct. The path bears to the right, behind the row of cottages, and another path veers off to the left, down to the sea; I can hear it, moving in the dark.

The path is overgrown with tangled evergreen hedging and leafless winter trees in the lane behind the properties, and probably not often used to access the back gardens. I follow Cynthia and she follows Joy as she counts the houses along, pushing back the bare branches that swing overhead, until we're right outside the back gate of Sarah's house. I'm beginning to feel sick again and I'm sure it's not just the hangover, although that's still banging away behind my eyes, too.

'We can't make any noise,' I whisper suddenly. 'The neighbour is a nosey old man, a proper curtain-twitcher, the sort who would listen out for intruders. He'd probably love to phone the police to report a break-in. I imagine he spends his time at his window looking for trouble.'

This thought is worrying, bearing in mind what we're doing, and I rather wish I hadn't brought it up.

The other two nod silently and Joy makes some odd hand gestures as if she's a deep-sea diver, pointing at the gate, before an OK sign and a thumbs up, which are the only ones I can actually identify.

She pushes the back gate open and we can see a little way into the garden. There's a shed to the left in the corner, but that's about all I can make out, as everything is covered in a thick layer of snow. I glance up to see if the curtains of both the neighbouring houses are closed, but away from the street lights at the front, it's impossible to tell. Somehow, I can still imagine his eyes trained on us and I shiver. It's so dark, I'm beginning to wonder how we're going to see what we're doing and also, what are we actually doing? I'm about to say that whatever happens, we can't break anything, but Joy is holding up one hand flat and pointing at the both of us. It takes me a moment, but then I understand – stay here.

She walks silently through the gate and behind the shed before inching herself along the fence panelling until she's swallowed into the black. I'd have walked a path straight up the lawn, but Joy is sneaky, clever, not leaving footprints. Not the Joy I've spent the last twelve hours with, but a capable woman, good in a crisis.

I lift one boot and then the other and rub my hands together through my gloves. I'm getting cold standing around, even with all of my layers, but at least I won't be identifiable. I pull my hat lower. Cynthia is wearing something in fur on top of her head. I imagine she was going for the look of the actress Julie Christie in *Dr Zhivago*, but it has more than a passing resemblance to a dead badger.

'It's good to see Joy taking charge, isn't it?' Cynthia whispers.

'When she has the chance,' I reply, raising an eyebrow in Cynthia's direction.

I immediately want to take it back, because I do know what she means, but she ignores the dig anyway.

'I doubt she gets much of an opportunity normally.'

'What do you mean by that?' I whisper.

'Just that I wouldn't be at all surprised if she's married to a controlling man.'

'Really? Has she said something to you?'

I think about the bruises I saw on her, the barrage of messages she got on her phone when we first got on the coach and how timid she is. Also, that childlike need for Cynthia's approval yesterday. I peer out to see if I can see her in the darkness, but she's walked too far into the gloom. All of a sudden, I feel protective of her.

'She did seem to get a lot of messages,' I say. 'But when we were leaving the ferry yesterday, she pushed the phone down between the seats – I mean right down, as if she were getting rid of it.'

'She probably doesn't want to be contacted while she's away; it's understandable,' she says.

I immediately remember Cynthia's own conversation with whoever Helen is; her daughter or sister, maybe a friend? Pretending to be ill not to have to go for Christmas. Cynthia is rather keen to extract information from others, but not so keen to give up her own secrets. It seems like both of these women are running or hiding from something, while I seem to be stumbling head long in, regardless of the consequences.

A light suddenly blinks at us from by the house. It swings around before stopping and shining on Joy's face, making her look ghoulish. It reminds me of Carol messing about with Dad's torch when she was young and irritating. She'd hide behind doors and leap out at me, the torch under her chin to make her features grotesque. I'd always pretend not to be bothered, but in reality, even though she was only little, I was still unsettled. Such a bag of nerves, my mother would often say about me. I wanted to suggest she might comfort me, that maybe that might help.

Joy is waving her hand, beckoning us forwards. We begin to trace her footsteps behind the shed, towards the house. I make every effort to walk quietly, but really we're making too much noise, the two of us stomping through the snow. As we get closer, I can finally see the shape of the houses and the curtains that are closed on the neighbours' windows. I allow myself a tiny moment of relief, then we're all standing on the doorstep, and that moment vanishes. Joy is triumphant, with a key in her hand and a huge smile on her face. The bright light is coming from the back of her mobile phone. Perhaps I imagined what happened on the coach.

'I found the key in a plant pot over by the patio chairs,' Joy whispers, pointing, and I follow her gaze to a clipped conifer in the shape of a bird with a hat of snow on its head. 'Classic hiding place. Not underneath the pot but on the soil, under the bird's bum.' She puts a finger to her lips and ushers me forwards. 'We don't all need to go in. We'll wait out in the lane; we don't want to draw too much attention, OK?'

I nod at her and take the key, but I really don't want to do this on my own. I could ask Cynthia to get it for me – I'm sure she would – but I'd probably never hear the end of it. Joy hands me her phone, too, and points at the torch. I take it from her and push the key into the lock, half hoping that it won't fit, but it slips straight in.

I look back at the other two, willing one of them to say how ridiculously stupid this is and to stop me from walking into the house, but Cynthia pats my shoulder, and then the two of them disappear back behind the shed and I'm left alone on the doorstep. Silently, I curse Tony for putting me through this, then I turn the key and push open the door.

Chapter Ten

Decoy

When I was ten, my best friend, Celia, and I broke into her father's shop. It was a family business that he'd run for years, just as his father had run it before him; a grocer's on the corner of Spring Rise. We didn't really break in – I mean, nothing was broken – although that was strongly refuted when we were caught. Celia had just taken the key from the drawer in their kitchen and we'd skipped Sunday school in search of something sweeter.

The punishment was worked out between her parents and mine – after-school cleaning in the shop for weeks; although I know for sure Celia's punishment came with a heavier hand. My mother was cold, but she never touched me, and my father wouldn't so much have squashed a spider under his shoe. I'd taken a chocolate bar, that was all, but I was grown up enough to understand it wasn't about that – it was the lack of respect, the mistrust.

I lost touch with Celia when we went to different secondary schools and I pushed the memory of that Sunday misdemeanour as far to the back of my mind as possible. If I could have, I'd have plucked it from my head and thrown it away, but then I had my mother to remind me when she was being particularly spiteful. Eventually, the aftermath died down, even she realised it was best not to keep highlighting her daughter's failures; it hardly looked good for her. I never talked about it again. Occasionally, though, it pops into my head, unbidden, even now, and the shame I feel is overwhelming. I still don't know why I did it. The chocolate bar was one I didn't even like that much. There was no reason at all for me to have done it.

Do I have reason now? Is this reasonable? Because suddenly, I'm not so sure.

I'm standing in a small kitchen, shining Joy's phone torch around like a criminal. Technically, that's what I am, again. I blame Tony entirely for what I'm doing now, in the same way that it was easier to blame Celia, sixty-six years ago. The light casts long shadows up the cupboards and along the ceiling, and the darkness seems to bulge behind me. I wish that the other two were still just outside the door, ready to rush in to help me if I need it. Just to see them behind the glass would be enough, but I feel the distance between us now, and they may as well be at the hotel for all the good they are outside in the lane. How long do you get for breaking and entering? I wonder. How old do you have to be to get away with it? Is there an upper age limit?

There's a cluttered but homely feel about the room. An oak table and four chairs sit in the middle with piles of magazines and paperwork taking up one end. Place mats set ready for a meal, a half-empty glass of water, a candle in a ceramic jar with a whiff of vanilla, and a silver salt- and pepper cellar in the shape of a cat and a mouse.

My breathing is slow and steady, even though my heart seems to be beating louder than usual. Not wanting to linger, I step out of the kitchen into a living room. I don't have time to take in all the details – I just need to get the letter and get out, but I can't help my eyes straying over the contents of the room. Expecting a bombardment of Tony, a presence of him here in this house, I'm oddly disappointed. There's no sense of him here at all. It suddenly feels as if the letter has no place here and, not for the first time, I'm confused.

There are two big comfortable settees and an armchair with colourful cushions that take up most of the room. A Christmas tree has been wedged in the corner, chock-full of decorations. It's a real one, I notice. The smell of spruce is overwhelming in this small room, but it isn't unpleasant. It comes at me like a blast from the past, a reminder of Christmases early in our marriage.

Shelving either side of the fireplace is rammed with books, and also ornaments that hint at stories of holidays and experiences. There are a number of photographs, too – some framed, others just leaning against each other. My curiosity gets the better of me and I take a step forwards, misjudge the distance entirely with only the light from the mobile phone, and catch my leg on the sharp edge of the coffee table, pain blooming instantly. I bend and rub at it furiously to stem the discomfort, then straighten up, focusing on what I need to do.

Leaving the living room through a door into a narrow hallway, I can see the front door ahead. My eyes go straight to the doormat, but there's nothing there. Panic begins to overtake the pain in my shin and I pick up the corner of the mat as if by some magic the letter has managed to squirrel its way underneath when I pushed it through the letter box. Ridiculous, of course it didn't. Someone has picked it up, which means someone came home, which means someone could be here right now.

Fingers of fear grip at me as I turn and hobble back through to the living room, my mission to get out as quickly as possible. But my eyes scan the area as I go, just in case I see it, and that's when I notice the cat curled up between two cushions on the settee. It lifts its head and eyes me curiously as I scan the items on the coffee table, but there's no letter.

There are cupboards built underneath the bookcases, but I squash the urge to open them and rummage. The chances of the letter having made its way in there is almost zero and as I so far haven't had any sense of Tony in this house, I certainly don't want to find some lurking inside. The kitchen, that's where letters end up.

I turn to walk out of the living room and the cat jumps down from the settee, stretching as it goes, and follows me. It yawns and a soft meow follows, and I can't stop myself from bending to stroke it. As my fingers find its fur, I make an instant and unexpected decision. I'm going to get a cat when I go home. An older cat, perhaps, a rescue one from the centre near me. After all, I don't have any allergies.

Stepping into the kitchen, I swing the torch around the cluttered worktops and across the windowsill. Plant pots, bowls of fruit, keys and cookery books. I turn to the table, remembering the pile of magazines I saw. There are letters on top and I will Tony's to be among them. I begin to flick through the pile. If it's here, it surely can't be far down. There it is! Sandwiched between a newspaper and what looks like a bill. I breathe out a sigh of relief as I reach out to pick it up. This was easier than I thought it was going to be. Don't crow too soon, I tell myself, just pocket the letter and get out.

As I turn to leave, I don't notice the cat begin to wind itself between my feet, its solid body suddenly wedged as I try to step forwards. I trip, knocking into the table and disturbing the glass of water, which topples off the side before falling to the floor with an almighty smash. There's a moment of ensuing silence before a creaking floorboard sounds from above. I'm frozen to the spot with the letter in my hand. Silently, without breathing, I slide it into my coat pocket along with Joy's phone, the torch still lit. Whatever else happens, at least I have the letter back.

'Hello? Is someone there?'

It's a man's voice, croaky from sleep, and then a light comes flooding down the stairs and into the hallway. How foolish of me to take the neighbour's word that no one would be home until this afternoon. I suppose he only said Sarah wouldn't be home; there was no mention of anyone else.

I'm not usually known for quick-witted decisions – goodness knows, Tony told me that often enough – and have no idea where this one comes from, but I bend and scoop up the cat from the floor, place him on the table where the glass had been. He looks unbothered, as if he's used to being handled by burgling pensioners. I sidestep the broken glass and the pool of water on the floor to reach the back door.

I hear the sound of feet descending the stairs and I don't

hang around but open the door as silently as I can manage and slip through. There's an agonising moment where I fumble with the key, but it finally turns and just as I pull it from the lock, light pours into the kitchen. Ignoring the pain in my shin, I duck below the window, also ignoring the creaking protest from my hips, and inch my way along the wall until I reach the plant pot. Dropping the key back in underneath the bird, I hobble round into the shadows behind the shed, and only then allow myself to look back.

Through the kitchen window, I can just make out the shape of the back of a man with the black cat draped over his shoulder like a baby about to be winded. I take a deep breath finally before my eyes travel up to the neighbour's house. Curtains have been opened in an upstairs room, to reveal the shape of a person framed in the window, arms folded and seemingly staring into the garden, or out at the sea, or at me; it's so dark it's impossible to tell.

Cynthia and Joy are waiting in the lane, huddled together against the cold. I bustle past them, leading the way back out from the tangled undergrowth. I don't look back – I can't bear the thought of seeing the figure in the window, still watching. I prefer to keep it as a figment of an overactive imagination. Adrenaline still pumps around my body as we come out and back to the end of East Street.

'Bloody hell,' Cynthia says. 'I don't think my heart has pounded this fast since I was a teenager. Please tell me you got the letter, Evelyn?'

'Yes,' I say, breathless. 'But only just.'

'Thank God for that,' she says.

'Let's just get back to the hotel.'

Joy looks shaken, even though this was her idea and she

seemed so in control before. Perhaps the reality of our crime has just dawned on her. Or maybe her hangover has arrived.

It begins to snow again, heavily, and I think about our footprints in Sarah's back garden, pray it will be enough to cover them.

Our walk back is laboured, partly because of the incline and also because the adrenaline is wearing off. This is the second time in about twelve hours I've walked this route in such cold weather and the pain in my shin flares again. I don't bother to mention it, though. Cynthia hasn't said anything about her knee, even though I've seen her struggling as she walks. I fill the other two in on what happened in the house.

'Do you think someone will think it's a bit weird when they find the letter missing?' Joy says as we stop for a breather.

'It was stuck between others, so maybe it's not been noticed, and to be honest, I don't care. I have it back, no one knows I broke in to get it other than you two, and that's all that matters.'

I sound convincing, but I can't help dwelling on the neighbour. I told him I posted a letter through their door and if Sarah or the man in the house tell him it's missing, he could, in theory, put two and two together, but hopefully by then, Christmas will be over and I'll be on my way home. I can put this whole sorry escapade behind me.

'Has it been opened?' Joy asks, and I pull it back out of my pocket to check. I hadn't even thought about that.

'No, I taped it up after I read it and it's still intact.'

'Thank goodness for the cat,' she says.

I nod, suddenly remembering her phone still lit up in my pocket. I take it out and hand it to her.

'I don't know how to turn the torch off, sorry,' I say. I hesitate before adding, 'I thought you left your phone on the coach, on the seat?'

She takes it from me, without catching my eye. Instead, she gazes over my shoulder, back down the road, and I don't think she's going to respond. I can just see the car park lights of the hotel ahead, and the thought of a cup of tea and some breakfast is appealing.

'I've left my husband,' Joy announces suddenly. 'This is a different phone – my new phone – so I can't be contacted.'

'You don't need to explain,' I say quickly. 'I didn't think before I spoke.'

'That's usually me,' Cynthia says with a low chuckle.

'It's OK, really. It's been a long time coming, but it's just… well, complicated,' Joy says.

We wait for her to elaborate, but she doesn't. In fact, her lips are clamped in a thin, tight line. She clearly doesn't intend to say more.

I reach out my arm and pat her shoulder awkwardly. Then just as quickly, I pull it away and push it into my pocket. We continue the last stretch in silence. Joy has given us something else to think about.

It's only six thirty as we make our way back down the driveway, a long time until breakfast.

Chapter Eleven

Not Quite the Needles

Alan is in reception when we get back. He's prowling around, talking into his mobile phone in a low voice, not dissimilar to a growl and quite different from his usual light-hearted and soft tone. When he sees us, he jabs at the screen with his finger before sliding the device quickly into the pocket of his jeans.

'Where on earth have you three been?' he asks, glancing at his watch as we begin stamping the snow from our boots and shaking out our coats.

His voice has lost the edge now, but I notice Joy looking at him apprehensively.

'Just out for a walk,' I say, guilt tripping off my every word.

'At this hour?'

'Problems, Alan?' Cynthia interrupts him, and he sinks into the nearest seat, running a hand round the back of his neck.

'Well, I don't need to tell you that this trip isn't quite what we all expected, do I?'

All three of us shuffle a little closer.

'The Get Go are going to the dogs, to be honest. Just got off the phone from my boss, who says he's heard a rumour that a few more staff members might be leaving today.'

'More?' I say. 'There are hardly any here as it is!'

'Probably just idle gossip, but it's the attitude of the man that gets me. He couldn't care less. Probably wouldn't even have bothered to tell me at all if I hadn't phoned him. Told me to get on with it! Can you believe it? That's how he runs his business.' He leans back in his armchair and lets out a long puff of air through barely parted lips.

'It isn't good enough,' I say, but only just get the words out, as Cynthia shoots out a hand and clasps my arm.

'Alan, it's fine, don't worry. This isn't all on you. We're all big enough and ugly enough to look after ourselves,' she says, and Alan looks up gratefully.

Good old rallying Cynthia! Joy seems to have collected herself, too.

'And anyway, you're leaving after this trip, so don't let them get you down,' Joy says, and Alan turns to look at her, his smile broadening.

Cynthia grips my arm tighter and it dawns on me that she wants words of encouragement from me, too. For goodness' sake – he's only got to drive the blasted bus.

'We'll manage,' is all that I manage.

'Thank you,' he says, getting up. 'You three are wonderful, a real tonic. Um, what do you think about our trip out later today? I say we should still do it if people are up for it, despite the weather. Well, you tell me what it's like out there?'

'Christmassy,' says Joy.

'Perfect day for a trip out,' Cynthia adds.

'Pitch-black and freezing,' I say, and hear a gentle tut from beside me.

There's a lightness in the air among the group as the coach winds its way to Godshill. Alan has turned on his microphone and is keeping up a constant and irritating chatter.

'The wonderful thing about the Isle of Wight is how diverse an island it really is. It has the most beautiful beaches, quaint villages, and then you turn a corner and there's—'

'The Cooperative Funeralcare services,' Sheila cuts in, pointing out of the window.

Amusement radiates around the coach as we pass the building.

'I was going to say unexpected rolling countryside, actually, but yes, there are also very useful services, too. It's also well known for its mild climate,' Alan continues as the wheels catch on a particularly dense patch of snow and it takes him a moment to regain control.

A ripple of titters ensues once it's clear we're not going to crash.

I tune it all out, my brain whirring with all that I've done. Now I have the letter back in my possession, my feelings are mixed. I've saved Sarah the trauma of reading it, but I've given myself the worry of being in charge of Tony's secrets again. Joy suggested that I rip it up and throw it away, but Cynthia said to hand it to the police. Neither of those options seemed right to me, so I've pushed it into the side pocket of my suitcase and stashed it in the bottom of the wardrobe. I've come an awfully long way and don't seem to have achieved anything.

The snow stopped falling before we left the hotel and now the sun keeps trying to find its way out from the tangle of clouds that scud across the sky. When it does, the snow sparkles like something from a perfect Christmas scene, although I don't feel Christmassy. Tired is all I can manage at the moment.

Alan swings the coach into a large car park surrounded by shops. He pulls in next to The Old Smithy café and parks up. I'm surprised how busy it is; we're not the only coach, but then it is Christmas Eve. There will be those who are out buying last-minute presents, I suppose, like Tony used to do. He'd usually come home in a frosty mood because he couldn't get what he wanted, as if Christmas had been brought forwards and he hadn't got the memo, choosing to ignore the weeks I'd spent reminding him. I'd long given up suggesting we could go together; he never seemed to be interested. He'd say he had something else to do, somewhere else to be, and of course now I realise, someone else to be with.

Alan tells us we have three hours to explore the village and have lunch before heading off to the Needles. After such an early start, I'm not sure if I have the energy for such a full itinerary. I'm almost hoping for a blizzard so we can head back to the hotel – someone said there was more snow forecast for later. I'm crossing my fingers. Perhaps I can stay on the coach and have a sleep, but no such luck.

'Right,' says Cynthia. 'Apparently, the Model Village is closed, which is a shame, but there are lovely gift shops and the pub looks nice for lunch.'

She's staring at the screen of her phone, looking up all the information. It reminds me that I should probably phone Carol when we get back to the hotel.

'Alan has asked me to join him for a coffee,' whispers Joy when we're off the coach.

The temperature has dropped again and I push my gloved hands into my pockets. I look to gauge Cynthia's reaction, because if I'm honest, it seems a bit premature to be having coffee with another man when you've only just left your husband. Cynthia is beaming; of course she is.

'Wonderful, enjoy yourself,' she says, and trying hard not to judge, I manage a tight smile.

Alan appears and offers his arm to Joy, and after a moment's hesitation, she takes it. I have that horrible gnawing feeling again in my stomach as I watch them walk away.

'I can't help but feel there's going to be trouble of some kind or another,' I say, and surprisingly, Cynthia nods slowly in agreement. 'What's the difference in their age?'

'Do you really think that's relevant?' she says, laughing, and I feel embarrassed to have asked. 'Actually, Joy's just seventy and Alan is sixty-six.'

'How do you know that?' I say sharply.

This woman is so mercurial. One minute she's thoughtful and caring, and the next she seems to be tripping me up for her own amusement.

'I find that if you ask a straightforward question, people tend to give you a straightforward answer. But seriously, I do know what you mean. There's something that Joy's not saying, but she's an adult, so we should leave her to make her own decisions.'

'You're pretty good at wheedling information out of people,' I say sourly.

'Oh, Evelyn, my lovely new friend,' she says, linking her arm through mine. 'I have absolutely no idea what you mean.'

We head for the pub slowly, our speed dictated by Cynthia's impending knee replacement and my own leg and hip pain. The tablets I took at the hotel have barely touched it. On the way, we pass a chocolatier. Cynthia decides to go in, but I choose not to follow. Instead, I wait outside, watching her animated conversation with the shopkeeper through the window. She can be very charming and manages to make most people smile. Almost not the same person as the woman lying into her phone at the service station.

There are several tea shops and cafés in the village, but Cynthia suggests there will be a better atmosphere in the pub. I know it's because she wants a drink and I'm beginning to think I might like one too.

When we push open the door and step inside, though, I have to agree with her choice. The place is homely, a lovely warm refuge out of the cold. Cynthia surprises me by ordering us both hot chocolates, sandwiches and large slabs of cake, and we sit in front of a roaring fire in comfortable armchairs. My head is beginning to feel better, but an afternoon nap would be nice after the early start. My eyes start drooping as the warmth begins to penetrate my limbs and the food registers in my stomach.

'So, have you thought any more about what to do with the letter?' Cynthia asks, dragging me awake.

'No, not really. I don't want to hand it to the police; I'm not sure it'll do any good now.'

'The way I see it is you've got two options and you have to pick the one you can most easily live with.'

I sit forwards in my chair and put my empty mug on the table. 'What are my options, then?'

'You can go back to the house, knock on the door and be prepared to have an honest conversation with this Sarah woman. See what she knows about Tony and Margaret, lay some ghosts to rest... Or you can enjoy the rest of your Christmas break and then go home and try never to think about it again. But no more sneaking around with that letter, because honestly, Evelyn, the only person who's going to get hurt is you.'

Alan takes the coastal road when we leave Godshill. I assume he does this so we can enjoy a view of the sea, but the wind has picked up again and the coach is buffeted from both sides along this exposed stretch. We're up high and some of the time we can't see the sea at all, but that doesn't stop every head on board straining to the left for the entire thirty-minute journey – and oohing and aahing when we do see it.

Alan talks about the beauty of the island, but right now, it seems a little bleak to me. We pass a couple of campsites and I shiver at the thought. When we turn a corner and the coach is rocked by another gust of wind, Alan points ahead to where we can just catch a glimpse of the Needles in the distance – a white expanse of chalk cliff face and three stacks out in the sea. I can't be the only person thinking we've seen them now, let's just turn back, can I?

We pass a lay-by with camper vans parked up, their owners cradling hot drinks while watching the waves, their hair blowing in all directions. I shiver again.

Suddenly, the sea is gone and we're into a tunnel of hedging, interspersed with thatched cottages, passing places and then eventually, a colourful sign: Welcome to the Needles.

'Why do they need a sign?' I ask nobody in particular. 'It's just some rocks, isn't it?'

'There's more here than just the natural wonder,' Alan replies over his shoulder. 'There's a lot of other attractions, too.'

He swings the coach round a bend and into a large parking bay.

'I just saw a sign for a teacup ride and Santa's grotto.' This is from Sheila, her excitement hitting me squarely in the back of the head. 'You can fill objects up with the coloured sand from Alum Bay, and there's a shop and a glass studio. I think they do demonstrations.'

I turn round to see her reading from a leaflet and my heart plummets.

'I thought we were just here to see some rocks,' I say.

'Where's your sense of adventure?' Cynthia asks me.

'Sense of adventure?' I hiss. 'You do remember what I did this morning? How much more adventurous do you think I need to be?'

'I'm not sure you're going to find adventure on the teacups,' laughs Joy.

And reluctantly, I get up and follow her and Cynthia off the coach.

After a trip to the ladies, the group splits up and Cynthia says, 'I'd like to see the Needles, and I'm certainly not interested in colourful sand and rides, to be honest, despite what I said before.'

'I'd like to give the grotto a wide berth, too,' Joy

says, and it's as if she's plucked the words from my own mouth.

I turn to smile at them both. Finally, we are allies, it seems.

'I'm afraid the bus that usually goes to the Needles isn't running.' Alan's voice looms from behind us. 'And neither are the chairlifts that take you down to the beach. It's out of season.' He looks apologetic, as well he should.

'So, you've brought us to the landmark site of the Needles and we can't see them, but if we want to mess about with some sand and see Father Christmas, we can? Do I have that right, Alan?' I say.

Cynthia reaches out her hand and places it gently on my arm again in her calming way. It doesn't work.

'I'm sorry,' he says simply. 'I thought you might enjoy everything else on offer here. I used to come with my children; it holds fond memories for me.'

'We're not children,' I say more sharply than I intend.

'It's fine, honestly, Alan. We can pop into the gift shop and buy some souvenirs,' Cynthia interjects.

'There is a viewing platform with a telescope,' he says. 'You can see the Needles from there.'

Cynthia's hand is still on my arm and she squeezes it when I open my mouth, so I close it again. 'That's great, thanks, Alan,' Joy says. 'What a lovely place to visit before your retirement.'

'Whose trip is this?' I begin to say, but Cynthia has propelled me round and is marching me away. I am tired and irritated, but I suppose that isn't Alan's fault.

Thanks, Alan,' she calls over her shoulder.

Joy joins us on the viewing platform a few minutes later and we take it in turns to look through the telescope. The lens is a bit scratched, though, rather spoiling the view, and eventually we abandon it in favour of our decrepit eyesight.

'How was your coffee with Alan?' Cynthia asks Joy.

'It was lovely,' she says, and there's that pink tint again, creeping up her neck. She draws her head a little further into the coiled scarf she has around her shoulders. 'It's probably too soon, though. I think Alan would like to find someone special to spend the rest of his life with, but I'm not sure if that's me and I wouldn't want to give him a false impression or...' Joy trails off, looking uncomfortable again.

I think about the way Alan looks at her and wonder if it's a little too late for that.

'Sensible to take your time,' Cynthia says. 'What about you, Evelyn? Any chance you might look for that special someone again?'

'No,' I say quickly, without giving it any thought whatsoever.

We stand for a while longer, staring at the three stacks of chalk with the lighthouse perched on the edge in the distance. We discuss the possibility of walking the bus route to get a closer look, because it does look enticing in all its rugged glory, but none of us has the energy.

'I'm just going to buy a postcard of the image,' Joy says. 'At least I'll be able to see it properly.'

Cynthia raises her phone and takes a photo before dropping it back into the pocket of her lemon duffel coat. 'There,' she says. 'I can zoom in later.'

'I'm really not sure why Alan brought us here with nothing worthwhile running.'

'I think you need to give Alan a break, Evelyn,' Cynthia says. 'He's just doing his best.'

I think about that for a moment and know she's probably right.

'I just feel… so disappointed,' I reply.

'What? Not to get closer to the Needles?'

'No, not really that.'

'It's not Alan's fault that you've been dealt a crappy hand, you know,' Cynthia says.

'I know,' I say. 'I shall make every effort to be more…'

'Kinder, nicer?' Cynthia asks.

'Sweeter?' says Joy.

'Tolerant,' I say, and a chuckle escapes my lips.

We stand, watching the waves spraying up the side of the lighthouse in the distance. Us three allies, side by side.

'Have we seen enough?' asks Joy, her teeth chattering, and both Cynthia and I nod. It's perishingly cold. 'Gift shop?'

Of course it's the last place I want to go, but wisely decide to keep my mouth shut.

The gift shop is busy. This might usually send my anxiety spiralling and I'm prepared to be overwhelmed. I stand near the door so I can make a quick exit if I need to, but oddly, I'm not experiencing any anxiety at all. I'm not sure where it's all gone? I broke into a house this morning and nearly got caught. In the last twenty-four hours, I've not been anywhere near what I would think of as my comfort zone and yet I feel surprisingly calm. I wonder again if it's the presence of these two women.

Idly, I glance around without much intention of buying anything – there isn't anything I need. Perhaps I could get Carol a tacky fridge magnet or a tea towel – she'd hate that. Or I could possibly buy her something nice; a peace offering for missing Christmas. I have a sudden vision of the next ten years or so of my life. A lonely existence in my isolated house, wandering around the meadow, stagnant, without even Tony coming home to punctuate my boredom occasionally. Then Cynthia taps me on the shoulder, holding a pretty picture made of sea glass, pulling me from my reverie.

'What do you think?' she says, turning it round so I can see it properly.

'It's very nice, but what are you going to do with it?'

'Well, I could hang it on the wall at home to remind myself of this eventful trip. Sometimes you need to think about making new memories,' she says as if she's read my mind. 'It's painful, but it has to be done.'

She turns away and puts the picture back on the shelf, but not before I notice her eyes glistening. When she's out of sight, I walk over to where she was looking. Reading the card stuck to the edge, I can see that all the pictures are made by a local artist. All box-framed artworks made from polished pebbles, sea glass and shells. One I notice in particular: three shell figures standing on the headland, looking at the sea. It's so reminiscent of the three of us just now that I pick it up, think about making new memories.

The predicted snow has returned as we all meet up by the coach, everyone keen to get on board now. It's falling heavily and a wind has picked up too, blowing the flakes across the car park. It's settling fast on the frozen ground, adding to what's already there. I'm sure it's not just me who's glad to be heading back to the hotel.

I turn to Cynthia and Joy, wanting to get something off my chest, something I should have perhaps said earlier.

'Thank you both for this morning. I appreciate your help in my'—I glance behind me—'delicate matter.'

'Goodness, Evelyn! First it's jokes and now we have gratitude from you, too. You truly are full of surprises,' Cynthia quips, and Joy tries to hide a chuckle behind her hand.

I bristle in the seat beside her. I don't know why I bothered if she's just going to make fun of me. She lifts her glasses and winks at me with a tilted smirk.

'You're very welcome,' she whispers, but I don't respond. The woman has an odd sense of humour.

The Welcome Rest sign is actually welcome this time as Alan turns onto the driveway, but as we pull up close to the front, I can see the car park is empty and the hotel looks deserted. Inside, it's like the *Mary Celeste* ship. Not a single member of staff in sight and then Liam appears, suddenly, from the dining room with the two young waitresses. There's a mixture of worry and also excitement on all of their faces.

'They've gone!' he says to us. 'They've all gone. Mr Jackson's resigned, and most of the staff have joined him and walked out!'

Chapter Twelve

The Place to Ourselves

When I told my mother I was getting married, it was fair to say she was shocked. When I told her I was three months pregnant, she didn't bother to disguise her disappointment until she found out that Anthony Pringle was the man responsible, and then she was overjoyed. Everybody loved Tony Pringle; he was charming and handsome, and he could make you feel like the most important person in the world. He could also make you feel as if you mattered so little to him that he could brush you aside in favour of a new car, a new venture – in fact, anything new. I understood this fairly quickly, but was hugely surprised when he said we should get married. There was no romantic proposal and I later found out that his mother had talked him into it. It also coincided with my father's business taking off in a big way. Tony, having worked at the factory for a few months, probably had his eye on the bigger picture.

I wasn't even sure if I wanted to marry him, but I wanted my baby. From the beginning I felt a fierce protectiveness towards the little seedling growing inside me. Maybe I just wanted to be a better mother than my own had been. When I voiced my concerns about marrying Tony, my mother had looked at me with a sense of disbelief. She did ask if Tony had forced himself on me and I said he was persuasive but that I hadn't really said no. She made it clear without ever saying it that I was lucky he'd agreed to stick by me; plain, sturdy Evelyn. So, like with most things in my life, I went along with it: my mother's whirlwind of wedding plans and my strained relationship with my future mother-in-law, who admitted she talked Tony into the marriage but still seemed to treat me as some sort of pariah who had stolen her son.

It's this that's on my mind as we gather in reception and Cynthia begins to organise everyone, dishing out jobs for us all. And we all just stand there and let her.

'So, there are thirty-eight guests and four members of staff,' she says.

Everyone is gathered around, hanging off her every word. Well, everyone apart from Barry and his wife, who I now know is called Brenda. They've scuttled off to their room, unsurprisingly, leaving an air of disgust in their wake. It feels like only yesterday that I might have done the same. It is only yesterday, and I still want to do the same.

'Better ratio than a primary school classroom,' Cynthia continues. 'Look, I suggest that the first thing we do is get in the bar and have a drink. Now, I'm not advocating stealing, so we'll account for all the drinks and pay on departure.'

'I think that as we've been put in the worst rooms in the hotel and the staff have all cleared off, we should do whatever we like,' I say, and watch as all eyes turn to me in surprise.

'Well, yes, but I'll leave a notepad on the bar; just jot down whatever you have,' Cynthia continues. 'Have you worked *behind* the bar before, Liam? I know you're a dab hand at serving in front of it.'

'I've never been allowed before. I think it's because I'm only sixteen. Mr Jackson liked to use older members of staff, but I think I'm legally allowed to serve alcohol.'

'I think that as the manager has jumped ship, we can all do whatever we want, like Evelyn says. It'll be like we're having our own little private party,' she says. 'But only if you're comfortable with it?'

'Yes, ma'am,' he replies in a terrible American accent, and then he touches his fingers to his forehead with a mock salute before disappearing.

'Right, everyone, go and help yourselves and we'll join you in a moment.'

We watch them all disappear like happy sheep until it's just Joy, Alan, Cynthia and me left in reception.

'Is this OK, Alan?' Cynthia asks, a little late in my opinion. After all, Alan *is* a representative of the coach company.

'Fill your boots. I'd say this is unprecedented circumstances,' Alan says. The Get Go have shown little consideration to you all and have made it clear that, mostly, they just want the coach back in one piece. You know, we could try and change the ferry booking and go home if that's what you all want? Although, the chances of getting a ferry this afternoon are almost zero and they don't run tomorrow.'

'I could put it to a vote I suppose,' Cynthia says.

'I vote no,' says Joy, so quickly, her words come out like a bullet from a gun.

'My vote would be no, too,' says Cynthia, and they both turn to look at me.

My immediate reaction is to say, let's just go home, but there is only one reason I came here, and so far that matter remains unresolved.

'Reluctantly, my vote is also no,' I say, and earn a broad smile from Cynthia.

'Right,' Alan says. 'You go and ask the others, but be clear it may not be possible, and in the meantime, what can I do?' he says.

'You can fetch the rest of the Christmas decorations,' Cynthia says. 'Then you and Joy are going to decorate the dining room, if you don't mind. I for one don't intend to eat my Christmas dinner without a tree.'

'What Christmas dinner?' I ask, remembering that we only have three teenagers to cook it, and that's if they plan on staying. I'm not sure the vote extends to them. They could just leave. I wouldn't blame them if they went home. I'm still a little tempted myself.

'The Christmas dinner that *we* are going to cook,' Cynthia says, and honestly, I don't even see it coming.

Of all the things I expected to happen on this coach trip, I didn't once envisage working in a hotel kitchen prepping turkey for thirty-eight guests - thirty-six of which voted to stay. Brenda and Brian began to make noises about leaving and Alan did offer to take them back to Fishbourne for the ferry — as it turned out they could take two foot passengers — but once they realised they'd be on their own the other side, they quickly and grudgingly changed their minds. So,

I'm in the kitchen and surprisingly, I'm enjoying myself. Liam is beside me exhibiting excellent knife skills as he liberates each bird from its limbs.

'It'll cook quicker and save a lot of time on the carving,' he tells me as if I'd never cooked a turkey before in my life, but I just smile at his enthusiasm.

He tells me he's studying food tech for GCSE, whatever food tech is. I assume it's a modern version of the home economics all the girls had to learn when I was at school.

'All we learned was how to sew and make our own aprons, how to lay a pristine table for dinner parties and how to make the perfect custard. Also, I remember being told always to wash up with one hand in the water and to use the other for momentum like some sort of odd hula-hooping exercise. I think it was a move designed to help keep our waists trim.'

'Jesus,' he says. 'What a waste of your time! We learn about the science behind food and ultimately, the skills that will enable us to go further in our catering career. I might have read that on my course sheet. I'm hoping to get into college in Newport. It's the only one on the island that does hospitality and catering, and it's OK. I had a look online at Leith's School of Food and Wine in London, but it's a bit out of my league,' he says with a resigned air to his words. 'I certainly won't be learning how to sew an apron or wash up one-handed.' He laughs now. 'I'd love to apply to *MasterChef* one day,' he says seriously, looking a little embarrassed. 'You know, the TV programme?' He lowers his head and attacks the meat with more gusto.

'I know it,' I say. 'I remember when Loyd Grossman used

to present it. They didn't go into fancy restaurants then. Everything was done under old-fashioned studio lights.'

'I don't know who that is,' he says. 'But I'd love to give it a shot, maybe one day.'

'You should,' I say, turning to him and laying my knife on the counter. 'Don't let anyone stop you from achieving what you want.'

'That's very profound, Mrs P,' he mumbles before reaching for a tray to place the turkey in. When he's covered it, he turns back to face me, composed now. 'Thank you, though; I'll remember that.'

He puts his hand up in a high-five gesture, which I've seen Carol's grandchildren do, and grins when my hand meets his. Then we both turn back to the matter in hand, a little embarrassed by the encounter, but I feel a fire in my belly that I haven't felt in years and I can't keep the small smile from my lips.

Later, once the Christmas dinner preparations are done and the dining room is decorated, Alan suggests going into town to get fish and chips for everyone. His proposal is met with an unexpected round of applause and a couple of people offer to go with him to collect it. We all agree to eat out of the paper to save washing-up and decide the bar is cosier than the dining room.

Once the men leave, Liam catches up with me by the lifts and pushes a key into my hand.

'Room four,' he says with a grin. 'One of the best rooms in the hotel. I've moved everyone who wants to, but I kept this one back for you. Do you want me to help you with your stuff?'

I'm actually no longer that bothered about moving

rooms, but he's so enthusiastic, and clearly enjoying being in charge, that I decide to go with it. I push aside the fact that I'm exhausted and follow him to my room, where he waits patiently while I shove all of my things back into my suitcase.

'It's a great room, much bigger than this, and the bed is huge,' he says as I try to push my toiletry bag into the side pocket of my case. 'It also has a much better view of the sea.'

The bag doesn't really fit and as I pull it back out, the letter comes with it. It falls to the floor like the dead weight it is, landing face up on the carpet. I bend to retrieve it, mortified the offending article is out in the open, but Liam is quicker and he hands it to me.

'There you go,' he says, giving it a brief look.

I don't mean to, but I snatch it from him. Even though I'm the only one who's read the contents, I feel sick; sick of it. Liam looks taken aback as I shove it into my bag, but he doesn't say anything and neither do I until we've left the room and he's pulling my suitcase back along the corridor.

'How long have you worked here?' I ask as we make our way, trying to get back to that natural easiness that was between us before.

'Just a year; kitchen duty, mainly, bit of gardening in the summer, but you can tell the whole place is mostly neglected. The reviews aren't great now. I don't like to be part of somewhere that's failing. It's for sale, you know, and I'd be interested to see what the new owners do with it, but I'll have to find somewhere else to work before I go to college. This was convenient, but not any more.'

We reach my new room and Liam takes great delight

in swinging the door open with a *ta-da*. It is a nicer room. For a start, it's warmer, in the main part of the hotel, and the soft furnishings look less threadbare, although anything would look plush after the previous room, to be fair. The curtains don't hang like limp dishcloths and the bed doesn't give me cause for concern. I doubt I might die in the night after being impaled on an old spring.

He's right about the view – the snowstorm has passed over and the sky is clear. The stars seem brighter here than they do at home, perhaps something to do with less light pollution. They're more visible, or maybe it's because I'm actually looking. The near-full moon casts an eerie glow on the surface of the sea and it moves as one huge iridescent mass.

Liam leaves me to unpack, the letter once again forgotten.

'God, I'm stuffed,' says Cynthia as the last of the fish and chip paper is pushed into bin liners.

We're all together in the bar and plenty of alcohol has been consumed, again. Now, tucked back in the corner, I get the sense that Cynthia wants to start asking questions again. I brace myself for the onslaught, but it seems that Joy is the target tonight.

'So, tell us more about your husband,' Cynthia says, and I wince at her directness.

Joy looks up warily, but the alcohol has softened her defences. I wonder if I should try to help her, keep her safe from the clutches of Cynthia's nosey mind, but then perhaps she does want to share some of her story. Perhaps I want to hear it.

'What do you want to know?' she asks.

'Well, how did you meet, what's he like, what went wrong?'

Cynthia really is on a mission and I expect Joy to clam up, but she seems to ready herself and then tells us.

'He was a customer in my restaurant, that's where we met,' she starts before being quickly interrupted by Cynthia.

'You had restaurant? Wow, I'm impressed,' she says. 'To think I've got you putting up Christmas decorations – I could use you in my kitchen.'

I roll my eyes at her words. She really has got some grand notions.

'Yes, a small French restaurant in Bristol where I was living at the time. It was a successful venture, probably my only achievement in all of my adult life.'

'Surely that's not true,' Cynthia chips in again.

'No, it really is, to this day,' Joy says brightly, too brightly.

Her eyes have taken on an unnatural glassiness and her tone is too upbeat for this conversation.

'What happened to your restaurant?' I ask.

'Oh, it sort of got in the way of my marriage and I gave it up. I decided I was spending too much time there, giving it all of my energy, and I hardly had anything left for home. Patrick, my husband, suggested I sold it so I could relax more and we could do things together. I put it on the market. I honestly didn't think I'd sell it so quickly, wondered if I might have a bit longer there, but we had an offer we could hardly refuse. We packed up and moved to Reading. It all worked out for the best in the end. It was the right thing for me to do.'

'That's awful, having to give up your business like that.

You must have found that very hard at the time,' Cynthia says.

'*Choosing* to give up my business. I got over it,' Joy says, draining her gin and tonic, the ice cubes performing a lonely rattle at the bottom of the glass. 'I was married – compromises have to be made.'

There's a matter-of-factness to her voice that doesn't quite hit the mark.

Cynthia gives me a quick glance, her expression unreadable. I can't help but think she's trying to impart something to me, but goodness knows what it is.

'Anyway, my marriage is over now and I'm looking to make a new start.'

'Good for you,' says Cynthia, raising her own glass.

There's an awkward silence for a few moments between us, as if an untruth has been released into the air above and no one wants to acknowledge it. I don't know whose it is – Joy's, Cynthia's or my own. Eventually, Joy excuses herself to go to the loo and as soon as she does, Cynthia pounces on me.

'Half of that is bullshit,' she says, and I'm surprised by her tone.

'What do you mean?'

'He *made* Joy give up her restaurant. That makes me so angry. Compromises have to be made? Give me a break! Don't hear the husband making any himself.'

'We don't really know that, do we? Perhaps she did want to.'

'Were you listening to the same conversation as me? He wasn't getting enough attention, that's the bottom line.'

'Well, maybe that is the case, but it's a long time ago now.

And Joy has left him. Perhaps she doesn't want the past dragged up. She might want to let sleeping dogs lie.'

'Like you, you mean?'

Cynthia's anger on Joy's behalf still simmers. I can see a vein pulsing in her neck.

'Evelyn, your husband ran over a cyclist, killed him and drove off. You want to track down the wife of that man and give her a piece of your mind for stealing your husband. You want answers – justifiably so, in my opinion. Why should Joy just accept and move on?'

Cynthia's accent seems to travel back up the country when she's had a drink, or if she gets particularly animated.

I sit back in my seat and study my hands in my lap, stare at the rings that have been on my fingers for fifty-eight years. Cynthia takes a gulp of her drink across the table from me.

'Sorry,' she says. 'I can get a bit carried away, can't I?'

'Yes, you can. It's different for Joy than it is for me. She knows what happened in her past, good or bad. Maybe leaving her husband is her recognising his faults and moving on. It's not for us to be angry on her behalf. I'm still trying to piece mine together.'

'You're right. I just get so irritated when people don't treasure what they have while they have it. I'm sorry if I upset you.'

'You haven't, but, do you know, I've been so centred on making sure this woman, Margaret, finds out about Tony's crime, I'd lost sight of the crime itself, and the poor man who died. What a mess.'

We sit in silence for a moment until Cynthia speaks.

'Did you never suspect anything? I mean, Tony and this other woman?'

'I knew Tony had another life without me – the same as I had a life without him. I didn't think further about it.'

She looks at me thoughtfully.

'Did you? Did you have a life without him?' she says gently.

I look up at her, surprised. Of course I had a life without him. What does she think I've been doing for all these years? And then it hits me, like a shard of something icy in my heart. Who am I? What *have* I been doing for all these years? It's a wild question that I don't think I've ever considered before and I'm not sure I'll be considering it now. I already know that the answer will be unsatisfactory.

Chapter Thirteen

Christmas!

Christmas morning and I wake with an ache in my chest and a longing for my son. It's such a physical pain that I have to lie still for a while until my breathing returns to normal. Time hasn't dulled the pain – I've just learned to wait for it to pass, to continue pretending that all is well.

My mother insisted we covered up the dates so it looked as if the baby came early rather than the fact I was pregnant when we got married. What a stupid, pointless façade we were all keeping up, and for what? Nobody believed us. Once he was born, I didn't care what people thought and anyway, they moved on to the next disgrace, the next scandal.

Stephen was my absolute joy. He was perfection and I was instantly smitten. Tony marvelled at me for a full twenty-four hours, the way that men seemed programmed to do after you produce a child, especially a son. It didn't last, of course. Life between us continued as before, but I didn't mind. I had my boy and that was honestly all that mattered.

I stare at the ceiling and force my mind to slip to other

things. It's Christmas Day and I don't want to entertain any more dark thoughts. I pull back the covers and wearily ease my legs out of bed.

Cynthia is in her element when I find her in the kitchen. She's wearing something close to an evening gown in midnight blue velvet and I'm thankful she had the foresight to cover it with an apron. Liam and one of the girls, Fiona, I think her name is, are there with her, both looking mildly terrified as she gives them their orders.

'Merry Christmas,' I call from the safety of the doorway, and Cynthia looks up at me over the top of her pink glasses.

She waves what looks like another list at me and I take an instinctive step back.

'Merry Christmas, Evelyn,' she says. 'I have fabulous news.'

She leaves the others putting sausages onto baking trays and walks towards me. Taking my arm, she pulls me away from the kitchen and once we're out of earshot, she begins.

'I've just heard the most amazing news from Liam. He told me that this place is for sale. I just looked it up online and you know what?' Her face is as lit up as the Christmas tree beside her. 'I'm going to buy it.'

'What? I didn't know you were interested in buying a hotel.' This is truly the last thing I was expecting her to say.

'I wasn't until I heard about this place. Just think what I could do with it. It could be amazing... well, once I've ripped down all those awful extensions and restored it to its former glory. There are lots of pictures of it online over the years. I'm going to make it great again.'

She's so animated, I don't want to bring her down from her cloud, but it seems so sudden and such a big thing to undertake. I tell her so.

'I hear you, Evelyn, I really do,' she says, but I'm not sure she really does. 'I've been looking for something since, well, for a while, and I think that this could be just the thing. I do need something in my life and this could be it.'

'Couldn't you get a dog?' I suggest, and Cynthia lifts her eyes towards the ceiling.

'I want a challenge, not a pet. I'm quite determined.'

'I don't doubt it,' I say. 'I suppose you won't be able to do anything about it until after the Christmas break, though. The agents won't be open, will they?' Perhaps by the time they reopen, she might have found some of her lost marbles.

'I sent a personal email this morning to the agent and they replied. I think he was surprised to receive an enquiry about it, to be honest. I was surprised they answered. I mean, who looks at their work emails on Christmas Day?'

'Desperate people,' I murmur, but she's not really listening.

'I think it's been on the market for a while. We've got a meeting before we leave on the 27th, in the morning, here.' She almost sings the words out to me, she's so excited.

'Goodness, no one could accuse you of procrastination,' I say.

'Right, we need to get going; we have so much to do. Where's Joy? Have you seen her this morning?'

'No, I got up and came straight down.'

'Come on, then, let's go and get her. I can't wait for her to hear my news.'

I don't really know why I feel such a sense of trepidation as we approach Joy's room, but I do. When Cynthia knocks on the door, I hold my breath, but Joy opens it relatively quickly and if she's faking her smile, it's a good one.

'Happy Christmas,' she says, pulling the door wider to allow us inside.

The room is a mirror image of my own, with similar furniture and identical curtains. Cynthia immediately sits down on the bed and proceeds to tell Joy about buying the hotel.

'Now I know you had a restaurant, I shall be looking to you for advice,' Cynthia says.

Joy looks momentarily stunned as if she can't believe Cynthia would consider such a purchase, but I then wonder if it's because she's forgotten how much she confided in us both last night. By the look on her face, it's all coming back to her.

It's a team effort to breakfast the thirty-eight guests and four staff members, including Alan. I notice that Joy seems to be avoiding him today and he looks a little upset. After we clear away the breakfast things, I decide to disappear to my room for a short while to phone Carol. It's with some reluctance that I pull my phone from my suitcase, though, but I forgot to phone her yesterday and I can hardly ignore my sister on Christmas Day.

'Hello, Carol,' I say when she answers. 'Merry Christmas.'

There's a beat of silence and I imagine her trying to decide how to play the conversation. She's probably secretly pleased that I'm not another of her house guests, she really has enough to do with all of her own family, but she still enjoys letting me know I've in some way inconvenienced her. There is truly no way to win with Carol. What I don't expect is to hear relief in my sister's voice.

'Evelyn! I've been so worried about you. Why didn't you call to let me know you'd arrived safely? I've been phoning you, but I assume you've had your phone switched off as usual.'

It makes me smile, the way she launches straight into admonishments, and I'm surprised as a wave of emotion takes me. I feel a very long way from home all of a sudden. I begin to tell her about the shabby hotel and how the manager and staff have walked out. She isn't impressed, even when I tell her about how Cynthia has us all organised with the food and Christmas decorations.

'It sounds to me like they're taking advantage of you. I don't even really know why you're on the Isle of Wight,' Carol continues. 'It's not like you to be impulsive and go off with no reason, and at Christmas, too. Perhaps you need to see someone, a grief counsellor or something.'

'I did have a reason for coming here, actually,' I find myself saying, and then stop. I could tell Carol I was lonely and didn't want to spend Christmas by myself, but she'd remind me that she'd invited me to stay with them. I could tell her I didn't want to be around anyone I knew or sit at home on my own, and that makes me think of Cynthia, for some reason. But I don't say either of those things. 'I found a letter in Tony's drawer,' I say instead.

'What letter?' Carol asks quickly, and it's there in the tone of her voice. I think she knows something.

'Is there something you're not telling me?' I ask her. 'Because it's a bit late for games, Carol.'

'What's in the letter?' she asks again, ignoring my question.

I get up from the bed, reach underneath for my case and take the letter from the pocket.

'I can read it to you, but maybe you've heard it before…'

'No, of course I haven't,' she snaps. 'I don't know anything about a letter, but I did think that Tony wasn't always entirely honest with you.'

I think about that for a moment, because my sister has never said anything like this to me before.

'Did you like Tony?' I ask, and there's a lengthy silence on the other end.

'I didn't dislike him, I suppose, but I think you'd have been better suited to someone kinder.'

'You once said he was my rock.'

'Did I?' she says. 'Maybe I meant it was better the devil you know.'

'That's just it, though. I didn't really know him at all. I'll read it to you.' I unfold the paper and sit back down on the bed.

My dearest darling Maggie,

I have something I want to tell you, something I need to tell you, but it's going to be as hard for you to hear it as it is for me to write it. Before I get too deeply into it, though, I first want you to know one thing. That is, how much I love you. You are truly the most wonderful woman I know and I can honestly say I've never felt as passionately about anyone as I do you. People use words like love and desire a lot, but I know they don't have even a millionth of what we share. I know you feel the same way, otherwise you wouldn't have agreed to spend the rest of your life with me, in whatever way we can.

And now to the situation that's been hanging over my head for a while. It's to do with your late husband

and I know you told me you didn't have the sort of relationship with him that you do with me, but I still think you may feel differently when you hear. I can't bear the thought of losing you, but I also can't live with this interminable guilt.

It was me. I was the unfortunate person who was driving the day he cycled out of that side lane without looking properly.

There, I've finally said it.

While you rage against the truth of this, please know that it was entirely accidental. There was nothing I could have done about it. I stopped, please know that I did that at least, but he was already dead and there was no more I could do for him. I panicked and fled the scene, which will haunt me forever.

And there's something else, too. The way in which we met. It wasn't the chance encounter you thought. I came to find you. I'd been riddled with guilt and wanted to see how I could make amends. I certainly didn't expect to fall in love with you, or you me, but of course, we did.

So there's the truth laid out before you and if I'm brave enough to send this to you, I'll finally know if you can forgive me.

Yours always,
Tony

'Bloody hell, Evelyn,' Carol says on the other end of the phone.

She clearly didn't know about the letter.

'And that's why you're there, on the island?' she continues.

'He was on his way to her with a ring when he died. I found the address in the back of his road atlas. She never got to read the letter because he didn't send it. He obviously decided to carry on the deceit. Perhaps he thought she'd go back on her decision to spend the rest of her life with him. Didn't get very long, did they!'

'What?' Carol says. 'No, Eve, that's not right, that makes no sense.'

'What do you mean? It's all there in black and white in his own hand,' I say, and listen to her big sigh down the line.

'I don't know what Tony was doing or where he was going when he died, but what I do know is that I saw him once with a woman he called Maggie. It was in Windsor. I'd gone to the theatre with a friend and you can imagine his surprise when we bumped into each other. He later told me that it was just a fling and he was sorry about it. He didn't want you to know; you weren't yourself and he didn't want to upset you further. I agonised over telling you, but I thought it might be too much for you to hear. He promised me he'd stop seeing her. He said she was nobody, that it meant nothing.'

'Well, it clearly didn't mean nothing, did it!' I shout. 'His letter proves that point very well indeed. I can't believe you didn't tell me about it. That's unforgivable. And when was this, Carol? When did you see him with this woman? Because quite frankly, I haven't been myself for fifty-one years!'

There's an ominous silence on the end of the phone and I begin to wonder if we've been cut off.

'It was in 1976,' she says finally.

Chapter Fourteen

Liam's Mum

In the kitchen, everything is in chaos. Fiona and Hayley, the other waitress, are heaving trays of potatoes into the oven, Alan and Joy are juggling vegetables, and Cynthia and Liam are dealing with carving all that turkey we prepared yesterday. I can't bear to be in a room with such hectic energy and the heat is overwhelming.

'I'm going to lay the tables,' I mumble, and without waiting for a response, walk out of the room.

I find tablecloths in the linen cupboard, which has been left open for us to take towels and toiletries from. We've had to help ourselves to everything. Cutlery I find in the long, low cupboards that run the length of the dining room, and as we've decided to make Christmas dinner a serve-yourself event, I leave the knives and forks with the plates on a table in the corner. I wonder briefly if this is a mistake, as the table is rather close to the other Christmas tree Alan and Joy found. It's not in much better shape than the one in reception and surely would only take a drunken nudge to topple it. I contemplate moving the table but can't be bothered to remove all the plates, so instead I decide to leave it to chance. People will just have to be careful.

Glasses I take from behind the bar and leave on a separate table. We've already got white wine in the large kitchen fridge and the red is open, *breathing*, Liam said, which at the time made me smile. There are boxes of Christmas crackers tucked right at the back where the little bottles of mixers are stored. A little dusty, but I can't imagine the gifts or jokes inside will have expiry dates. I drag them out and begin to count them, and then I give up. If there aren't enough, tough luck.

Straightening up, I walk over to the bay window and watch the snow as it continues to fall. It hasn't stopped since we got back yesterday and is layering up on what was already there. It makes the view more appealing, not being able to see the potholes in the car park and the rubbish in the borders. I lift a finger to the pane and draw four numbers in the condensation on the glass: 1976. What was I doing in 1976?

We'd been married for twelve years then, which means it was five years of not having Stephen and the wound had been just as raw as it had been five years before. I wouldn't let Tony anywhere near me; the thought of him touching me in any way terrified me. I couldn't bear the idea of having another child, but the grief was crippling.

I was taking treatment for depression and had been asked to step down from the school. I wasn't officially dismissed, but I couldn't work with the children any longer. I was apparently becoming too attached to some of them, being too emotional in school, and the parents had begun to complain. Had it been too much for Tony? Did he choose another life for himself while still clinging on to the one he already had? I wished I could ask him – the letter only tells one half of the story.

I'm desperately fighting the urge to go back to my room and crawl underneath the covers. Instead, I pick up a wine glass and walk to the bar. I pour a large measure and knock it back in one go. Heat sears down my throat and fires up my insides. A wave of nausea takes me for a moment and I hold on to the bar until it passes. Closing my eyes, I wait for the alcohol to hit my system and when it does, when I can feel my limbs loosening and jaw softening, I pour myself another.

'Hello?'

Voices call from reception and when I look through the doorway, there are three women and two men standing there, stamping snow from their boots and pulling their arms from their coats. They're all wearing colourful Christmas jumpers; an array of fluff and sparkle, and both of the men have Santa hats on. Good grief!

'Yes,' I say tentatively. 'Can I help you?'

The wine has softened the edges of my words on my empty stomach and I wish I hadn't spoken.

'We're Fiona's parents,' says one of the women, touching the arm of the man standing next to her. I could have guessed as much. Fiona and her mother both have the same auburn hair.

'Hayley's parents,' the other woman says and her husband gives a little wave.

'I guess Liam's mine then,' says a petite woman, on her own, with a warm smile.

One of the dads steps forwards as if to shake my hand and without thinking, I take a step back. I'd forgotten that we'd offered to invite them so they could spend some of Christmas Day with their children.

'OK, I'll just get someone,' I say, and rush off towards the kitchen to find Cynthia.

I don't want to make small talk with these people – that's her forte.

The chaos has calmed a bit in the kitchen and things seem under control.

'The parents have arrived,' I hiss at Cynthia.

'Well, offer them a drink and go and talk to them,' she says, turning to look at me, brandishing a roll of tinfoil.

I still have the second glass of wine in my hand and Cynthia eyes it.

'Starting early, and without me?'

I ignore her question. 'Do I have to? I'm not very good at small talk.'

'I'll go,' says Liam, wiping his hands on the towel tucked into his apron.

He disappears out of the room and Cynthia hands me a wooden spoon.

'Can you stir the gravy, then, while you're enjoying your tipple,' she says.

Tipple? If I finish this glass, I shall probably be drunk.

Cynthia taps a fork against the side of her glass and the sound rings out across the dining room, cutting through the chatter.

'I want to thank everyone for all they've done today,' she says as she surveys the room.

Her eyes sweep the guests as if checking to see she has everyone's attention. She's queen of her castle, with a paper crown and an audience, completely in her element. I realise my thoughts are a little churlish, but I want to say to her, *It was just Christmas dinner, you know*.

'Thank you to the parents,' she continues. 'Not only for coming to join us today, but also for raising such fine and hard-working people. They're a credit to you.'

I look across at where Liam, his mum, and Fiona and Hayley's parents are sitting. Cynthia's speech is over the top as far as I'm concerned, but they all seem to be lapping up the praise. To be thanked for being a good parent – what a thing. Reaching for my glass, I find it empty and the bottle is too far away, so I press my hands into my lap and wait for Cynthia to finish.

The parents all seem content in each other's company; perhaps they're friends. I suppose this isn't such a big island, after all. Liam's mum is petite with wispy blonde hair, and I register that her son must get his height and thick dark curls from his father. I watch them for a moment, how easy they are with each other, how they smile and share conspiratorial looks. It makes my heart hurt.

Cynthia finally finishes speaking and there's a short round of applause.

'The Queen's Speech!' calls Alan from his seat next to Joy, who elbows him in the arm.

'I know Cynthia goes on a bit, but she's hardly up to Her Majesty's standard.'

This is from Barry, who's the only one who chuckles at his own joke, and even Brenda looks a bit taken aback. Personally, I think it's tame for him.

'No, I mean it's nearly three. We should listen to the Queen's Speech,' Alan says. 'Let's go into the bar and put the telly on.'

People are starting to move now and I decide to gather plates, begin to clear up. I didn't do as much as the others to get this meal to the table and the idea of hiding in the kitchen with the washing-up appeals. I have no wish to hear any more speeches today. As they all move off with their paper crowns askew, weave their way towards the bar, I collect the plates either side of me and pick up a half-finished bottle of wine. No one seems to notice.

The kitchen is a disaster and there's a tiny moment where I contemplate leaving it and swapping my hiding place for my bedroom. Guilt stops me, though – and the idea of being alone and idle with my thoughts. They're a whisker away from spiralling out of control. I turn on the radio that sits on the windowsill and find some classic Christmas music. After pouring a fair measure of wine, I set to work.

I scrape plates into the food waste and plunge the crockery into scalding water. I go at the baking dishes with scouring pads and scrub cutlery until it shines. I try really hard not to imagine that it's Tony under the burning water that I'm annihilating. I manage about half an hour of this manic cleaning before I'm interrupted.

'Party for one?'

Cynthia appears in the doorway with Liam and his mum just a step behind her. My solitude is broken and I have to force a smile to my lips.

'I was just telling Liam's mum about my plans for the place and saying that he's welcome to carry on working here when I officially become the owner.'

I stifle a sigh. It seems impossible that she only heard about the opportunity this morning. I can't be the only one fed up with hearing about her plans for the hotel.

'Well,' she continues with a curiously direct look at me. 'Meet Liam's mum… Sarah.'

It takes me a moment to comprehend the look and Cynthia's meaning, and then it hits – Sarah. Of course it's probably just a complete coincidence. It's only a name, after all.

'They live just down the road, near the sea, in East Street.'

My mouth has dried up and when I attempt to swallow, it comes with an audible gulp. Luckily, Sarah either doesn't notice or is just too polite to show her surprise at my witless behaviour. She steps forwards and I raise my hand like a robot, just in time for her to take it, to shake it.

'It's lovely to meet you,' she says. 'And it's so nice of you all to take such trouble with lunch. I was trying to get Liam to come home, forget the place entirely. He has no obligation to the management – they certainly didn't think twice about him or the other two when they abandoned ship – and I've got a few choice words I wouldn't mind sharing with them.'

'I couldn't agree more,' Cynthia chips in. 'So unprofessional.'

'I'm glad now, though, that he talked me into letting him stay on. I think it's been a great experience for him, thanks to you ladies and all of your hard work.'

'We should be thanking you! Liam is an absolute credit to you.'

'That's so kind of you to say,' Sarah says, sliding an arm around her son and drawing him towards her.

He just grins knowingly, not remotely embarrassed by her display of affection.

'Right, well, good luck to you, Cynthia. Hope it all goes well. I'm sure you'll make a great success of it.'

And then they're gone. And I just stand there, mute, watching the woman who's home I broke into, the daughter of my husband's lover, walk out of the door. I reach over to turn off the radio and finish the washing-up in silent thought.

Upstairs, I make a cup of coffee and settle back on the bed with the letter. I read it again, but this time with fresh eyes and the knowledge that it was written, not recently, but many, many years ago. I search my brain for a time when Tony must have had the accident that killed Margaret's husband, but all I can think about is that he instigated a meeting with her because of his guilt. What sort of a person would do that? An arrogant one, I assume: Tony.

I can picture him trying to make amends for his crime, because it was a crime; leaving the scene of the accident, failing to phone the police or for an ambulance. He might have been sentenced for dangerous driving. Maybe he was drunk and it wasn't quite the accident he suggests. Then I remember his car, years ago, with a dented bonnet. He told me he hit a concrete post in a car park, or something like that, and I believed him. More likely, I wasn't really listening to him. How could a concrete post cause a dent on top of the bonnet?

He told me he took the car to a garage to be fixed but the garage owner offered to buy it from him. He came back with a completely different car. And I just accepted everything he told me. And the reason I did that was because I didn't care.

I had no interest in Tony and what he did. For a moment I wonder what it was like for Tony to be married to me.

I pick up my phone and toy with the idea of calling Carol. My fingers hover over the buttons and I imagine telling her what I'm planning to do, ask her what she thinks, but then I put it back on my bedside table. She knew Tony was seeing someone and she didn't tell me. How can I speak to her after that admission? I should be furious with her, but honestly, I don't even seem to have the energy to muster that up.

And what about Sarah? The thought has been hovering around the periphery of my mind all afternoon. How old is she? Who's her father? Every time I try to conjure an image of her, it slips away. All I can remember is her fair hair and slight frame, neither of which says Tony Pringle.

What I do know, though, is that I won't be able to leave the island now without talking to her. Yesterday, when she was just a faceless name, I may have been able to return home and cease to wonder about her and Margaret, what their true connection to Tony had been, shut it tight in a box with all of my other unwanted thoughts, but not now. Now that I've met her – and I have to assume that she is the resident of forty-eight East Street and that it isn't just a coincidence – I have to follow it up. I don't really have any other choice.

Chapter Fifteen

St Mary's Hospital

When I wake on Boxing Day it's to the sound of rain pattering against the window and running off the flat roof below. I pull back the curtain and see that the snow is disappearing fast. The lawn is becoming visible again and the untidy borders, too. Everything looks tatty without the snow to cover it in its pristine blanket. It feels like Christmas is over and then I remember that tomorrow we go home. It's that thought that galvanises me. I came here for a reason and so far, nothing is resolved.

I have a quick wash and clean my teeth. I dress in my navy trousers and grey blouse and secure my gold pendant back around my neck. Joy's deftness with the hot brush is still just about holding on and I brush my hair tentatively so as not to disturb her efforts. I contemplate make-up and decide on just a bit of face powder to take the shine from my skin and a thin sweep of pale pink lipstick. I stare at my reflection in the mirror, turning my head this way and that way until I've seen enough. I don't need to impress anyone. I check my phone, but there's nothing from Carol, of course.

Breakfast is in full swing downstairs and I feel guilty that I haven't contributed. Cynthia waves me away with her hand when I try to apologise.

'Liam and Fiona did most of it. Hayley's not in today. I'm organising a whip-round for them; they've more than deserved it. Why don't you come and get something to eat? There's plenty left and I'm about to tuck in.'

We help ourselves to sausages, bacon, eggs and mushrooms, and take a seat by the window. I stare at my plate, unsure whether I'll be able to eat it. I have butterflies at the thought of going back to the house.

'Where's Joy?' I ask. 'Has she been down?'

'Yes, she popped down earlier, but only for paracetamol. Too much vino yesterday.' Cynthia laughs. 'But then didn't we all. Don't forget the trip to the theatre tonight. Our last night; it's gone too quickly.'

I watch her tuck into her breakfast with fascination. She's gone low-key today, dressed in a simple grey tunic top and leggings, a silver chain around her neck; elegant. Cynthia is someone who enjoys life, it seems, and I suppose I admire her for it. She embraces whatever she's doing with an enviable enthusiasm. The woman who was annoying me on the coach only two days ago is disappearing, or rather, I've become more accepting of her. I think that says more about me than it does about her. Following her lead, I pick up my knife and fork and begin to eat.

'I'm going to the house today,' I tell her between mouthfuls.

'Do you want me to come with you?'

'I think it's best if I do this on my own.'

When I leave the hotel an hour later, the rain has eased, but hasn't stopped, so I push up my umbrella and make my way through the puddles on the driveway and out onto the main road. It's the third time I've made this journey and I'm hoping it'll be the last. A woman walking her dog passes me on the other side of the road when I reach East Street. She calls out a cheery 'Happy Christmas' and I raise a hand in response. And now I'm at the gate again, but I'm far more nervous this time, perhaps even more so than when we broke in.

Checking my watch, I see it's ten thirty – hopefully not too early for a Boxing Day call. I don't want to intrude. Then again, when was the last time I knocked on a stranger's door at Christmas? This will most definitely be a first. And why am I concerned about intruding when I have a letter in my bag that could blow their world apart?

Margaret... this thought comes up fast after I'd so successfully managed to push her name to the back of my mind. I might be meeting her. Perhaps that was where Sarah was on Christmas Eve, picking her mother up, bringing her home. But that can't be right; why didn't Margaret join us for Christmas lunch? And didn't her neighbour say she was staying with a friend? I'm beginning to worry about my hasty breakfast as I swallow hard and step forwards to knock on the door.

As it swings open, I feel as if I've made a terrible mistake. Sarah is standing in front of me and I can't think of a single thing to say.

'Can I help you?' she asks as I lower my umbrella. 'Oh, you're from the hotel, aren't you? Is there a problem? Is it Liam? Is he OK?'

I watch the worry flood the woman's face and finally find my voice.

'Liam is fine as far as I know; this is nothing to do with him,' I say.

The woman smiles tentatively, looks a little bemused.

'What can I do for you, then? Do you want to come in out of the rain?'

She's being so nice, I almost can't bear it. She steps back, allowing me access to her home, and the guilt of having been here already is overwhelming.

'Thank you.' I walk inside, popping my umbrella down, where it begins to drip onto the mat.

We hover awkwardly in her small hallway. She doesn't invite me in any further. She waits. She wants to know what this is about. I take a breath and without knowing what I'm going to say, I begin to speak.

'I know you introduced yourself to me yesterday, but can I just check, you are Sarah, aren't you?'

'Yes, I am,' she says, the confusion giving way to something else, something as yet indefinable.

'May I ask you if your mother is Margaret?'

I watch her eyes narrow further into irritation.

'You can ask, but I'd probably want to know why you were asking,' she says.

'My husband knew someone called Margaret and I wondered if I have the right person.'

'Well, that would depend on who your husband is,' Sarah says with an odd smile, as if this is some kind of game. It must certainly seem that way to her.

'Anthony Pringle,' I say slowly and watch as Sarah's face darkens. Clearly, I have the right Margaret.

'Why are you here? What do you want?' she asks, her tone now tight and controlled.

'I want some answers. Is she here?'

I try to peer over her shoulder towards the living room, the one that only two days ago I was creeping around in the dark.

'I want you to leave. I have nothing to say to you,' she says and leans past me to open the door.

'If she's here, then I have some things I want to say to her.' I try again but I know I sound desperate and possibly deranged. Liam's mum is glaring now as I take a step back over the threshold, out into the rain. 'I just want the truth,' I try one last time, but Sarah has her hand on the door, ready to close it.

'You want the truth? The truth is that Tony Pringle was the worst thing that ever happened to my mum,' she says and slams the door in my face.

As the rain falls steadily down on me, I remember too late that my umbrella is still in her hallway.

The coach is hurtling down the driveway when I get back to the hotel, splashing through puddles as it goes. I step quickly out of its path, glad I'm missing whatever excursion there is today, but Alan pulls up next to me and the door hisses open.

'Evelyn!'

Cynthia appears, looking alert and organised, and I wonder what she has planned now. I intend to get in a bath and get back into bed. This day hasn't gone how I hoped it would and wallowing is all I have on my mind now.

'Joy's had an accident,' Cynthia says, and that does get my attention.

'What happened?' I step up onto the coach and see Joy huddled in her seat with a wet towel over her arm.

'A burn in the kitchen. We're going to the hospital; it looks nasty.'

Alan has closed the door and begun to drive again, and I'm thrown down into a seat.

'Oh, I was just going back to the hotel,' I say.

'No time, sorry.' Alan says. 'We really need to get Joy seen to as soon as possible.'

I do wonder if both Alan and Cynthia are being a little bit melodramatic, but when I glance again at Joy, I see her face is ashen and she looks close to tears.

'I hope you're not in too much pain,' I say.

I'm not very good in a crisis, especially not a medical one. I hope no one asks me to do anything.

Alan takes the turning into the hospital at an alarming speed and I just catch the sign that reads St Mary's in huge blue letters on the building. It looks more like an airport than a hospital. There's a brightly coloured cone on the grass to the side of the building. It's unexpected; I wonder what it's supposed to symbolise.

'We'll get Joy out here, and you can go and find somewhere to park this thing,' says Cynthia.

'Righto. I'll meet you inside as soon as I can.'

Joy gets up, but her reluctance is written in all of her movements. Perhaps she doesn't like being fussed with. Cynthia can certainly take a situation over, but when we get inside and Joy takes the towel away for an initial consultation, I can see that she was right – it does look nasty. Joy begins to whimper as the staff member tries to take down her details and she doesn't seem to be that forthcoming.

'This is all so unnecessary,' she says, but they obviously don't agree and after insisting on Joy's particulars, she gets taken into a cubicle for treatment and we walk back to reception to wait.

This Boxing Day waiting room has the feel of a Monday morning in our surgery. The place is full of people who, to my mind, don't look ill at all. There's a woman in a wheelchair with a cardboard sick bowl in her lap. It's empty and she's having a very animated conversation with the man sitting next to her. One lad has a bandage on his foot, but he's so engrossed in his phone that he doesn't hear his name being called. Others are coughing and some are even asleep. No wonder they took Joy in so promptly – they can obviously recognise a true casualty when they see one.

'How did it go at the house?' Cynthia asks as she lowers herself gingerly onto a plastic chair.

Her knee must be troubling her again.

'Not well at all,' I say, sitting beside her. 'Actually, it was a complete disaster. As soon as I mentioned Anthony Pringle, Sarah threw me out of the house, and I only made it in as far as the hallway.'

'Oh, Evelyn, I'm sorry. At least you know you have the right person.'

'She said that meeting Anthony Pringle was the worst thing that ever happened to her mum and then she shut the door in my face.' Resting my head back against the wall, a weariness overtakes me and I close my eyes for a moment. 'I didn't tell you, but I spoke to my sister yesterday and she said she remembers seeing Tony with a woman called Margaret many years ago. At the time he underplayed it, apparently, said it was a fling, that it meant nothing, that he didn't want me to know and he'd stop seeing her.'

'So it's an old letter then, I assume. It's not likely to be written recently, is it?'

'Not recent, no. I doubt it, anyway. It seems Tony and Margaret have been a thing for a long time, or certainly they were a thing a long time ago.'

This fact cuts a lot deeper than I thought it might. A wave of shame takes me. Shame that I wasn't enough, shame that my husband wasn't enough, either. And then there's the thought of Sarah again, bubbling away inside my head.

'I want to ask you something, but it's a little delicate. Does Sarah look like your husband? Now we know the letter is old, is it possible she could be his daughter?'

I whip my head round at Cynthia's words, her thoughts aligned perfectly with my own.

'I don't know,' I say. 'God, I hope not. I mean, she doesn't look like him, but maybe she takes after her mother. Of course I don't know what Margaret looks like.'

Cynthia pats my hand, which is clenched in my lap.

'You have a sister, then. That's nice – I only have two brothers. I always wanted a sister.'

'She kept it from me. She knew that Tony was seeing someone and she didn't say.'

'Perhaps she really believed him when he said it was over. Maybe she thought she was protecting you by keeping quiet. Sometimes people do the wrong thing for the right reason. You know, you can just leave this all behind tomorrow when we go home. Get rid of the letter, brush it all off and move on.'

'I could do that, of course. I could have not booked this trip, I could have destroyed the letter back at home and pretended that everything was fine, but I didn't. I've spent my life allowing others to tell me how things are, what's going to happen and how I should feel about it, and I've had enough. Sarah holds the truth now, like another gatekeeper, pushing me away. But it's my story, too, and no one's allowing me access to it.'

The anger begins to swell inside me. All that's been taken from me, all I've just had to accept, everything I've allowed to happen to me. It rises in my throat like it's going to choke me.

'I can't just brush this off, Cynthia. Secrets fester, they find a way of creeping into everything that you do – this needs addressing. You should know that as much as anyone.'

'What's that supposed to mean?' she says.

Her look of concern has shifted to surprise and because the anger is still stuck in my throat, I finally say it.

'I heard you on your phone in the service station, pretending to be ill, lying to Helen?'

I regret the words the moment they leave me and pollute the air between us. Only three days ago I might have taken a tiny pleasure from exposing her, but now it's as if I've slapped her hard in the face.

'You don't know what you're talking about, Evelyn,' she says so quietly that I can barely hear her.

I open my mouth to say something, anything to make amends. A strangled sorry just about leaves my lips, when Alan appears, and I'm not even sure if she heard me.

No one has anything to say on the journey back to the hotel and the silence is pronounced in the cavernous space of the coach. Joy has a dressing on her arm, some painkillers and advice about what to do when she gets home. She hasn't uttered a single word since we left the hospital. Perhaps the shock has settled. Cynthia bundles her inside and I meet Liam coming out of the lift as I walk through reception.

'I'm off home, Mrs P,' he says brightly. 'I won't see you before you go tomorrow, so I shall say goodbye now. I hope you enjoy the theatre and meal out later. Oh, and a big thanks for my tip. That's if you contributed, of course.' He laughs, zipping up his coat and pulling his rucksack onto one shoulder.

'Yes, of course I did. You deserve it for not leaving us in the lurch. I wish you all the luck with college. I really hope things go well for you.'

It seems so strange to be having this conversation with him now I know who his mother is, who his grandmother is. I desperately want to know if he met Tony. Did my husband get to play with this young man when he was a boy? In fact, I have so many questions that it's almost a relief when he finally waves and disappears out of the door.

Will Sarah tell him about me turning up on their doorstep and ranting like a madwoman? I really feel as if Liam and I had made a small connection, although I'm not stupid enough to think he's nice to everyone he meets, but he was very kind to me. The thought of him thinking badly of me, on top of my encounter with Cynthia, is too much. That thought I can't bear.

Chapter Sixteen

Sleeping Beauty

I'm in no mood for a visit to the theatre and yet, I manage to rally and troop out of the hotel and back onto the coach with everyone else. In just seventy-two hours I've become part of this group. We've become quite the little club. Unfortunately Cynthia still isn't talking to me, I have a feeling that might be it with her; I don't think she'll speak to me again now. And that is upsetting, because we're going home tomorrow.

Joy has also made the effort and seems to be putting on a brave face, despite her obvious pain.

'It's not that bad,' she says quietly when I ask her how she is. 'I just don't like hospitals, that's all.'

Cynthia steps onto the coach behind me and stands in the aisle for a moment looking in my direction. She's ditched her simple attire now in favour of a dress that probably wouldn't look out of place on the stage tonight. I'm trying not to look, but I'm sure those are pink bows on the sleeves. I have my head turned steadfastly to the window, but I can see her in the reflection. I wonder if maybe I'm wrong and she wants to say something, but before I can turn my head, she pushes her point a step further when she chooses to sit next to Joy. My hot breath mists the window and I can no longer see her or anything else.

The restaurant has a function room attached to the side of it and we move through the busy, buzzing atmosphere of the main restaurant to get to it. It's sterile and a bit chilly, a sort of lean-to conservatory with too many windows. I imagine it's like a greenhouse; cold in the winter and unbearably hot in the summer. There are a couple of blow heaters in the corner and I gravitate in that direction, keeping my coat on regardless.

The whole party seems subdued, and I suspect it's because it's the last night and in less than twenty-four hours, everyone will be back at home. I for one can't wait. This whole Christmas trip hasn't worked out at all. I didn't even want to come in the first place, not really, and I've achieved absolutely nothing.

I take a glance around the table and watch as people fiddle with their cutlery and sip at their drinks in relative silence. It doesn't help that we can see the main restaurant through a window. Family parties enjoying themselves, raising glasses, laughing. Or perhaps it's just because we're all exhausted. It hasn't exactly been a relaxing holiday, doing all our own cooking, being frogmarched around by either Alan or Cynthia. I'm determined to try to enjoy the meal this evening as I haven't had to cook it myself, but when it comes, a pre-booked Christmas dinner, it's not a patch on our own efforts yesterday and I wish I'd thought to have chosen the fish dish instead.

I push a flaccid sausage wrapped in bacon through a smear of congealed gravy and choose something green to spear my fork into. It must have once been a broccoli floret but now closely resembles something you might find floating on a pond. I slide it into my mouth anyway and wash it down with a glug of warm white wine. I'm actually impressed that they've managed to get the wine to this temperature, what with the room feeling like the inside of a fridge. I drink some more. When we get to the theatre, I plan to sink down in my seat and go to sleep.

I can't help it, but my eyes keep drifting to Cynthia. The silence stretches between us across the table like a taut elastic band. It's beginning to annoy me now, but she seems unperturbed, having a muted conversation with Sheila on one side of her and a short tubby man on the other. She refuses to look in my direction. Her silence and cold shoulder is far worse than her usual incessant chatter. I keep my head down and ignore my impulse to call across the table, tell her she's being silly. Cynthia will talk to me when she chooses to, if she chooses to, but if she leaves it too long, I may not be prepared to listen.

Sleeping Beauty is the pantomime at the theatre in Shanklin and my heart sinks when we pull up outside. Any idea of a quiet sleep in my chair disappears at the sight of the razzmatazz that greets us. There are bright lights and a colourful billboard, a person dressed like a circus master handing out programmes, encouraging everyone inside with his booming voice, while Christmas music filters out from a speaker on the pavement. It's going to be awful!

I look around at the faces of the group, filing off the coach behind me, and there's a mix of different levels of excitement. Some shuffle along without much enthusiasm while others seem quite keen; even Joy has managed to muster a smile, despite her injured arm. Then Cynthia climbs down with a face like a smacked backside and it's this that makes me rally. If she's going to be like that, I shall have a nice time, even if I have to pretend.

We make our way up the steps into the theatre and I watch Cynthia struggling. She has a gloved hand on the rail and she's pulling herself up painfully slowly. That's what she should have bought in that gift shop, a bloody walking stick. I move forwards to offer her my arm – despite everything, I don't like to see her in pain – but Alan gets there first. It's probably a good thing, as it wouldn't have been pleasant to hear her turn me down.

There are pre-performance drinks in the foyer and I choose a gin and tonic, hoping it'll help me to enjoy the show. I went to a pantomime once, years ago with Carol and her girls. Tony didn't come and I can't remember where he was. It hits me that I'll probably have to believe that all those moments Tony was absent from our marriage, he'd have been with Margaret. I'm trying to remember if I enjoyed the experience at the theatre before. I'd definitely have railed against the outing.

When I look back and allow myself to remember, I used to do a lot with Carol and her children. I was invited to most events. I always thought it was a way for my sister to show off her perfect family, but was she really just being kind? Was it worth the gloating, inviting someone who you knew didn't really want to be there – sour-faced old Auntie Evelyn? Another wave of shame sweeps through me and I have a sudden longing to speak to my sister, but of course, my phone is switched off, back at the hotel, in my suitcase, and then I remember her deceit. That, I realise, hurts most. Whether I like it or not, Carol is the most important person in my life now, the only person in my life now, and that feels ruined.

There are lots of children buzzing around their parents' legs, darting in and out, desperate to go in and watch the show. It's so lovely to see the excitement on their faces. And then there's the large contingent of pensioners, too – mostly us, of course, from the coach party – and I wonder what it is about pantomimes that elicits such a response from the elderly and the very young. Then I realise it's probably the assumption of a lack of sophistication. I make my way into the auditorium with the others. I feel a trepidation, but I'm sure it's mixed with a little excitement.

We're seated in a block together, but I manage to keep clear of Cynthia. In truth, I'm not bothered who I sit next to, but I'm grateful to the man who introduces himself as Arthur as he pats the seat beside him and I even manage a small smile. There's nothing worse than being the last to be picked. I do wonder if I've made a mistake, though, when he pulls a large bag of chocolate balls from his pocket and proceeds to tuck into handfuls of them with the telltale chomp of his dentures.

I sink into my seat and close my eyes as the lights go down and the curtain goes up. I could easily go to sleep; it's dark enough in here and comfortable. And then the performance begins and any thoughts of sleep are torn from my mind. The stage is dazzling, lit up like Christmas and New Year rolled into one, and that's before the cast walk on. Arthur offers the packet to me and I take a couple, settle

THE SECOND CHANCE HOLIDAY CLUB

back, sighing into the chocolate as I push it into my mouth. The music begins.

By the interval, I'm wiping tears from my eyes and my sides hurt from laughing. My throat is hoarse from shouting at the stage. I can't believe how thoroughly engaged in the whole production I am. Arthur orders us another drink and we go back in. I notice Cynthia looking at me from the queue for the toilets and I offer her a small smile. She quickly looks away, but not before I notice acknowledgement on her face.

We gather back in the foyer after the show and the whole group seems energised. Who would honestly have thought that dressing up in ridiculous outfits, prancing around on a stage and singing silly songs would have us all so engaged? I feel buzzy, and it's not just the two large gin and tonics I've consumed, although that has helped – it's the laughing. Something I haven't done in a long time; laughing until you're crying. Such a fine line between the two.

'Enjoyable, wasn't it?' I say to Cynthia as she tries to get past me.

I'm determined now to be the bigger person, but she doesn't get the chance to respond, because Alan steps up in front of us.

'I've had notification from Wightlink ferries that they've postponed tomorrow's crossing.'

A groan rises from the group and settles over our heads, dampening the joy that had been there only moments before.

'But it's not the end of the world, people. The crossing has just been put back by a few hours. We won't be leaving the hotel until tomorrow afternoon now. It's all to do with the weather and it'll be blowing a gale in the morning.

That's obviously not their official terminology, but you get the idea.

'It does mean that if you have someone picking you up from our final stop, then you'll have to let them know to come for you later. It also means you have a more relaxed morning ahead of you. You can pack at your leisure – that's after you've cooked your own breakfast, of course.'

This instigates a chuckle from most of the party, which a couple of days ago it wouldn't have. I, however, envisage a frosty morning at the hotel followed by an equally chilly coach journey. It does give me an opportunity to go back to speak to Sarah, though. If I try to jump straight in with an apology for this morning, maybe she'll talk to me. One thing I said to Cynthia at the hospital comes back to me: I will get to the bottom of this one way or another.

The hotel seems bleak when we get back and most head into the bar for a nightcap. Joy catches up with me before I step into the lift.

'Evelyn, what's up with Cynthia? She's hardly said a word all evening.'

'I don't know,' I lie. 'Maybe she's sorry to be going home tomorrow.'

'It can't be that. She'll be back here in no time to get started on the renovations.'

'Renovations? I didn't know she was doing anything like that; she's not mentioned it,' I reply innocently.

Joy raises a hand to her mouth in mock outrage.

'Evelyn! I can't keep up with you. Just when I think I have the measure of you, you do or say something funny or surprising.'

We say goodnight and I step into the lift with something

akin to a glow inside me. I can be unexpected, funny, surprising. I have a broad smile on my face as I walk to my room.

Sleep won't come and I toss and turn for ages. The clock on my bedside table is bright, illuminating the whole room, and I stare at the ceiling for long enough to drive me mad. Throwing back the covers, I slide my legs round and sit on the side of the bed. Then I reach underneath and take my phone out of my case. It's too late to call, but I switch it on and try to navigate to the screen that allows me to send a text message. I've never sent one before and it takes me a while to work out how. I push the buttons for Carol's number and begin to tap in the words:

Dear Carol,

I know it's late. I'm coming home tomorrow and would love to see you. Went to a pantomime tonight. Reminded me of you and your girls. I look forward to catching up and sorry for cross words.

Love Evelyn.

Perhaps Carol will think me surprising, funny, unexpected. I think I need her more than I care to admit. I press the button to send and a message pops straight back onto the screen. For a moment I think that Carol has responded, then I read it:

Message sending failed.

Chapter Seventeen

The Calm Before the Storm

All night the wind howls and the window frames rattle as if the storm is trying to get inside. I don't sleep, but instead my mind tumbles in its own little tempest. By the time the small hours limp towards daybreak, I'm finally ready to give in. My body has carved out a comfortable shape on the mattress and my eyes are heavy, but I don't get long. The sounds of the hotel waking up take over from the battering outside. The downside to being in the warmer and more comfortable part of the main hotel means you're privy to most of the goings-on downstairs. Something that Cynthia would be wise to address.

Pushing back the curtains, I can see the waves are wild with white crests and the trees that are already bent over in their exposed location are bowing lower still. The tarpaulin that was covering some gardening equipment below now flaps from the far corner of the lawn, pushed up against the hedge. Alan was absolutely right about the weather and I for one wouldn't want to be on a ferry this morning. But when I consider what else I have planned, I do wonder if a force nine gale in the Solent would be preferable.

I waste time in the shower with a cap over my hair and then spend a lot of time packing my suitcase. Tonight I shall be back at home. I'll have a meal for one in front of the television and then... well, then I shall probably just go to bed.

I begin checking drawers that I haven't used and opening cupboards that I've already cleared. I get down on my hands and knees – a mistake – to check under the bed and then spend an agonising few minutes trying to get back up again. I'm avoiding going down for breakfast and seeing Cynthia, although one of the many things drifting in and out of my thoughts through the night was that I owe her an apology. She wasn't the one being childish – I was. I upset her – I am in the wrong. Unexpected and surprising Evelyn Pringle, who I barely know myself.

I make a coffee from the provisions on the table and tuck into a packet of bourbon biscuits in the dish, forgetting a little late that I'm not that keen on them. Then, when I feel I look respectable enough, I pick up my coat from the bed. I don't take the letter this time. Maybe its presence in my handbag yesterday made me twitchy. I do have the ring, though. Maybe I'll throw it in the sea.

As I reach out my hand towards the door, there's a sudden tapping from the other side and I open it to find Joy.

'Morning,' I say as brightly as I can manage. In truth, I'm just glad it's not Cynthia. 'How's your arm?'

There's the telltale bulge of bandaging underneath her sweater and she seems to keep it tucked close to her body.

'Honestly? It hurts a bit more today than it did yesterday, but I've got some painkillers, so I'll be fine,' she says. 'I'm not looking forwards to the crossing later though. I hope the wind dies down. Don't really want to go home at all to be honest.'

She looks tired, like she had as little sleep as I did last night. Her hair isn't its usual perfect self and she barely has any make-up on. Either she's in a lot more pain than she's letting on, or there's something else bothering her — something other than a rough crossing. But then, there has been something else bothering her this entire trip. She's been in good company with me and Cynthia – there's been something bothering us all.

'This weather will die down, don't worry. If your arm is bad, though, you could go back to the hospital? There's still time before we leave to catch the ferry. I'll go with you, if you like?'

'No,' she cuts in quickly, decidedly. 'I mean, it's not that bad, really, but thank you. Look, I came to tell you that you have a visitor.'

'Do I?' Who on earth would be here to see me? God, I hope it's not Liam, come to tell me to stay away from his mother.

'It's Liam's mum, Sarah. She said she'd like a word, if you have time?' Joy shrugs. 'Looks like she might have saved you a journey,' she says, looking at the coat draped over my arm.

I thought I'd have the walk to prepare what I'm going to say, but now, I'm just going to have to hope something comes to me. Throwing my coat back on the bed, I follow Joy to the lift.

Sarah is sitting at the corner table where, just four nights ago, I also sat and told Cynthia and Joy about Tony. It gives me hope that it might be the perfect place for some kind of confessional. She stands when she sees me approaching and now I'm unsure how to do this. Do we shake hands? Surely we don't hug... In the end, Cynthia's card opponent, Sheila, walks over with some coffee for us and Sarah takes the opportunity to sit back down.

'Thank you,' I say to Sheila, surprised. Then she hovers and I see the true motivation for her kindness – she wants to know what's going on. 'Thank you,' I say again, staring at her until she turns and slowly walks away.

I sink into the chair opposite Sarah and clasp my hands together in my lap.

'Where to begin?' I start and smile, a small welcome gesture. 'I'm sorry I came to your house out of the blue yesterday. It must have been a shock and I wasn't exactly polite.' I take the coffee cup from the table, offering her a chance to respond.

'It was a surprise, to be honest. I thought I was done with Anthony Pringle. You were the last person I expected on my doorstep. I was rude, though, and I'm sorry for that.'

'I realise that one of us needs to start at the beginning, or at least the beginning for us, and for me it starts with Tony's death,' I say and gauge Sarah's reaction.

Judging by how she was when I mentioned his name yesterday, I doubt very much that she's going to break down in tears. She does indeed look fairly straight-faced about the news.

'What happened to him?' she asks without emotion.

'He had a heart attack a couple of months back; he didn't suffer.'

She shrugs at that, as if she couldn't care less whether he suffered or not.

'So, what happened, after he died? What made you come to see me?'

I take a sip of my coffee and realise that Sheila has put sugar in it, and actually I'm glad. Placing the cup back on the table, I decide to be honest.

'He was found in his car on his way to Portsmouth. He had your address and a ticket for the crossing. He also had a ring in his pocket. I didn't know what it all meant, and then I found the name Margaret in with his things and I made a few assumptions. I came to the island to find out the truth.'

It feels good to get the words out. And also embarrassing to think about what my assumptions were. Bigamy, Tony on his way here to propose to Margaret. That ship had long since sailed.

'What sort of a ring?' she asks, of all the things she could ask.

I take it from the side pocket of my handbag and place it on the table in front of her. She doesn't pick it up, but I can see her lip trembling.

Suddenly, we're interrupted by Cynthia and her agent as they walk into the room. Cynthia is expressing her concern about the structure of the building while throwing her arms wide, waving her hands in each and every direction, enjoying being centre stage as usual. And is that a business suit she's wearing? Sarah gets up from her seat.

'I'm just going to pop to the loo,' she says and narrowly misses one of Cynthia's arms in full swing.

'I'll wait for you?' I say, catching her eye, making sure she's coming back.

She nods.

'Sorry, Evelyn, we're interrupting,' Cynthia says as she sweeps past the table.

It's the first thing she's said to me since the hospital and I wonder if she even meant to speak to me or whether it's from habit.

'You know this hotel is a rundown money pit, don't you?' I say to her, but make sure the agent is in earshot.

He's scribbling things down in a notebook, but he looks up at my words.

'I mean, personally I wouldn't touch it with a barge pole, to be honest, but if you're thinking about it, you'd certainly want to get it for a knock-down price. Just think of all the work you'd have to do to get it up to any kind of decent standard.'

Cynthia has her back to the agent and she's looking at me with barely concealed amusement. Her eyes are twinkling and it reminds me that I quite like bossy, happy Cynthia, not that I'd tell her that.

'You have a point,' she says. 'Maybe I'm being too hasty.'

'Well, why don't we go back to where you talked about taking the lower-storey extension down and I'll tell you my idea for a wedding venue,' chips in the agent, and Cynthia sweeps him back out of the room without another glance in my direction.

I pick up the ring from the table and twirl it round, watching the diamonds twinkle. I don't notice Sarah coming back into the room, but when I glance up, she's there watching me.

'They always said you knew about them,' she says, sliding back into her seat, and I place the ring back down. 'Because it sounds now as if maybe you didn't. To be honest, it was one of the things that shocked me most about the whole situation – the thought that you knew and went along with it. I hated you for that.' She looks up at me and shrugs. 'Not that I knew you, of course, and now I realise I only knew what they told me about you.'

I let that wash over me for a moment, feeling a nip of anger biting. That I might have known about them, that I knew and went along with it, that I knew about a crime, an affair... no, not an affair, a whole other life, another family – how horribly distasteful.

'I didn't know anything about them. I still know very little about them.'

'This was my mum's,' Sarah says, picking up the ring from the table. 'I thought it had been stolen when she was in hospital. It didn't occur to me that Tony would have taken it. But I suppose it makes sense, as he was the one who bought it for her.'

The question that had been bubbling inside me evaporates. That's the second time she's called him Tony, not Dad. I desperately want to know if Sarah is Tony's daughter. And yet, as I sit across the table and take in her petite features – her small, pointed nose and slight curved ears just visible where she's tucked her blonde hair – I think, no, she's not Tony's daughter. And there's nothing about Liam that says Tony Pringle, either, and I'm happy about that. One of the worst things Tony could have done to me was to have a child with another woman after losing Stephen, but it's more than that now, I realise. I don't want Liam to have anything to do with Tony Pringle. He has such a quality about him that I'd like to be nothing whatsoever to do with my husband. But I'm concentrating on the wrong thing.

Why would Tony steal Margaret's jewellery? Why was Margaret in hospital?

Guests have started banging about, bringing down their suitcases ready for departure, even though we're not leaving for ages. There's a buzz in the foyer and some people drift into the bar with talk of lunch and what can be rummaged up. Barry and Brenda are making demands to anyone who will listen, but people have learned to avoid them. Nothing good can come from an interaction with those two.

I want to move our conversation elsewhere, somewhere private. We're not remotely finished; we've barely started. For a moment I think about inviting Sarah up to my room, but that seems odd and it would mean starting the conversation again, and I'd rather not jeopardise what we've begun already. Getting up, I turn to the group directly behind me.

'There are plenty of leftovers in the kitchen, you know. You only have to help yourselves – no need to stand on ceremony here.' I smile encouragingly at them and begin to make shooing motions with my hands, which seem to be going unnoticed. Cynthia would have them out of here in a moment. 'The dining room is free for anyone wanting to mill about.' I try again. 'Or those comfortable chairs in reception? Look, I'm trying to have a private conversation here, can you all just shove off.'

I hear Sarah try to disguise laughter behind a bout of coughing, but she seems to be the only person who's listening to me. For one horrible and perhaps silly moment, I wonder if Cynthia has asked them *all* to stop talking to me, but I do know that's ridiculous. And then it becomes clear why everyone's attention is diverted. There's a commotion in the foyer.

Chapter Eighteen

A Serious Matter

Through the window I can see a police car parked outside the front door and two officers walking across the car park. Inside the hotel, everything slows and then stops. The chatter dies instantly and the ensuing silence is deafening. Everyone's attention is caught, thirty-eight pairs of eyes trained on them as they walk into reception. I make my way to the bar door for a better look, Sarah momentarily forgotten. Cynthia was in the middle of saying goodbye to the agent, shaking his hand, and he now looks as if he doesn't want to leave; whatever is transpiring here is clearly far more exciting than whatever he has planned next.

'Pensioners' drugs bust?' Sarah asks.

She's walked over to join me and is leaning on the door frame watching, but I'm so surprised to see the police here that her joke is lost on me.

'Seriously, though, what's going on?' she says.

'I have absolutely no idea.'

'If Liam was working, I'd be worried, but luckily he's at home, I hope.'

'Is the manager here?' asks one of the officers in a surprisingly high voice.

A voice better suited to his female companion. It seems at odds with his bulky physique and the beard that's a touch longer than acceptable.

'No,' Cynthia says, stepping forwards. 'He left with most of his staff on Christmas Eve. I've just put an offer in on the place, so I'll be the new owner soon,' she says to a ripple of interest from the guests and a large smile on the agent's face.

Oh, God, here she goes...

'I'm not sure that's relevant, madam, and should you all be here without proper supervision?'

This is from the other one – the female officer with a tight ponytail that hangs down from under her hat. In any other situation, I might be amused that her voice is lower than his, but nothing about this situation is funny. I watch as Cynthia bristles.

'We're not a bunch of unruly toddlers, officer, and are quite capable of looking after ourselves, thank you very much.'

I can see irritation in the grim set of her mouth, but the police don't seem remotely bothered.

'Yes, I'm sure you are, but what I'm not sure about is the insurance.'

The agent tucks some papers into a leather bag and slings it over his shoulder.

'I'll be in touch,' he says to Cynthia. 'Best I get out of your way.'

He catches the eye of the male police officer, who waves him away, and he disappears out of the door.

Sarah taps my shoulder and points out of the bar window. There's another police officer walking around the outside of the hotel, holding on to his cap against the gusty wind. He stops when he gets to the doors that lead into the back of the kitchen and he begins peering in through the glass.

'What is going on?' Sarah whispers into my ear, and I shrug, but there's a sliver of something chilly in my arms and I rub my hands together.

Could this be about Tony? The police aren't mind readers, I tell myself. How could they possibly know about something that happened over forty years ago? I'm being paranoid.

'What is it we can do for you, exactly?' Cynthia asks. 'We're leaving this afternoon, so there's nothing more to worry about with regards to insurance and we promise not to cause any damage before we leave. I can assure you, we're all law-abiding citizens.'

That starts a ripple of amusement among some, but the policeman narrows his eyes.

'We're here on a serious matter,' he says. 'We're looking for a Mrs Joy Wilson.'

I wonder for a moment if it's to do with her burn and the hospital. Perhaps it's a health and safety issue. Just as quickly, my thoughts flash to an image of us breaking into the house the other day; it was Joy's idea, after all.

Coincidentally, she chooses that exact moment to step out of the kitchen with a tray of sandwiches in her arms. It's almost as if her ears were burning, or maybe she caught sight of police person number three prowling around outside.

'Anyone want something to eat?' she says. 'I've done turkey, ham and…'

Cynthia is trying to gesture to her to go back into the kitchen, but she's not being very subtle, flicking her hands about as if there's a fly bothering her. It's a pointless gesture anyway, because as soon as Joy sees the police, she drops the tray on the floor, scattering sandwiches everywhere, meat and mayonnaise flying. She starts to walk towards them as if she's expecting them, but her legs buckle, probably because of those blasted heels she insists on wearing. The policewoman catches her arm and it's an odd thought, but it's such a shame that Joy is apprehended under the Christmas tree that she decorated herself.

'Be careful,' I say, striding forwards. 'She's injured her arm.'

The policewoman glares at me, but Cynthia beams and I realise that being in her good books is no bad place to be. Then a pair of handcuffs are produced.

'Joy Wilson, we are arresting you on suspicion of the murder of your husband, Patrick Wilson. Anything you say will be…'

In the first seventy-six years of my life I'd never been in a police station, and then Tony died and somehow this is my second visit in as many months. We're going to miss the ferry, I've had to abandon my conversation with Sarah and I'm not sure that either Cynthia or I have anywhere to stay tonight. Joy will be OK, because she'll probably be in a cell. She has a solicitor with her now and they've been talking for hours. Cynthia and I have been outside waiting for her, but nobody is telling us anything.

'Do you think they're questioning her about the break-in, too?' I ask, handing her another cup of coffee from the machine.

It's our fourth cup and I think we're both a little keyed up. Cynthia takes it and puts it straight onto the empty chair beside her.

'No, I don't. Even if they knew about it, which they don't, they'll not be interested in someone letting themselves into a house with a key to retrieve a letter posted through the door.'

I keep hold of my cup for warmth. People keep trailing in and out of the main door and it takes so long to swing shut that it's chilly in here. I rest my head back and look at the clock on the wall for the millionth time. The hands have inched round to five thirty.

'They'll be on the ferry now,' I say, and Cynthia grunts a response.

She gets up to pace again but soon sits down, her knee unable to take it.

'How long are they going to keep her in there for?' This isn't the first time I've asked this and Cynthia doesn't respond. 'Do you think she really killed her husband?' It's not the first time I've asked that and there's nothing from Cynthia this time, either.

Seeing Joy bundled into the back of the police car earlier was shocking. It was like something from a television drama, and not a very good one. We had to make quick decisions and Alan drove us to the police station. He also stayed for a while, but then he was asked to move the coach because it was blocking an entrance. And anyway, as he said, his main responsibility had to be to the passengers and getting them to the ferry. He did look upset, though. I don't think he likes the idea of Joy being questioned by the police any more than we do.

He came back with our luggage an hour later, said the hotel had been locked up and he had to get everyone to Fishbourne. I could tell he was, even then, wrestling with his decision, but this waiting area could hardly accommodate thirty-eight pensioners.

'Are you coming or staying?' he asked us.

Then, to my eternal shame, I hesitated, because honestly, there was nothing I wanted more than to get home. Cynthia, of course, cried out a firm 'Staying!' and I was only just a couple of seconds behind her. So, here we are, in the police station, with three sets of luggage and Joy's other phone, which I remembered about at the last moment. I popped back on board with the pretext of saying goodbye to everyone, which surprised them, and I hardly got much more than a few half-hearted waves from most of the miserable bunch, but then I slipped my hand between the seats and pulled it out. I put it in my pocket, where Cynthia suggested it stayed. I was proud of myself for my quick actions at the time, but she said it would have been better to have left it on the coach. I think she's probably right, because I suppose if it has any evidence on it, I've brought it right to them. It feels heavy resting against my leg.

'The way I see it,' Cynthia says now, 'is that we should assume she didn't kill her husband, but if it turns out she did, then we should assume she had a good reason. That's really all there is to it. And as for missing the ferry, well, I have a hotel to buy, so it's fortuitous, and you, Evelyn, have a conversation to continue. There's a reason you're here, or had you forgotten?'

Of course Cynthia is right, but I still feel as if I've been admonished. She starts tapping on her phone and I rest my head back again. My stomach gives a low grumble, but with poor Joy in there being interrogated, I don't feel as if I should mention it.

'Cynthia?' I say, suddenly leaning forwards in my chair. 'I want to say sorry.'

She stops tapping and looks up, one eyebrow raised.

'I'm sorry for the way I spoke to you in the hospital. It was unforgivable.'

'Not unforgivable,' she says quietly. 'Shall we say no more about it?'

'OK.'

I rest my head back again and she gets on with whatever she was doing on her phone. A sense of peace settles over me.

'So, first it's jokes, then gratitude, and now I find out you also do apologies. What an unexpected person you are, Evelyn Pringle.'

My head snaps up, but she's tapping away, her own head down with the ghost of a smile on her lips.

A side door opens and Joys appears, flanked by two officers. She looks exhausted and we both jump up. Her solicitor says something to her and she nods slowly, her expression all shock and surprise, but relief floods her face when she turns and sees us.

'You stayed behind for me,' she says, wiping a hand across her eyes.

'Of course we did.'

'We've got your things,' I say, motioning to all our luggage cluttering the waiting area.

'I've just got to fill in a form to say where I'll be staying etc,' her voice cracks and tears spring to her eyes. 'But I don't have anywhere to stay,' she says, wiping her sleeve across her face.

'Come on,' Cynthia says, taking her arm. 'I'll help you.'

They walk to the front desk and Joy begins to write as Cynthia explains something she reads from her phone. I hang back and wait for them, but it doesn't take long and they're soon ready to go.

'Let's just get out of here,' Cynthia says, and the three of us gather our suitcases and walk into the chill evening air, glad to be out of the police station. 'I've found a hotel with availability. It's a chain place, which means it'll be more anonymous. We don't want some nosey guest house owner asking questions, do we? And it's walkable,' she says, slipping her phone into her handbag. 'Come on – I'll lead the way.'

We pull on our coats and gloves and follow Cynthia down the steps and into the high street. It's become dark since we've been inside and Christmas lights compete with car headlights in a dazzling display. Cynthia leads us round the back of the station, past the car park and onto a side road, towards the gentler lights of the quayside. For a few minutes, as we fall into step with each other, we're silent and I remember Joy's phone still in my pocket. Pulling it out, I think about handing it back to her, but then I remember she was actively trying to get rid of it. Taking a sidestep closer to the edge, I let it fall from my fingers into the water, where it lands with a barely audible splash.

I watch the boats bobbing in the icy water, their masts swaying in the breeze. The gale of this morning has dropped as if it were never there. And yet, I can't help but feel frustrated about that fact. If the weather hadn't been as bad as it was this morning, then we'd be home by now. I'd be stretched out in Tony's reclining chair with a hot chocolate and the remote control. Instead, I'm heading for another hotel with the bossiest person I've ever met and a woman who may or may not have murdered her husband.

Chapter Nineteen

Crosswords

Cynthia insists on paying for the room herself and it's just one room, with a double bed and two singles: a family room. There's even a teddy bear on each pillow. It's actually quite a nice room, all clean lines, neat furniture, straight curtain poles and... I press down on one of the beds. Firm mattresses. I don't need to say it, but it's much nicer than The Welcome Rest.

I heave Joy's suitcase onto the bed and give her ownership of the double. She hasn't said a word since the police station and now she slips off her shoes, crawls onto the covers and curls up in a foetal position next to her case. I wait for Cynthia to choose which bed she wants, but she disappears into the bathroom, so I flop down on the one nearest the window. I should probably phone Carol, let her know what I'm doing...

God, what am I doing? These women are strangers, really, and I've chosen to stay with them instead of getting the ferry home. Who's to say there won't be another storm? How long might I be here for? Why did I let Cynthia guilt me into staying? I wouldn't have had to look at her disappointed face for long if I'd chosen to go with Alan and the others. I'm the weak woman I always thought I was.

Cynthia closes the bathroom door behind her. 'Well, I don't mind if anyone wants to say it; this is so much nicer than The Welcome Rest.'

A rush of warmth and admiration for her honesty hits me, takes me by surprise, makes me smile. She's a strong, fearless woman.

'I really need to come up with another name for the hotel,' she continues. 'The Welcome Rest is terrible, and I need to distance myself from its, no doubt, negative reviews. Let's do names in a hat later, see what a bit of brainstorming can do.'

'It might not be so bad if it was accurate.'

'You're right, Evelyn. Maybe it's supposed to be ironic.'

'It's just lies,' I say, which makes her grin.

'Joy?' says Cynthia gently. 'We're just going to pop out and get some food. I assume you don't want to come, but is there anything you'd like? They don't offer room service here and I doubt any of us can be bothered to go down and sit in the restaurant.'

Joy lifts her head from her pillow and offers us a wan smile. 'Thank you, both. I really do appreciate you staying with me. There's nothing I need thank you.'

Cynthia and I retrace our steps along the quay, past the police station and onto the high street. Our pace is laboured now. We're both tired and hungry, and the cold breeze isn't helping our spirits. If I could magic us back into that warm hotel room, I would. Eventually, we find a convenience store, where I pick up a basket from the stack by the door. A quick glance around and I realise we won't be getting anything substantial in here. Everything looks a bit grubby.

'We should try to find somewhere bigger, somewhere that sells actual food instead of all this outdated tinned stuff?' I say irritably.

'I'm not walking another bloody step unless it's in the direction of the hotel! It's not outdated, anyway,' Cynthia says, taking the tin of peach slices from me and putting it back on the shelf. 'We can get what we need here; certainly enough to fill us up for now.'

I glance down at the fresh vegetable section and grimace. 'Look!' I say, turning my nose up at a couple of limp lettuces.

'For God's sake, Evelyn! We're not buying bloody veg. You do have some airs and graces, don't you? I can't understand why you don't just muck in, get involved – it won't kill you.'

'Airs and graces? What about you? *I'm buying a hotel. Listen to all my renovation plans,*' I mimic. 'All you've done so far is sign a form, and I'll bet you'll be telling that poor man at the till *all* about it.'

She stares at me, agog. Here we go again – she'll probably stop talking to me. I wonder how long I'll be sent to Coventry for this time.

She narrows her eyes. 'Are you hungry, Evelyn?'

'Yes, I am.'

'Do I really sound like that?'

'Yes, you do.'

She turns away and picks up a large bag of crisps, then after she drops it into the basket, she picks up another.

'You get some cheese and crackers, and I'll get the

wine,' she says and disappears into the next aisle, leaving a harumph in the air behind her.

We leave the shop with a couple of bags of provisions. It's hardly a meal, but I doubt any of us have the energy for much more this evening, especially Joy. We try to pick up our pace on the way back. Neither of us say it, but we don't want to leave her on her own for too long.

'This hotel is just for tonight,' Cynthia says. 'I barely dare tell you after your little show in the supermarket, but I've been messaging the agent and the owner, and I've got him to agree to us staying back at The Welcome Rest until the end of the week. God, I'm sick of that name. We really do need to come up with something else.'

'You don't really sound like that, Cynthia,' I concede. 'You're right – I'm just hungry and being disagreeable.'

'Oh, I think perhaps I do,' she says, and we fall into a comfortable silence as we walk.

'The end of the week? You think we could be here that long?' I ask eventually.

'Joy's solicitor told her that she'd see her on the 1st, back at the police station, five days from now.'

I let that information settle; another five days here. I suppose Carol would say that there's nothing stopping me from coming home. If I phoned her, she'd probably book me a ferry. In fact, she'd probably come and pick me up from Portsmouth. We walk a bit further and we're back by the quayside, the breeze nipping again now that we're closer to water.

'So,' I say, 'we'll be here for New Year, then?'

Cynthia doesn't stop walking or even look at me, but her

shoulders visibly relax and I somehow know that if she was testing me, then I've passed.

'New Year,' she says. 'We could have a little party, just the three of us.'

'Why are we allowed back to stay at the hotel? After what the police said earlier, shouldn't we be a bit wary, I mean about the insurance?'

'It'll be fine. My offer's been accepted and I told him I want to do some measuring up. Really laid it on thick about what needs doing and negotiated the price accordingly. To be honest, I don't think he cares. The agent really shouldn't have told me, but the owner's wife is very ill and he wants to get rid of the place. He's lost vision, apparently.'

'I think he lost vision the minute he started installing all those plastic windows,' I say, and she chuckles. 'Are you really sure about this, Cynthia? It's such a huge step. Have you done anything like this before?'

'No, I haven't,' she says, 'but you know, a huge step is exactly what I need in my life right now. And there was a time, not so long ago, that I wanted a guest house by the sea, or something similar. I'm a sociable creature, you know, and I thought it would be just the thing for us, for me. Doesn't life have a way of throwing a grenade into your plans and turning everything on its head when you least expect it?'

'Yes,' I say quietly.

I want to ask her more, why she needs a huge step in her life right now and who is the other person in us, and maybe she might have told me, but we're back at the hotel and we lug our haul into the lift.

I open the wine and we drink it from plastic cups we find

in the bathroom. It's room temperature, cheap, white and has a slight soapy taste. We all agree it's awful. There are no plates or cutlery, but we're past caring. Cynthia pulls a couple of pages from the local paper she bought and we use those instead. I delve my hand into the crisps and make a pile on top of the sports pages. We break chunks off the cheese and drop cracker crumbs on the bed covers.

I push myself back until I reach the headboard and kick my shoes onto the floor. It feels warm and cosy here with just the three of us after days surrounded by the whole coach party. No one knows we're here apart from us and somehow that thought is comforting. I know I need to get in touch with my sister, let her know what's going on, but for now, I'm content. It's the best I've felt in ages.

'Three across, six letters, lucrative student left out.' Cynthia has her eyes on the pages of the newspaper, bits of cracker and crisp brushed to one side.

'Earner,' I say confidently. It just comes to me.

'Yes, well done! I've never been too good at cryptic crosswords,' she says. 'I can just about manage an easy teatime one if I can be bothered.'

'My brain begins to shrivel when I'm asked questions like that,' says Joy. 'I'm sure it doesn't work properly. I'm OK with a word search and that's about it.'

'Here's an easy one, then – three and seven letters, passionate.'

I gulp down some wine and shove a few more crips in to stop myself from answering, give Joy a chance. Cynthia has turned the page, though, her eyes drawn to something else.

'I don't know,' Joy says, despondent. 'See, I told you I was

THE SECOND CHANCE HOLIDAY CLUB

thick.' She rests her head back against the board and closes her eyes, her wine cup still clutched tightly in her hand.

'According to this, there's a hotel near mine that opened late summer and they're offering reduced prices on lunches between Christmas and New Year. It's my direct competition – we should go and check it out. It looks nice enough.' Cynthia lifts up the page to show us the picture, a spray of crisps with it.

'It looks OK,' I say with little enthusiasm. The wine has taken the last of my energy and the rubbish we've eaten hasn't helped. I begin to gather the edges of my paper until I've folded the wrappers and crumbs inside, then I lean over the edge of the bed and drop it into the wastepaper basket. 'I hope you didn't want to read that,' I say.

'Shall I make us a reservation for the day after tomorrow?'

'What day is that?' I ask. 'I've lost track.'

'It's the 27th today, so the 29th.'

Joy's eyes flick open, but she keeps her gaze on the wall. 'So, New Year's Day is five days from now,' she says.

'Yes, ages away,' Cynthia chips in quickly.

'Not actually that long,' I say, thinking about going home, too late to pick up on Cynthia's cue.

She cuts me a look that brings me back up to speed.

'Well, I suppose five days is quite a long time.'

I'm not very good at this. Cynthia rolls her eyes and dumps her paper in the bin on top of mine. She levers herself off the bed and opens the other bottle, ignoring my hand over the top of my beaker. She takes it from me and fills it anyway, and perhaps my resistance is only half-hearted. Joy holds hers out eagerly, for the same treatment.

'Did I tell you I used to own a dress shop in Covent Garden?'

Cynthia lowers herself back onto her bed and I wonder if I can pretend to be asleep.

'How wonderful,' says Joy. 'When was that? Recently?'

'God, no. Years ago, in the Seventies. You should have seen the sort of stuff that I sold. I had a partner and we'd buy fabrics, old clothes, anything we could get our hands on, and transform it. Leslie was a whizz with a sewing machine and I was good with the customers. We patched, fringed and tie-dyed absolutely everything. It was fun.'

Joy has swung round on her bed, engrossed, and I can now see why Cynthia started this conversation. Anything to avoid talking about today.

'Did you sell flares?' Joy asks. 'I used to wear bell-bottom trouser suits. Can you imagine wearing anything like that now?'

I think about Cynthia's alternative dress sense and choose to keep my mouth shut.

'We did sell flares, yes, in the most glorious colours. I've always had an eye for fashion.'

'When did you stop?' I say. I couldn't keep it shut for long.

'Oh, Evelyn, give it up. You've already used up your one joke for this year; you'll have to wait for next year for another one.'

I glance across at her. She's smiling into her wine and I lean back, smiling, too.

'You two are so funny,' Joy says, laughing.

'So, tell us about Bristol and your restaurant,' Cynthia says.

I give her a sharp look, wondering if just as she's livened things up, she's killed them, although that feels like a poor choice of thought in the present circumstances. Joy doesn't seem to mind, though.

'I bought the place when it was run down,' she begins, pulling her knees up to her chin like a child. 'Pulled the whole place to bits, redecorated, reimagined and created a French restaurant. My chef was French,' she says, looking across at us. 'So the food was authentic.'

Is she blushing? She looks wistful and I wonder if she's remembering the restaurant or the chef.

'Guillaume; he asked me to marry him once. I think I should have said yes.'

She stops suddenly as if she's woken from a dream or been slapped. Perhaps she's remembered her husband, the man who made her sell her business and move away. The husband whose murder she's spent the afternoon being questioned about. Why are we talking about flares and bloody restaurants when we should be talking about *that*? Oh, God! Please let's not start talking about that.

'I used to work in a primary school,' I blurt. 'Springfield Primary School,' I add unnecessarily.

'Were you a teacher?' Cynthia asks. 'You have to have a lot of patience for that.'

'No, not a teacher, but you might be surprised how patient I can be,' I say pointedly. 'I was predominantly a teacher's helper; reading with the children, music and movement, that sort of thing.'

'When was that, Evelyn?' Cynthia asks.

I'm startled by her question, as if she's trying to catch me out. I'm beginning to wish I'd kept my mouth shut.

'Late Sixties, early Seventies,' I say cautiously.

'Oh, I thought you meant recently. I didn't think assistants were a thing back then – maybe parent helpers?'

'They weren't really a thing, no,' I say quickly. 'Ours was a small cottage school and a bit exceptional, I suppose.'

My mouth feels dry. I lift my beaker to my lips and finding it empty, I place it on the cabinet beside my bed. I can almost see the cogs working behind Cynthia's eyes as she grapples with the next question. I close my own and wonder if I'd actually like her to ask me, and if she does, what I might tell her.

'We should play a game,' she says unexpectedly. 'A would-you-rather game.'

'I don't know what that is,' I say, and glance at Joy, who looks similarly perplexed.

'You know, would you rather a free lifetime supply of chocolate or a free lifetime supply of the best sex ever? That sort of thing.'

I choke on a mouthful of wine and Joy snorts. Then with no prompt from either of us, we both say, 'Chocolate,' at the same time. Cynthia hoots with laughter.

'Actually, can I say crisps instead?' Joy says. 'I'm not a huge fan of chocolate.'

'You can have whatever you want,' says Cynthia, wiping the tears from her eyes.

'Would you rather...' Joy pauses to think. 'Would you rather all the guns in the world disappear or a self-cleaning home?'

'Good one, Joy, but obviously I'll have to go with disappearing guns,' Cynthia says.

'I'll take the clean house,' I say, and both turn surprised

eyes on me. 'Well, some people are fundamentally bad and will just use fists or knives, or cricket bats. If you'd said that all people would be lovely and kind and have no urge to hurt each other, I'd have gone with the same, but as it's just guns, I'll take the clean house.'

'That's very smart, Evelyn,' says Cynthia, her accent creeping in again with each sip of wine.

'I shouldn't have asked that,' Joy says quietly. 'I've fallen into that age old trap, haven't I.'

'Internalised misogyny?' Cynthia asks. 'Why should we always be thinking about cleaning our bloody houses!'

'Well, yes, that and I've made Evelyn suggest she likes guns.'

'I do not,' I say, curtly. 'But, I will admit to liking a clean house.'

'Oh, God! Sorry, you two, it was only supposed to be a fun game,' Cynthia says laughing.

'I'd have thought it was a game designed to provoke a discussion, and in that case, it's worked,' I say. 'Where were you born, Cynthia? I keep hearing a northern hint to your voice.' I decide to change the subject.

'Ripon,' she says. 'I was born in Ripon.'

Her accent is clear and true Yorkshire. Obvious now she's using it.

'Why did you drop the accent?' asks Joy. 'It's lovely.'

'I moved down to London when I was seventeen to go to RADA – the drama school, you know? – and they told me pretty quickly to drop the voice. If I wanted to get any part in anything on the stage, I couldn't sound like a northerner, apparently. I never really made it though, anyway. It turns out you can change your accent but not your face.'

'What was wrong with your face?' Joy asks.

'I just wasn't pretty enough to be on the stage; they were looking for something else. I did get a couple of small roles in television dramas, but that was it. I felt so guilty, though, after my mother saved so hard to send me, that I ended up working in a biscuit factory so I could pay her back. Then I moved up the ranks to the office and then... well, then I moved on to other things.'

She laughs lightly and it's easy to see her remembering. She reaches for her cup and finishes it.

I imagine Cynthia in drama school. Of course, it fits in with her larger-than-life personality perfectly, but not to have made it is such a shame. I can also imagine her in a biscuit factory, in a shop in Covent Garden... in fact, anywhere. I get the impression that Cynthia doesn't say no to anything. 'Seize the day' must be her motto. So far removed from my own, which is probably 'stick your head in the sand until it all goes away'.

'Hot-blooded!' Joy suddenly shouts from the bed next to me.

'Sorry?' I say, but Cynthia is giggling.

'Passionate, three and seven letters,' Joy says triumphantly.

'You're not as thick as you first thought,' Cynthia says. 'Come on – let's get this finished.' She empties the last of the wine between the three of us.

We settle back again and take our conversation down to simple things: television programmes we like, holidays we've been on and places we want to visit. It makes me realise that my travel aspirations have been rather inadequate as I listen to the other two talk about some of the exotic locations they've either been to, or have plans to go to. Getting the

300 bus into town is as far as I've ventured for ages. But, look at me now; I've crossed a body of water, stayed in a hotel, made friends. It's a start, but it's not enough. Where *do* I want to go? I very much want to be able to astonish Cynthia and Joy by sending them a postcard from a far flung place. My mind begins to bubble with the possibilities.

We talk about books and gardening, films and food we like to cook. We manage to navigate our way around all difficult topics. We don't talk about letters to dead husbands' lovers or brushes with the law, and we don't mention telephone conversations and lies to loved ones.

We talk, we drink and then we sleep.

Chapter Twenty

Helen

In the morning I wake, disorientated, and it takes a moment to catch up with where I am. My mouth is dry and I realise I didn't even bother to clean my teeth last night. The room smells of cheese. Cynthia is snoring, a soft gentle sound rolling around the back of her throat. Turning my head, I can see that Joy has curled back up in a ball again, sleeping silently like a cat. I stare up at the ceiling, where a slit of sunlight splits it into two like a crack. It must be late if the sun is up, but then we were still talking at three. I glance at the bedside clock and see it's eight thirty.

It's the 28th of December today and I can't believe we're still on the island. I muse over the fact that we've been here for only five days; it seems like half a lifetime. But remembering what we've done in that time almost makes me dizzy. And besides, we're going to be here for four more. I'm actually glad that Cynthia has arranged for us to return to the hotel, despite the comfort here in this room. It's closer to Sarah and really, we have so much more to say.

As quietly as I can, I get out of bed and shuffle into the bathroom. My hips ache from all the walking yesterday. Reaching a hand behind the shower curtain, I turn the water on full and while I wait for it to warm up, I clean my teeth. There's a handrail and I use it to pull myself over the lip of the bath. With the hot water on my skin, I begin to unwind the knot of tension I woke up with. The thought of what I came close to talking about last night brings a lump of fear to my chest. I have to be more careful when I drink – it loosens my tongue. I need to keep a tighter lid on things; I can't afford for everything to unravel.

The reception staff order a taxi to take us back to the hotel. The agent has left a key for us in a box, which is useful but lax. The owner obviously can't be bothered with the place any more. He probably couldn't believe his luck when Cynthia showed up to take it off his hands.

'So, you're going to do some measuring up, are you?' I ask Cynthia, who looks at me as if I'm mad.

'What, with no tape measure?' she says, laughing. 'I just wanted to get us back here, and it's no skin off the owner's nose if three old ladies stay for a couple of days.'

'Four days,' Joy says suddenly. 'It's four days until I have to be back at the police station. The post-mortem will be done and the results will be back by then.'

This is the first time she's made any mention of her situation since we left the station last night and it seems to stop both me and Cynthia in our tracks. There's a horrible silence, which I'm concerned Joy might fill with other things I have no wish to hear.

'Let's get inside and get the kettle on, shall we?' I say, and pushing open the door, we all walk in.

It feels as if we're trespassing as we step into the foyer and close the door behind us. I imagine the police turning up and kicking us out, and even though Cynthia assures us it's all above board, I don't really believe her. The space seems cavernous now without the bustle and chatter of the other guests and I wonder if we should have stayed where we were, but once Cynthia locks the front door and I make a pot of tea, we settle in pretty quickly.

Cynthia takes us on a tour, pointing out what she plans to do with the place, how she's going to pull some of it down to restore it to its former glory. In a cupboard behind the bar we find photographs of how it looked in the 1930s when it was first built and I begin to see what she means, and how good it could actually be.

'I'd like to have fewer rooms and make more of the garden, maybe think about a grand conservatory on the side where that ugly extension is now. Obviously, a hotel is only as good as the food it serves, so I'd like to get someone special on that front. Lots to think about,' she says, and I notice her looking speculatively at Joy.

Cynthia shows us the owners' accommodation, comprising a two-bedroom annexe with a bathroom and kitchenette. There's a cosy sitting room with French doors leading out onto a private garden with a view of the sea. Much like the rest of the hotel, it needs work, but the potential is here. I feel a stab of envy for a moment – Cynthia has plans, exciting ones. But I have no desire to run a hotel; I don't want to run anything. I let the moment pass, because honestly, I'm happy for her.

'This is so wonderful,' Joy says. 'To have such a vision and a plan at our time of life is really something special.'

It's as if she's taken my thoughts straight from my head.

'I'm seventy-eight,' Cynthia says. 'Older than you both by a few years. And I really feel if I don't do this now, I never will.'

She sits down suddenly in a chintzy armchair and sighs. It's a deep, ragged noise that sounds like it's been dragged out of her by force. It almost makes me jump.

'Are you OK, Cynthia?' I ask.

'No,' she says. 'But I'm going to be.' Both Joy and I sit down opposite her on a small peach-coloured settee, and I imagine Joy is holding her breath like I'm holding mine.

'We're the three widows,' she says unexpectedly. 'We could start a band,' she laughs, but it's a dry, hollow sound that really isn't her.

'You had a husband, too?' Joy asks. 'I thought you were single, to be honest. I thought women in their seventies who laughed as much as you were always single. It's the married people I know who look like life is passing them by. God, I'm so sorry, Cynthia, that's very insensitive of me.'

'Don't worry. I tend to agree with you usually,' she says. 'My marriage was one of those unexpectedly wonderful ones – the kind everyone thinks they're going to have until they find out that very few are. Ian died just over a year ago before Christmas.'

'I'm so sorry,' I say, feeling her grief radiating from her.

'He had cancer, as so many do, and it was devastating watching him die. I'd have traded places if I could, not to see him suffer like that. Death isn't kind for everyone,' she says.

My thoughts go to Tony in his car, gone in a painless flash, and I feel angry for a moment.

'We have children, a son and daughter, and they had to watch him like that, too. It broke me. That first Christmas was excruciating. It had only been a month and it was so raw for us all. I went to my daughter's to spend it with her and my grandchildren. My son, James, lives with his boyfriend in Spain and after weeks at his father's bedside, I couldn't blame him for not coming home for Christmas. My daughter, Helen, wanted to get out family photos and cry over them, and all I wanted to do was die. So I went into self-preservation mode – upbeat, jolly Cynthia – and Helen wasn't impressed.

'We've barely spoken in a year and I fabricated an illness so I wouldn't have to go through another Christmas like that.' She stops and looks at me. 'That was what you overheard, Evelyn; me lying to my daughter. I know it's selfish, because maybe she needs me, but I haven't got anything to give her. She has her husband and children, though; she's not alone.

'I know she doesn't understand why I'm not whooping and wailing like she is, but if I started, I don't think I'd be able to stop. Do you know, Ian wanted to be buried, but after he died I chose to have him cremated, because I knew that if he had been buried, I couldn't guarantee that I wouldn't dig down and crawl in beside him.'

Fat, silent tears have begun to slide down Cynthia's cheeks and Joy scoots off the settee and crouches beside her, her hands on Cynthia's. I'm stuck in my seat, powerless to move as a deep-rooted pain of my own takes hold. I fully understand Cynthia's yearning. Tony had wanted Stephen's body to be cremated for exactly that reason and I'd railed against that decision. I've regretted it ever since though, because wouldn't it have been better to let him fly in the breeze across the meadow than be buried in a box in a churchyard that I never visit, because I want to dig down, too?

Cynthia is exhausted and goes to lie down on the bed in one of the annexe bedrooms after our conversation and Joy ushers me into the main kitchen. She wants us to cook a lovely lunch for Cynthia. She knows her way around this kitchen by now and sets to work rummaging through the fridge, picking out things that have a now-or-never date on them. It only just occurs to me that no one has restocked since we arrived, so we need to be careful what we use.

'Where did you learn to cook?' I ask Joy, thinking about Liam.

'I went to a catering college in Bristol,' Joy tells me as she deftly slices vegetables for a ratatouille she's making.

I become her sous chef and rush about collecting whatever she asks for as she chops, sifts and stirs.

'I was thirty-five when I went and the oldest there,' she continues.

'What made you leave it so late to go? Was it a change of career?'

'No,' she says. 'I grew up with just my dad after my mum left when I was eighteen. She couldn't cope with dad's illness any more. He had Huntington's disease and it had progressed considerably when she left, so, I became his carer when it was just the two of us. It meant that I couldn't get a proper job, just a part-time stint as a waitress in a local restaurant. I loved the buzz in the kitchen and we did alright – we just bobbled along together until he died twelve years later.'

'Goodness, that must have been very difficult for you,' I say. Honestly, I'm appalled that her mother left her to it.

'It was hard at the time and I did miss him, but I also felt as if I'd missed out on the chance of a career in something worthwhile. It took me a few years to pluck up the courage to apply to the college, but eventually I did, using the money my dad had been squirrelling away for me. Some say it was selfish of him to keep me at home, but I needed him as much as he needed me.

'Anyway, I'd always dreamed of running my own restaurant and after I qualified, my great aunt died, leaving me some money. Overnight, I suddenly had options I'd never had before. I bought that rundown place I told you about and transformed it. Ran it for eight years until I met Patrick and, well, things changed after that.' She stops slicing suddenly and spins round with the knife in her hand. 'I didn't kill him, you know,' she says, and instinctively I take a step back.

She quickly puts it down on the counter, looking abashed.

'I thought I'd have a marriage like Cynthia did with Ian. That was how it started, but he changed, or maybe I did, it's so hard to remember clearly.'

'You could start again, like Cynthia. Maybe not leap into buying or even running a restaurant, but what about working in one to start with, see where it takes you?'

'Thank you for saying that, Evelyn, but I'm too old. No one would give me a second look. I can't compete with the youth in the kitchens now.'

I wonder if perhaps she's right. Who indeed would employ a seventy-year-old woman? Which means that just as she's free yet again, it's actually too late. It makes me think about

Liam and then about Sarah and how much I want to talk to her, to put this thing to bed before it's too late. Tomorrow, I decide. I'll go and see her tomorrow. I don't have a phone number for her; I'll have to just chance it and turn up.

We have lunch at the little table in the apartment, choosing to by-pass the dining room in the main hotel. I've laid the table with the nicest cloth I could find and some crystal wine glasses that were hiding at the back of a cupboard. I've also found some candles, which I light as Joy brings in the food. Cynthia is delighted with our efforts although understandably, she's more subdued than usual. We tuck into goat's cheese starters followed by the most delicious pie with ratatouille and then crème caramel for dessert. We don't talk about Tony or Patrick or Ian. We raise our glasses to ourselves and to moving forwards, but I'm left feeling a bit like I have nowhere to go.

Chapter Twenty-one

Phone Calls and Lies

There's a touch of snow in the air again as I begin my walk to Sarah's house, but it floats around in the breeze and doesn't settle. It's the fourth time I've made this journey now and I'm pretty sure my feet alone know the way. We slept in the apartment, Cynthia insisting on the pull-out sofa bed, leaving the two bedrooms for Joy and me. We have the whole of the hotel at our disposal, but by some sort of unsaid understanding between us, we closed the door on it.

The apartment is cosy, if a little cold away from the stove, and Cynthia is stamping her mark on it because, after all, it'll be her home. The thought of taking on something this big terrifies me, but Cynthia seems to take it all in her stride. She wants to keep busy – I can see that now. It's obviously her way of coping.

It's three days until the end of the year and I quite like the idea of being with Cynthia and Joy to see in the new one. It'll be unusual for me to celebrate at all, but I imagine whatever we do will be low-key; after all, Joy has to be at the police station the next day. Apart from her outburst in the kitchen yesterday, there's been nothing more, and when I broached the subject with Cynthia, she said we should leave it alone, that Joy would tell us what she wanted to, when she wanted to. Even though I do believe her when she says she didn't kill her husband, it seems strange not to talk about it.

My nerves are beginning to trouble me the closer I get to East Street. I wonder what Sarah has told Liam. I push open the front gate and approach the door, take a deep, reassuring breath and knock, pushing the memory of the last time I was here to the back of my mind.

'Evelyn,' Sarah says, surprised.

I watch as she rearranges her face to accommodate me.

'Hello, Sarah. I hope you don't mind that I've come – it all got a bit mad the other day and we didn't get to finish our conversation.'

She hesitates but then pulls the door back, inviting me into her home.

'Come on in,' she says. 'I'll pop the kettle on. What happened with your friend and the police?'

'Oh, just a misunderstanding,' I say, stepping inside and closing the door behind me.

I bend to slip off my shoes, holding on to the wall for support.

'Don't bother – we never worry about that sort of thing here,' she says. 'Oh, and that's yours.' She points at my umbrella, now folded and leaning against her shoe rack.

'Thank you,' I say, taking off my coat and hanging it over the banister at the bottom of the stairs, then I follow her through the living room and into the kitchen.

I try again to catch a look at the photographs on the bookshelf, but Sarah's too quick and I haven't earned enough trust yet to start nosing around.

'Tea or coffee?' She flicks the switch on the kettle.

Her kitchen is homely in daylight, but I still have a horrible flashback to when I was last in here.

'Whatever you're having would be lovely, thank you. Is Liam home?'

'No, he's gone to some mates for a gaming session.' She rolls her eyes affectionately. 'They'll be shooting bad guys and trashing cars, or some such nonsense. I have to be grateful that he's only doing it on-screen.'

'What about his dad, is he here?' I ask but wonder immediately if I've overstepped the mark. I think I need to let Sarah lead this.

She looks round at me, hand paused above a mug with a teabag dangling from her fingers.

'God, no. Dean? He hasn't lived with us for years.'

So in all probability, it was Liam upstairs that morning. I can only be thankful he didn't get downstairs quicker – I'd have scared the poor boy half to death.

'I'm sorry, that was rude of me to ask. It's really none of my business.'

'It's fine. Liam sees him occasionally when he's on the island, but Dean has a girlfriend in France, so it's not that often. They get on, though; they get on well. But Dean has a bad habit of disappearing. Basically, Liam just knows that his dad isn't that reliable and not to expect more than a flying visit.'

There's a moment when her sharp eyes lock on mine and I realise she could just as easily be talking about Tony. Then she turns back, drops the teabags in both mugs and fills them with water.

'Have a seat,' she says, placing my drink on the table, and I pull out a chair, lower myself onto it.

'So, Tony died,' Sarah says, getting straight to the point. 'He had a fair innings, then. And it was his heart?'

'Yes,' I say. 'He was in his car, on his way here. Did you know he was coming?'

'I knew he wanted to come. He phoned me and I told him to stay away. That was about two months ago, the last time I spoke to him, but I hadn't seen him for many years before that.'

It's so odd to hear this woman talking about Tony in such a matter-of-fact way. A phone call, a conversation, a ticket, a ring. None of this is matter-of-fact to me and there's still the most enormous elephant in the room.

'You said that Tony was the worst thing that ever happened to Margaret.' I'm determined to force her name into the conversation. 'What did you mean?'

'Exactly that! It ruined us as a family, all the lies, the deceit, which I doubt she was capable of until she met him. How much do you actually know?' Sarah asks me as she places her mug back on the table.

'I know that Tony was in love with Margaret and on the day he died, I *thought* he was coming here to propose to her with that ring. I obviously now know that's not the case. I didn't know you existed – I assumed I'd find Margaret here in this house when I arrived. I don't know if Margaret and Tony were still together when he died and if she knows that he's actually dead.'

Some truth at last, but not all of it. I won't give her the

letter. In fact, I make an instant decision to destroy it and make sure no one else ever reads it, either. Only hurt can be caused by it now. She then stretches her hand across the table and surprises me by laying it gently on top of mine.

'Oh, Evelyn,' she says. 'You really don't know anything at all.'

Embarrassed by this gesture and the words that accompany it, I pull away, bury my face in my mug, while Sarah gets up and paces the kitchen.

'You have to remember that I don't ever talk about Tony any more. I cut him and Mum from my life when I was seventeen. They lied to me and I wanted nothing to do with them. I packed a bag and left home.'

I can see her fingers trembling as she reaches for her mug again.

'We don't have to talk about this, Sarah, if it's too much for you.'

'You've come a long way to hear it, Evelyn. How can I possibly deny you the truth?'

She walks over to the sink and leans back against it before she begins to speak again.

'I was six months old when Tony met my mum. It was 1973 and we were living in Norwich. My father was killed in a hit-and-run when Mum was pregnant with me and after that we were on our own until Tony turned up.'

She looks at me properly then, maybe to gauge my reaction, and I have to hold on to my breath and my breakfast. The year 1973 was two years after we lost Stephen and Tony was in Norwich to meet the love of his life.

'Obviously, I didn't know anything about this at the time because I was just a baby, but that's the truth as I know it now. Anyway, Tony arrived on the scene and he and my mum... is it OK just to be honest with you?' she asks, and I nod.

This is why I've come, after all. I want to hear this and will just have to deal with the fallout after.

She continues, 'They fell in love, I guess, and Mum and I moved from Norwich to Chesham.'

I baulk at this new piece of information. Chesham is just five miles from my home. Tony moved his family for convenience.

'I had a new pop-in daddy. That's what I called him as I got older, apparently.' Sarah laughs, a small mirthless sound leaving her lips. 'So, we just started again as a family, but one that wasn't like many others.'

'So, did they make you think Tony was your father? How did that work? What about friends? Family?'

'We'd moved, don't forget, over one hundred and thirty miles, and Mum had been pretty solitary, anyway. The friends she had before, she dropped. She didn't have a great relationship with her brother, my uncle David. My grandparents lived in America. She was an easy target for Tony – and as for me, well, what child really questions their situation? I took everything I was told to be true. Tony worked away at his factory and was a very busy daddy, so only came home occasionally. Where did *you* think he was when he wasn't at home?'

'Well, supposedly he was often away at furniture fairs or talking to suppliers, sourcing new materials around the country. I guess now he wasn't, really, because the factory was mostly run by others, and eventually, it began to fail without proper management. I didn't realise how bad it was until it was too late. Weekends he was often away fishing or golfing with friends. He went to antiques fairs, too, and he must have done some of that, judging by what was said about him at the funeral.'

'Mum collected a few antiques,' Sarah says quietly. 'I believed what I was told to begin with, but then later I started to ask questions.' She walks back over to the table and sits down opposite me.

'I was about fourteen when I found out he wasn't my real father. I'd become a bit of a nosey teenager, had been going through cupboards and drawers. I'm not proud of snooping, but something didn't feel right at home. It was like I was in a TV drama – we were all acting at being a family.

'Being adopted had become the latest horrible slur at school. Saying to someone they were adopted was like calling them fat or ugly or geeky. I was convinced that I *had* been adopted and looked for evidence. I found nothing personal in the bedside drawer on Tony's side.'

She stops again and looks at me before sliding her eyes away. Yes, I want to say, yes, this is excruciating to hear, but I don't. I let her continue as I drain the last of my tea.

'It was like he just had overnight things in our house and it was suddenly glaringly obvious that he didn't really live with us, not properly. Hardly any post ever came for him, but when it did, it was a reminder that he didn't have our surname, Waters. I always knew they weren't actually married and I had Mum's name, but she'd told me it was because she was a modern woman, not that it was legally impossible.

'When I tried to talk to Mum about it, she just kept saying

about him working a lot and it was easier for him to sleep at the factory sometimes. But I had a dogged determination and wouldn't let any of it drop. One day I was on a coach on a school outing and I saw Tony with a woman – with you, it turns out,' she says, and I draw in a sharp breath.

'With me?' I repeat.

'Yes, just walking along the street. I thought he was having an affair.' She barks out a laugh and throws up her hands. 'How ridiculous! I mean, how messed up! Of course, I went straight home to tell Mum and that was when they had to admit the truth. They told me about my real dad dying just before I was born, about Mum and Tony getting together, and that because he didn't have any children, he wanted to think of me as his own. They said he had a wife who was ill, like ill in the head. Sorry, Evelyn, this must be painful to hear. Tony said how could he leave her when she was so poorly, but his need to be with my mum was too much for him. He said he'd found a family who needed him; a widowed woman and a fatherless child.'

A prickle of ice begins to start in my fingers and travels up my arms to my face. Sarah moves pretty quickly and puts her arm around my shoulders, but I can't feel it. I hate him. I actually have absolute hatred for this man Sarah is talking about.

'Are you OK? I'm sorry to have to spell it out, but I think it's better to know, don't you? Do you want me to continue?'

'There's more? How can there be any more?' I ask, but of course there is – I have a whole letter's worth of more.

Sarah gets up again and flicks the switch on the kettle for another round of tea. She takes my mug from me before rinsing it and popping in another teabag.

'Things started to disintegrate between me and Mum then. I had no respect for her, carrying on with a married man, whatever the situation, and even less respect for Tony, who I thought was just probably enjoying the best of both worlds. I just wanted to get away. I started sleeping over at friends' houses quite a lot and I think Mum and Tony were relieved to have me out of their hair. Then, just before my seventeenth birthday, I overheard Tony on the phone.'

I find that I'm holding my breath suddenly, because I have a horrible feeling I know what's coming.

'He was talking about my real dad and about the hit-and-run accident. I don't know who he was talking to, but he admitted to being responsible. When I challenged him after, he denied it, said I was hearing things, that the police had reopened the case after another cyclist was killed on the same stretch of road. He said he was helping with enquiries. I knew he was lying; he always made the mistake of thinking I was as gullible as my mum. The whole thing was completely implausible.'

My blood seems to have cooled again and makes me shiver as it runs icy through my veins.

'What happened?' I ask quietly. 'Did you approach your mother?'

'Oh, yeah, I told her everything I'd heard, and do you know what? She said I was mad and that ever since they'd told me the truth about my real father, I'd been cold towards Tony and that now I was making things up to make him look bad. She said that she wouldn't entertain the idea. I knew then that she'd side with him no matter what I said. That was the week I packed up and left.'

I'm gripping hold of my mug so tightly that when I let it

go, it falls over onto the table, spilling out the dregs from the bottom.

'I'm sorry,' I manage, and Sarah grabs a cloth to mop it up.

'No problem,' she says, dumping it back in the sink. 'I shouldn't have just come out with it. I guess it's a bit of a shock for you. I keep forgetting he was your husband. I always thought you knew.'

'I didn't,' I say quietly, my head spinning.

She re-boils the kettle and takes my mug from the table. Doesn't ask if I want another drink, just drops another teabag in from the caddy. She's like a chain-smoker, lighting one cigarette from the last. Eventually, she does sit down and toys with the corner of a newspaper.

I have to tell her about the letter, I realise. It would be cruel not to.

'May I ask where Margaret is now?'

'She had breast cancer – eight years ago, my uncle David told me. She wanted me to know so I could get myself checked out. I decided to break the years of silence and go to her, make some sort of peace. I couldn't let her die without seeing me. It felt like the right thing to do. I did it for her. I saw Tony at the hospital briefly – yes, they were still together then – but I didn't speak to him and she died the following day. I never saw Tony again.'

I let those words sink in. Margaret is dead. It brings me no comfort.

'I have to tell you something that to be honest, I wasn't going to. But now, after what you've said, what you've been through, it would be wrong not to.'

'What else?' she says warily. 'What else did Tony do?'

'He wrote a confessional letter,' I say slowly, and watch as she lowers herself into her chair. 'He admits to being responsible for the accident that killed your father.' I let that settle for a moment. 'Please don't think I knew. I only found out any of this after he died. I'm so sorry he denied it when you confronted him – that should have been the time when he took responsibility for what had happened. I can only guess that it was to stop your mother from chucking him out. He should never have let it come between you and your mum. I really didn't know my husband at all.'

Sarah gets up from her seat and begins to rinse our mugs under a trickle of water before upending them on the draining board. She stares out of the window into her back garden, her eyes fixed on one spot.

'Have I done the right thing in telling you?'

'Yes,' she says, turning to me, wiping a finger underneath her eye. 'I'm glad to know I'm not mad, that what I heard on that phone call was exactly what I knew it was. So many times over the years I thought that I could have misheard, as Tony said I did, and that I walked away from home on a misunderstanding.'

'There was no misunderstanding. It was all Tony, please remember that. He had an innate sense of entitlement – a need to control and have what he wanted at all costs.'

'It was her, too. She chose to believe him over me. They deserved each other.'

There's no bitter edge to Sarah's voice, just a sadness and perhaps a resignation.

'I don't understand why he wrote it down, though, if he never intended to admit to it,' she continues.

'I think maybe that *was* his way of admitting it. Of course, we'll never really know. Do you want to read it?'

'No,' she says quickly. 'Do you have it here?' She eyes me nervously.

'No. No, I don't.'

'I guess there's no point doing anything about it now anyway; they're all dead, after all,' she says.

It's true, I realise. A toxic couple who no longer exist, almost as if they never did. Only Sarah and I will carry the scars of Tony's deceit – and her scars run much deeper than mine.

'I'd burn it, personally, move on. I did, many years ago.'

'Something I don't understand is why Tony was coming to see you – why then, particularly? What did he say on the phone?'

'He thought he was dying. He wanted to atone, I suppose, give my mother's ring back.'

'He was dying?'

'He said he was having chest pains. I told him to go to the doctors and never phone me again. It sounds heartless now, I guess, and maybe if I had spoken to him properly, he might not have attempted to make the journey.'

We sit in silence for a moment and I digest all that's been said. An overwhelming sadness grips me as I imagine Tony trying to play daddy to Sarah, play-acting as a husband and family man. I think about that plaque on the side of the library in memory of a well-loved man who did so much for others. He didn't really exist. How could he leave me when I was so poorly? He'd never have left me, because I was the one with all the money.

Chapter Twenty-two

The Stepmother

I leave East Street in the wrong direction. It could be the sound of the sea that's pulling me. It could also be that the thought of going back to the hotel is overwhelming. There's a block of garages at the end of the street. Graffiti decorates a couple of the doors, some actually quite artistic, if you like that sort of thing, but also there's a splattering of unfortunately legible wording with what Gary wants to do to Joanne. For a moment I think it's a dead end, but then I see the lane continues. After squeezing through the bicycle barrier, I'm out onto the seafront, trying to breathe through the building rage.

I'm so angry with Tony I could scream. The utter arrogance of him is unbelievable and yet completely so at the same time. To come home to me and slide his feet into his slippers, sit at the table and watch me place a meal in front of him, make small talk, very small talk, and to carry all that deceit with him... No wonder Sarah thought I was complicit. And there's the thought. Was I complicit? The act of never asking him about where he was for 50 per cent of our marriage. That thought hangs heavy. I watch the waves draw back and pull away, dragging knotted seaweed, sand and stones with it. The sound is soothing, the monotony calming. Eventually, the chill begins to dampen the rage and I turn to begin the walk back.

My legs are stiff and my fingers frozen, even inside my gloves. I begin to wonder if I'll be able to manage the journey. I have my mobile phone in my bag – Cynthia's insistence – and I contemplate calling a taxi. Of course my phone isn't smart, or certainly I'm not smart enough to use it. I won't be able to look for a number I don't have. I notice a couple over the road who look as if they're heading for the pub on the corner of the street.

'Hello?' I call as I make my way over to them, but I'm not quick enough.

The man already has his hand on the door and they don't look round but disappear inside. I reach the pub and hesitate, my own hand on the door. A woman should never walk into a public house on her own. My mother's words come at me from across the years. Sorry, Mum, but this woman needs a lift.

'What can I get you?' the barman asks as I approach.

The couple who walked in before me are already being served further along the bar and at the other end, an old man sits with a newspaper and something close to the colour of treacle in a pint glass.

'I'd like the number for a taxi, if you have one, please.'

'No trouble,' he says, pulling a card from behind the till.

As I take it from him, my hand begins shaking violently.

'I got a bit cold out there,' I say, embarrassed by my weak body, my age declaring itself.

'Why don't I phone Bill and you take a seat? Can I bring you over a coffee or a cup of tea to warm your hands? You look frozen, love.'

'Actually, a coffee would be very welcome.'

There's a table in an alcove near the window and I pull out a chair, confident I can see when the taxi comes. My coffee appears moments later by a young girl with the most elaborately plaited hair I've ever seen.

'Taxi will be about half an hour,' she says. 'I hope that's OK. He's got a drop in Shanklin and then he's going to come for you.'

I take a note from my purse that more than covers the cost of the coffee and tell her to keep the rest. Then I sit back with the cup in my hands, my fingers beginning to warm. I have an urge to speak to my sister.

'Carol?' I say, my voice breaking as the call connects.

'Evelyn, at last, you've switched your bloody phone on!'

I think back to the message that never sent the other night when I was trying to reach out to her. How she probably thinks I've been ignoring her after our last conversation.

'I thought you were supposed to be back on the 26th, but it's the 29th now. Are you still there, on the island? I've been over twice to your house, but it's clear you haven't been back. What's going on?'

'I'm fine, Carol. Yes, I'm still here at the hotel. Something happened to one of the guests and two of us decided to stay back to help.'

'What happened? This isn't like you, to be so... I don't know, bold, I suppose.'

I think for a moment about telling my sister about the police visit and the real reason we've stayed behind on the island, but it really isn't my business to tell and that might be an adventure too far for Carol to take.

'There was an accident. A woman burned her arm and has to go back to the hospital on the 1st to have the dressing removed.'

It's not a complete out-and-out lie, but I still manage to stumble over the words.

'Really? Why can't she just get it done at her own hospital, or surgery, for that matter? It makes no sense. I hope they're not taking advantage of you.'

'Of course they're not. And I'd know all about that – I've had a lifetime of it! The two women I'm with are actually very nice, but listen, that's not important right now. I've been back to speak to Sarah, Margaret's daughter. I've got to the bottom of all of it. Well, most of it. Of course I'll never know what truly motivated Tony, but I have the facts at least.'

'And?' Carol asks, her voice softer now.

'Sarah was six months old when Tony dropped into their lives. She's forty-nine now.'

'So it was the woman I saw him with? It had been going on a long time, then?'

'Yes, Sarah found out he wasn't her real father when she was fourteen. They let her think for all that time that he was, when the mostly absent and longed-for figure wasn't even the real deal.'

I begin to repeat what Sarah has told me and Carol listens quietly as I try to get the words out. It feels surreal, sitting in this pub, unravelling the threads of my life, because this story doesn't feel as if it belongs to me at all.

'So, Margaret's no longer in the picture, then?' Carol says when I stop talking. 'That's a relief, I suppose, in a sad way. I had a horrible image of you and this woman having a slanging match in the street.'

'Hardly, Carol. Not really my style. I'm more the suffer-in-silence type.'

'Silence, you say?'

I take another warming sip of my coffee and listen to my sister chuckling on the other end of the line. Oddly, it's the closest I've felt to her in years.

'She knew about me – Margaret, I mean. Tony was honest about that from the start, apparently. But listen to this, Carol. Margaret told Sarah that I knew all about them and that I accepted the situation – can you believe that? I mean how horrible and delusional. It's why Sarah was so frosty towards me to start with. She thought that there was a big secret and she was the only one excluded. The poor girl really had her whole world blown apart.'

'Why on earth would they tell her about you?'

'Because Sarah saw me and Tony together one day. Sarah got the impression they thought it would make them look better. If I knew about them and condoned it, how bad could they really be? They didn't account for her to have been horrified at the thought. They told her I was ill and that Tony still needed to look after me. Christ, Carol, they painted me as Bertha Mason, the mad wife in the tower from *Jane Eyre*.'

'I just can't believe that Tony would have sunk so low, to play you like that. When you needed his full support, after Stephen, he offered it to someone else,' she says. 'I wish I could have been there with you. What a thing to have to do on your own.'

'I needed to do it on my own to be honest, Carol. This whole trip has taught me a few things, and not just about Tony's lies. I'd really like to come and see you when I get back, if that's OK?'

'Of course it is. When are you back?'

'We're getting the ferry on the 2nd January at about two fifteen. Cynthia has organised it all. I think you'd really like her, and Joy, too. I sent you a text message, by the way. I don't think you received it though.'

'A text message, very impressive, but no, sorry, I didn't. Not to worry though. What did you want to say?'

'Oh, you know, just this and that. Nothing really.'

There's a moment of silence on the end of the line and I pick up my coffee and finish it. The silence stretches and there's so much we should be saying to fill it, but maybe it'll be better in person.

'I'll speak to you when you get back then, shall I?'

'Yes, OK,' I say and wait for my sister to hang up.

Cynthia and Joy are in the kitchen in the annexe when I get back, and there's a meal laid out on the table – another wonderful creation from Joy.

'Perfect timing,' she says when she sees me.

'We thought we'd eat early and then get tucked into some board games. I've found Scrabble, Monopoly, a couple of packs of cards and loads of jigsaw puzzles,' Cynthia says, dishing out large slabs of lasagne onto our plates.

The rich smell of oregano hits me as I sit down and my mouth waters.

'Sounds good,' I say, happy to be absorbed in something other than talking about the story of my life, which feels as if it's been razed to the ground today.

'Want to talk about how it went at Sarah's?' Cynthia asks me, as if she's misread my mind.

'It went fine. We've got things sorted. I just spoke to my sister and relayed it all. Do you mind if I tell you another time? I'm pretty exhausted with it all, to be honest.'

'Of course not,' says Joy. 'I'm sure it's the last thing you feel like doing now.'

'You can tell us tomorrow,' Cynthia says, tucking into her meal.

I can't help but smile at her. Joy picks at hers, lost in her thoughts, and by the time Cynthia and I have cleared our plates, she's eaten next to nothing.

I make a pot of tea and Cynthia lights a fire in the stove. I settle on the sofa next to Joy and Cynthia takes the armchair, all thoughts of games momentarily forgotten. My eyes become heavy as the smokey warmth reaches me from the fire. The gentle rustling and crackling helps me to sink further back until I could just drift off. It's been the longest of days and will take me some time to process.

I can sense Joy beside me; twitchy and tapping her fingers on the arm of the sofa. I open my eyes and she pushes herself up, walks towards the fire and stares into the flames before lifting the curtain to look out into the early evening darkness. Cynthia watches her while she drinks her tea. I have no room for anything and leave my cup abandoned on the table.

'Are you OK, Joy?' she asks, and Joy turns to us both, anguish clear in every line of her face and each movement of her body.

She comes to sit down, letting the heavy curtain fall behind her. She picks up her cup but puts it straight back down without bothering to take even a sip. She turns her attention to her fingernails and begins nibbling. I usually find adults doing childish things abhorrent, but with Joy, there's something heartbreaking in her actions.

'Do you want to talk about it?' Cynthia tries again.

'I lied to the police.'

There's no longer any droopiness to my eyes. I'm wide awake, alert, and I have to stop myself from shuffling away from Joy along the sofa. It's a natural reaction of mine, to take flight when I sense danger. Not Cynthia, though, it would seem.

'Oh, well, we've all done that. I wouldn't worry too much. I'm sure they expect a certain amount of liberty-taking in an interview situation. I once told a policewoman who was questioning me about some stolen dresses that I hadn't been anywhere near the warehouse in question when the items went missing. Of course I had, because they were all in a box in my basement. I'd walked out with them in a suitcase.' She pauses long enough to look up at us both, and I throw a glance at Joy, who looks bemused. 'Perhaps a story for another time, though,' Cynthia says.

'My husband, Patrick, had a stroke three years ago. It was a major one and left him heavily dependent on me. Carers came to start with when he finally left hospital. They'd bustle in, all jolly, "Come along then, Patrick, let's get you sorted."'

Joy's voice takes on a sinister note as she mimics the carers and brings a chill into the room despite the roaring fire. I change my mind and pick up my tea with a sudden urge to cling to something.

'But then it was down to me. He didn't like strangers in the house. His kids hardly ever came, either. They don't like me; they think I stole their dad.'

'You have stepchildren?' Cynthia asks, and I'm annoyed with her for interrupting.

Joy may not finish her story if Cynthia keeps butting in.

'Yes, two grown-ups... well, grown up in age only. They both behave like spoiled children. Marcus is, I don't know, late fifties, and Stephanie a little younger. They treat me like a Cinderella to their ugly sisters instead of a wicked stepmother. Frankly, it's pathetic, and Patrick would always indulge them, take their side, talk down to me in front of them.'

'And when they weren't there?' Cynthia interrupts again, and I scowl at her, but she ignores me.

'Oh, yes, far worse when they weren't there.' She pauses for a moment and stares into the fire. 'I was planning on leaving him. I'd managed to squirrel away some money and was thinking about going to stay with my sister in Canada, but of course he then had the stroke. What sort of woman leaves her husband when he most needs her?'

'Plenty of men do it,' I say, surprised at my words and the strength of my voice.

'Hear, hear,' says Cynthia.

'I thought it would turn the tables on our relationship. I thought I could handle it, him, if he needed me. I thought he wouldn't be able to intimidate me, to hurt me any more.

Well, it turns out I was wrong. Even from a prone position in bed, he still managed to scare the shit out of me. Well, not any more, though.'

I suddenly feel that chill again and I'm keen for Joy not to finish her story. I already know it doesn't end well for her husband and nasty images come to me: a pillow over a face, a sharp knife in the heart.

'It would have been fine if it hadn't been for his kids. They were the ones who sold the police the story of the evil stepmother, sowed that seed of doubt, when really it could have all looked so innocent.'

'What did you lie about?' Cynthia asks the question that I'm too scared to.

'I told them that he was alive when I left the house, which may or may not be true, but I didn't tell them that he was dying when I left the bedroom.'

There's a loud crack from the fire and both Cynthia and I jump.

'I think perhaps you'd better enlighten us, Joy, because it rather sounds like you may have aided your husband on his way out of this world and I'm sure that's not what really happened... is it? To be honest, if it is, we could do with some time to get your story in order,' Cynthia says, and it's the first time I've seen her looking uncomfortable.

'I didn't kill him!' Joy says.

'What, then?' I ask. 'What happened, exactly?'

'I'd just had enough. I had to care for all of his physical needs because he refused to have a professional in the house after the initial couple of days. He'd hurt me when I helped him into the shower. I'd end up with friction burns on my wrists where he'd grip and twist. He'd pinch me when I helped him into bed and he'd kick out when he was frustrated. I've been covered in bruises for years. I never go swimming any more because I don't want anyone to see them. I'm so ashamed of myself.'

'Why should you feel ashamed?' I ask. 'He should be ashamed.'

'Because I chose to stay with him,' Joy answers simply. 'He wasn't always so physical, but when he became ill, it was his last ability to hurt me, because he didn't really have the words any more. The stroke had stripped him of those. Anyway, I'd finally had enough, decided to organise long-term care for him, get him into a home. Get rid of him, I suppose. But the waiting list for the local homes were endless and his kids were calling me selfish – how could I treat their father in such a disposable way?

'Then I found his will. He'd left everything he owned, equally, to his children. It wasn't as if I wanted his money, but to know that I meant nothing to him was that final nail. So I just booked the first thing I could find – this Christmas trip, actually – then rang round for an emergency carer, packed a bag, messaged my stepdaughter to say she should visit her father because I was leaving and went upstairs to tell him I was going.

'He was incensed and unable to get up to stop me. I'd got to the door before he went quiet. He was struggling, I could see that, and I did go back to him, but by then I think he was unconscious.'

The silence when Joy stops talking is incredibly loud. It seems to be ringing in my ears. Cynthia is quiet for a moment, processing, and then she gets up out of her chair, with some effort, and pokes the fire with a length of kindling.

'Well, you're right about one thing, Joy,' Cynthia says with her back to us. 'You didn't kill him.'

'I didn't help him, either.'

'No, but perhaps it wouldn't have made a difference, anyway.' Cynthia picks at her fingernail for a moment, deep in thought. 'Joy, when the police questioned you the other day, did you mention to them about his controlling behaviour?'

'No, I didn't think to – I was just so upset.'

'Good, don't. It gives you a motive.'

I can't believe we're having this conversation. I'm out of my depth.

'So, did the carer find him, then?' I ask.

'No. Stephanie did,' Joy says, looking uncomfortable. 'The carer messaged me to say she couldn't come after all as she was ill and I replied that it was no problem and his daughter was on her way. I was on the coach by then. And then the messages from Stephanie started. She said she didn't have time to play nursemaid and I was his wife, so I should just stop moaning and get on with it. I didn't respond. In fact I turned my phone off.'

That was the barrage of messages Joy received that day as we left on the coach, I realise. No wonder she pushed her phone down between the seats.

'I should have gone back then, but I'd finally escaped – I couldn't go back!' Joy begins to cry now, her tiny shoulders moving up and down with each sob. 'I didn't want him dead. I didn't want him at all. And now, when the police find that phone, they'll know I read the messages, that I knew she wasn't on her way.'

Cynthia puts her arm around her friend and Joy sobs openly.

'The only thing is, Joy, the police will be able to see that you read the messages on Stephanie's phone, not yours. But you can say you left it at the service station, or where you picked the coach up. Maybe it was stolen and the thief read the messages, not you.'

'But I have an app to track my steps. It shows how many, where, when. As soon as they plug it in and charge it, they'll know where that phone has been. And before the coach left back for the mainland, it was within close range of me.'

'But, if your phone was switched off, no steps will have been tracked. I think that's how that works,' Cynthia says.

'Joy, that's not going to happen. They won't find it now,' I say.

'They will. As soon as Alan cleared the coach, he'd have found it and probably handed it in. He's so proper like that.'

I think about his chain-smoking in car parks, rather improper to my mind, but try to focus on the matter in hand.

'Well, it's a good job I took it before he left, then,' I say, and they both turn to look at me. 'I dropped it in the sea.'

Chapter Twenty-three

Job Offer

Cynthia reminds us that we're going out the next morning and she's booked a taxi to drop us in the village. I'm pleased. This annexe is beginning to feel claustrophobic and people are becoming a little too honest.

I immediately get up to find my coat and shoes, wondering why I automatically do whatever Cynthia tells me to. Glancing across at Joy, I see reluctance on her face.

'Do you think it's OK for me to be out and about?' she asks the room, not making eye contact with either of us.

'You tell us,' Cynthia says. 'Are you a danger to the public?'

I cut her a sharp look. After what Joy said to us last night, it's too close to the mark. I look to see what impact those words have on Joy. Surprisingly, there's the ghost of a smile on her lips and I wonder how Cynthia does it, how she manages to judge the situation so perfectly and come out with just the right words when needed.

'I think the public will be fine,' Joy says quietly, the smile still hovering. 'I'll just use the bathroom quickly and get my coat.'

We abandon the breakfast dishes and after a flurry of activity, Cynthia locks the front door to the hotel with barely suppressed excitement. I know it's not the thought of our day out but the prospect of her soon to be acquiring all of this. Taking a step back, I look up at the great monstrous pile of bricks and rather wonder at her enthusiasm.

It's a short distance down the hill into the village in the opposite direction to the sea. Right at the centre there's a large, lit and decorated Christmas tree in the middle of a green next to the church. There is a row of pretty thatched cottages and what looks to be an old forge with metal artwork hanging on the wall outside, and a sign advertising their craft. An imposing manor house sits just opposite the church with Georgian windows, clipped box hedging and the promise of a beautiful display of wisteria come May. Further along the lane there's a small village store and then the welcome lights of the hotel that I assume we'll be visiting for lunch in a short while. The village is charming – the sort of place I'd imagine a film crew recording a cosy murder mystery.

It's such a short drive, we really should have walked, but the air is still furiously cold, certainly too cold to be spending much time outside. The taxi driver drops us off at the church and suggests we phone him when we want to be picked up, then he drives away. Cynthia proceeds to drag out a book from her bag and begins to make notes. She's wearing what looks like a very old fur coat in an odd shade of tabby, with her dead badger hat. Her suitcase must be like the Tardis with the amount she's stuffed in there.

She's managed a different outfit for every day we've been here, sometimes changing twice in a day. No walking stick, though. She continues to struggle along on her knee.

'What are you writing?' I ask as I take in the church.

The stone porch has been decorated with holly and ribbons, and there's a huge wreath on the oak door. A low stone wall separates it from the road and some of the larger gravestones are just visible over the top. I give a little shiver that has nothing to do with the perishing temperature of the air.

'I'm just making observations about the area,' Cynthia says, pushing open the iron gate and beginning down the pathway to the entrance.

Joy raises her eyebrows at me and shrugs. We both follow behind her, like a couple of happy sheep.

I take a glance at the gravestones, some so old they barely stand. I take a deep breath of the icy air and wait for the despair to overwhelm me, but it doesn't come. In fact, I have a strange lightness in my body that surprises me. Joy is holding back at the gate, but Cynthia has disappeared inside. I walk back towards her, where she's leaning against the wall. Perhaps she's trying for nonchalant, but her eyes look wild and her fingers are entwined in a knot.

'Are you OK?' I ask her, and she gives me a sharp nod in response. 'I have to say, I don't usually like churches that much, but this one is different. It seems calming somehow, I don't know,' I laugh. 'Bit silly, really.'

'Maybe it's because you're not on your own, or maybe because you don't have a loved one here.' Joy loosens the grip on her fingers and then pushes them down inside her pockets. 'I'm a bit nervous about going back to the police station, to be honest. About what's going to happen, what the post-mortem might say. Maybe they'll find out he was barely human at all.' She lets out a dull laugh and it cuts through the air like a rusty bell.

'Whatever happens, we'll be with you. I'm sure everything will be fine. You're innocent, Joy,' I say, forcing myself to believe the words. 'And they'll see that.'

'Why don't you like churches?' she asks.

I lean my back against the wall next to her and fold my arms across my chest for warmth, and also for comfort. I can hear magpies chattering in the tree above us, but I don't chance looking up to see how many. I could just tell her – I could just speak the words. Doctor Graham would say, what's the worst that could happen?

'I had a son,' I say. 'He was seven years old when he died and he's buried at our local church.' I don't look at Joy but stare at some moss growing in the cracks of the stone wall. 'What Cynthia said about wanting to climb in beside her husband... well, I feel like that, too, only with my son. In fact, I've felt like that every day for fifty-one years. I don't go to his grave. I know how awful that sounds, but I can't bear it. I had to be sedated after the funeral, I was quite mad with it all.

'Do you know, Joy, I've been in such a state of utter despair for all these years, with the occasional bout of complete anger, it's exhausting. I never talk about him. I failed at my job and failed at my marriage, too. No wonder Tony wanted another life with another woman. I was no wife at all.' I look up now and Joy takes my hand, squeezes it gently.

'Evelyn, I can't begin to imagine how awful that was for

you, to lose your little boy.' She wipes a tear from her cheek, but my own eyes are dry. 'You might find that if you can go to your church and see his grave, it might help you. But you know he's not really there – it's just a marker of his precious little life. What's his name?' she asks, and the question is unexpected.

People don't usually ask, preferring not to engage in that sort of difficult conversation.

'His name is Stephen,' I say, and she slides an arm through mine and pulls me a little closer.

We turn to see Cynthia appearing from the dark doorway of the church and she's chatting to a man. I notice the white flash of his collar – the vicar.

'As for marriage,' Joy continues, 'it's supposed to be a partnership. It sounds to me as if Tony jumped ship before you'd even left the harbour.'

I think about this as Cynthia begins to walk towards us, the vicar disappearing back inside the church. After speaking to Sarah yesterday, I recognised another layer of unpleasantness in the man I married. He really should have just left me and married Margaret, made at least one honest decision.

The hotel is smaller than The Welcome Rest but far grander. It's lit beautifully at the front, with carefully clipped bay trees either side of the door and window boxes festooned with winter blooms. It's far more welcoming on the outside and when we walk through into reception to the sound of a log fire crackling and tasteful music filtering softly through the air, it's certainly more restful, too. We're greeted cheerfully and taken through to the dining room, all the while Cynthia scribbling furiously into her notepad. The waiter keeps giving her furtive glances and I wonder if he thinks she's a restaurant critic. Suddenly, I have great hopes for our meal.

'So, is this the sort of look you want to recreate?' Joy asks as we begin to look at our menus.

Cynthia orders a bottle of champagne and insists she's treating us all to lunch. We know better by now than to waste time arguing with her. What Cynthia wants, Cynthia gets.

'Sort of,' she says. 'You know, Ian and I were going to buy a hotel once. We'd talked about it for ages and became obsessed with looking online for what was available. We never quite got round to it, though. Our kids needed our help in one venture or another, Ian's job, or mine, got in the way – general procrastination, really, thinking we had all the time in the world. I'm determined to do this for Ian and for what could have been. I think he'd be very proud of me.'

I take Cynthia's hand across the table. 'He would have been very proud. I'm sure I can speak for Joy and say, *we* are very proud.'

'Hear, hear,' Joy says.

Cynthia's lip starts to quiver and she bashes away a couple of tears with the back of her hand.

'Thank you,' she says quietly. 'So, I do want this type of warm atmosphere, but with my own touch,' she continues after composing herself. 'You know, I want to reduce the number of rooms and create a large conservatory. Obviously, I want to modernise and update, and I'd like to offer retreats for writers and artists. Yoga, too, maybe with a resident expert to take classes. But not just privileged old women like us – I want to help aspiring younger people, too. Perhaps offer affordable places to those less fortunate.'

Her eyes are shining with excitement and then she thinks of something else to add to her list and goes back to writing it down. The waiter arrives with a bottle, and my thoughts return to Sarah and to unfinished business. Something has been gnawing at the back of my mind, something I might like to do, but I push the thought aside for now. This is Cynthia's moment.

Once the glasses are poured, Cynthia clears her throat in an overly obvious gesture and says, 'There is one thing that I don't have and badly need, though.'

'Money?' Joy chips in. 'Because all that's going to cost you a small fortune.'

Is she going to ask us to invest? My heart sinks at the thought.

'No, not money. I'm ashamed of how comfortably my late husband left me. I'm talking about a chef. I need someone who really knows their artichokes from their kumquats.'

'Well, that's me out, then,' I snort. Mostly, I'm relieved that Cynthia has the means to do this on her own.

'Joy, I'd like to offer you the position. But before you turn me down,' she says, raising a hand in the air, 'I'd like you to know that obviously, I realise you have a situation that needs resolving. And I have no idea whether or not you'd even want to move to the Isle of Wight, but please know that you're my number-one choice.'

She lifts her glass and automatically, we do, too. We clink them together and an appealing sound rings out. Joy clears her throat.

'Thank you, Cynthia. I'll let you know after my visit to the police station,' she says quietly.

We're silent for a moment as we sip our champagne. I glance across at Joy and her face is set in resignation. As lovely as the offer from Cynthia is, I can't help but feel that Joy has something else to worry about now – turning Cynthia down.

'In other news, we've been invited to a watchnight service late tonight. The vicar there is lovely and very welcoming. It's a service to remember what we've done throughout the year and also to look forward to a new year and a new start. Maybe put some ghosts to bed and make plans for the coming year. I think it could be very cathartic for us all. What do you think?'

'I'm not much of a churchgoer, to be honest,' I say, and Joy nods in agreement.

'OK, no pressure. Let's just have a think about it.'

I already know we'll be going. Cynthia will talk us into it and like lemmings, we'll follow. I suppress a smile, because in truth, I don't even really mind now.

'Right, I'm going to have the salmon to start, then the lamb shank. If I can squeeze it in, I might have the raspberry panna cotta for dessert, as you're buying.' I raise my glass in Cynthia's direction.

'Blimey, I think we'd better forget the idea of a taxi – we're going to need to walk this lot off,' she says.

Our walk back isn't brisk. I'm uncomfortably full after three courses and the alcohol has only added to the discomfort. The chill bite in the air does help to liven my senses, though, and I pull as much of it into my lungs as I can. Cynthia links her arm through mine and Joy's, part in friendship and part because she's still not brought a stick. The woman is a nightmare, but I already know I'm going to miss her when we leave the day after tomorrow.

'Evelyn, have you ever thought about teaching again? Even in a small way, you could, you know?'

'Funnily enough, I did give it some thought a little while ago. They ask at our local school for reading helpers sometimes. I've wondered whether that could be me.' I wonder now if I might be a little drunk.

'They'd be very lucky to have you,' Joy says back in the annexe, I make my excuses and go and lie down. I blame it on the heavy lunch, but it's more the weighty conversation I had with Joy in the churchyard. Thinking about Stephen is exhausting, but talking about him cuts much deeper. I lie on the bed and close my eyes, think about getting through the church service tonight, and try not to listen to Cynthia and Joy talking about me on the other side of the wall.

Chapter Twenty-four

Fireworks

It took me many years to understand fully that the problem with my mother wasn't me, it was her – and surprisingly, it was Carol who told me. I'd always had a difficult relationship with my mother. I wasn't clever enough, pretty enough, quiet enough, and at the same time wouldn't speak up enough. I wasn't enough full stop. To her, I wasn't worth the sleepless nights, the sagging middle, the loss of her youth, although that had been through the war years.

She once said that being stuck at home with a child was unfulfilling. She stopped short of saying I'd been a mistake, although she had said it in every other way possible. By the time she had Carol, though, she'd remodelled herself into a perfect Fifties housewife and mother straight from the pages of her favourite *Woman & Home* magazine. It was too late for me and her, though – the damage had been done.

She did love being a grandmother, though, and adored Stephen. She enjoyed telling me how to parent and I enjoyed ignoring all of her advice. When he died, she was distraught, as we all were, but my mother reserved the right to be more upset than anyone else. *Her* grandson had died. Not my son – always *her* grandson. After the funeral, when everyone was eating the finger buffet that Carol had organised, I had an argument with our mother. I told her that it should have been *her* funeral, not Stephen's – a vicious thing to say, but I meant it. It was the first time in my life that I'd ever said anything unpleasant to her. She said I'd be lucky if she ever spoke to me again, and I said I'd be luckier if she didn't.

A few days later, Carol came to see me, to talk about Mum. I thought she'd ask me to apologise to her for what I said, but she didn't. Instead, she told me that our mother had a problem that was all about herself and nothing to do with me. She didn't highlight what the problem was and I didn't care anyway, but she suggested I didn't waste any energy on her and to concentrate on myself, and healing. Of course I didn't do that, I didn't heal, but slipped into a depression that was so monumental, it took years to come out of it. One thing I did take from what Carol had said, though, was I didn't waste any energy on my mother from that day onwards.

I'm thinking about this now in Cynthia's annexe. It's because of the New Year service we're going to and the themes that it raises: redemption, forgiveness, resolutions. My mother had few redeeming qualities and I resolve, as I do every year, not to forgive her for letting me down.

The church is welcoming with candles lit and Christmas wreaths on the ends of each pew. A beautifully decorated tree dominates the inner porch to the side of the bell tower and some classical music plays gently through hidden speakers. It's not at all what I imagined. My expectations leaned towards a chilly church with someone banging out tuneless hymns on the organ. I hold back by the door next to Joy, tentatively touching the spines of a pile of hymn books while Cynthia sails down the aisle like a blushing bride in search of her new-found friend, the vicar. She's sporting a glittery pink jumper with wide black trousers, catching a few looks.

'I'm networking,' she says into the air as she goes.

It seems like neither the time nor the place to me. It amazes me how Cynthia's knee can support her better after a couple of glasses of wine.

'The best kind of pain relief,' she said as she was knocking them back before we left.

I'm not so sure I agree.

The atmosphere is warm, much warmer than the hotel. I wouldn't want to say to Cynthia that her whole building is seriously cold. She must realise, unless she's particularly thick-skinned, and I wouldn't put it past her. It's fine if we stay in front of the stove in the annexe, but moving around the place proves to be a toe-curlingly chilly experience.

The aroma of mulled wine, or certainly the spices from it, circulates in the air around us now and I notice a woman with an urn on a table behind me, cups laid out, perhaps ready for after the service. The vicar's wife, possibly, but when I glance down the aisle to see Cynthia laughing outrageously and hanging onto his arm, I rather hope she isn't.

Joy is particularly quiet, which is hardly surprising, what

with her visit to the police station looming tomorrow. I pick up a couple of books and service sheets and suggest that we go and hide somewhere at the back of the church. We sink onto the hard wooden pews and Joy leans forwards, unhooks an embroidered cushion hanging from the pew in front. The stitching is worn where many knees have touched it. She lifts it up and pushes it underneath her backside. She was already taller than me and now even more so. I look up at her.

'I think those are for praying,' I say.

'I am praying – praying this will all be over soon,' she says, trying to sink down in her seat, impossible now she's on all that padding. 'I hate church services. Honestly, Evelyn, I really didn't want to come. I'm only doing it for Cynthia, but I don't like it.'

'At least it's warm in here,' I hiss as Cynthia slides in beside me and the service begins.

In the end, it's not nearly as bad as I thought it would be. Singing the hymns was actually uplifting and made me feel a little joyous. The vicar didn't drone on too much and most of what he spoke about was relevant. Redemption came up a lot, which was to be expected, and I kept glancing sideways at Joy, but she sat stony-faced, her bitten fingernails picking at the pleats in her skirt. Cynthia looked a little like a child on Christmas morning, hanging off every spoken word and nodding in rapt agreement, saying amen every time the vicar paused for breath. I was sure she was going to start raising her hand in the air and twice I leaned in to tell her to calm down. She ignored me on both occasions.

When the collection plate came round, she enthusiastically threw in a substantial wad of notes and the man collecting gave her a look of awe as he recognised a parishioner who would cheerfully donate their life savings to the church fund. Tony always used to go on about the brainwashing that went on inside churches, although how he'd know was a mystery, as he'd only ever set foot inside one twice before: on our wedding day and for Stephen's funeral.

Perhaps that's what he meant; he'd been brainwashed into marrying me. And there it is again – the idea that actually, Tony may well have been a regular churchgoer. Perhaps he and Margaret often joined the congregation of a small tucked-away church, somewhere that no one knew them. How could I possibly know? I realise I'm going to have to put the idea of them to bed, so to speak. I can't spend the rest of my life comparing what I thought I knew about my husband with a guess at the reality. It'll drive me mad. I think I'm going to have to stop thinking about him at all.

'This mulled wine is delicious,' Cynthia crows, completely over the top and perhaps a bit drunk.

I'd be amazed if she wasn't with what she's tucked away this evening. It's five minutes to midnight and the congregation has collected around the trestle table, now bulging with wine and nibbles, to see in the New Year. It seems very un-churchlike and much more like a private soirée, but I like it. I imagined we'd be seeing the New Year in back at the hotel, but this is surprisingly nice.

'Apparently, there are going to be some fireworks on the green just after midnight,' Cynthia continues, with a definite slur of her words now. 'So, grab another wine while you can to keep you warm.'

She reaches forwards for another handful of nuts and

another glass as the vicar begins the countdown: ten, nine, eight...

My thoughts drift to what I was doing this time last year. I was alone, because Tony wanted to go to the golf club party and I hadn't wanted to join him. I'd been in bed by ten fifteen. I was often in bed early, never wanting to join Tony in whatever he was doing. A sudden sadness for my failed marriage sweeps through me and I wonder how high I should raise my hand for my part in its deterioration.

Seven, six, five...

I look at my companions and see the possibility of a different sort of life; one filled with friendship and sharing. I could step out of the darkness I've built around myself and embrace something new, but perhaps that's the wine talking.

Four, three, two...

I lean forwards and take two glasses of wine from the table and hand one to Joy.

One.

'Happy New Year,' I say with as much enthusiasm as I can manage.

We troop outside and through the graveyard to get to the green. I keep my eyes averted from the headstones. The fireworks are a little disappointing, although it doesn't stop Cynthia from whooping with delight as each one soars into the night sky. Joy remains quiet, spending more time looking down than up at the display. I'm glad when it's over.

'There's just one last thing I'd like to do before we leave,' Cynthia says before turning back to the church.

We follow her inside and I squeeze Joy's arm when she lets out a little sigh. There's a pile of candles just inside the porch and a lighter, too. Cynthia picks it up and lights one before sticking it into a hole on a shelf next to many others. She closes her eyes and bows her head in contemplation, although what with her swaying slightly, it's hard to know if she's thinking or if she's fallen asleep.

'For you, darling Ian,' she says as if in answer to my question.

She hands the lighter and a candle to me, and I almost don't take them. I know what she wants me to do and why she wants me to do it, and I'm not sure I want to. Then I remember my thoughts inside the church and my part in my marriage.

'Forgiveness is important if you want to move on,' Cynthia says.

I light the wick and stand the candle next to hers, close my eyes but don't bow my head.

'Tony,' I begin out loud. I want the others to bear witness to my words, because after this, I have no wish to repeat them or even think about them again. 'I understand why you sought love with another person. I wasn't the wife I thought I'd be, but you were a selfish man and ruined many lives. Not just the poor man you killed, but Sarah, too. Because of your lies and deceit, she lost that special bond with her mother and I'm going to do a small thing to help her and her son on your behalf. I'm going to give them some money, Tony. Now rest in peace.'

'I'm not sure that was quite what I had in mind,' Cynthia says, taking the lighter from me and handing it to Joy. 'But I hope you get some comfort from it.'

'Yes, yes, I will.' I smile at her.

Joy takes the lighter but reluctantly and it's several

seconds before she lights a candle. She places it into the space next to mine and folds her arms firmly across her chest.

'Do you want to say a few words?' Cynthia asks her gently, but Joy shakes her head.

The vicar is making his way back towards us, no doubt to lock up the church for the night, and Cynthia rushes over and begins to gush about the service again. It's while she's engaged with him that I notice Joy step away from me. I watch as she leans back and snuffs out her candle between her fingers.

Chapter Twenty-five

Paper Aeroplanes

The taxi drops us off outside the police station at ten forty-five in the morning and we file inside without a word between us. Once again, Cynthia and I are left in the waiting area as Joy disappears into the bowels of the station, her efficient-looking solicitor following behind.

'She ate nothing but her fingernails this morning,' I say. 'God, Cynthia, what's going to happen to her?'

'I have every faith in the police and the criminal justice system. We'll be walking out of here with a rightly free woman in a short while.'

'I wish I had your faith. You hear such terrible stories of people being wrongly convicted.'

'Perhaps, but in this case I'm confident that justice will prevail. Now, I'm going to get us both a tea and you're going to tell me what you're going to say to Sarah this afternoon.'

I phoned Sarah before we left the hotel. She was surprised and I hope pleased to hear from me. I asked her if I could see her before I left for the ferry in the morning. She suggested meeting for a coffee this afternoon and I really hope I won't have to cancel. If the outcome here isn't as Cynthia predicts, I'm not sure I'll just be able to disappear. Cynthia arrives with two cardboard cups of tea, a groan leaving her as she sits down beside me.

'When are you getting your knee sorted? You can't possibly start renovating a hotel with pain like that?'

'I have an appointment for my pre-op in a couple of weeks' time, so not long after that, hopefully. They're trying to get me in for a cancellation, but you know how these things work – slowly.'

'Will your daughter come and help you after? Perhaps you could go and stay with her?' A loaded question from me, and maybe a little foolhardy, bearing in mind what happened the last time I brought it up, but I hope we've moved on from all that now.

'I don't think so. I doubt Helen's forgiven me for not going to hers for Christmas and I very much doubt she believed I was ill. I'll pay for a local carer to pop in to help me in those first couple of days. Someone's got to help me get my knickers on,' she says, laughing. 'Evelyn, do you think I'm a selfish person, not to go and comfort my daughter when she needed me? I keep thinking about how much she misses her dad and with me not there for Christmas as well...'

'I think you're the complete opposite of selfish, actually. Your reason for not visiting Helen was all about self-preservation and completely understandable, to my mind.'

'Thank you for that – you're a good friend.' She pats the back of my hand.

'Don't leave it too long to reach out, though. From experience, if you don't say how you feel now, the years go by and you never do. Resentment builds and it's hard to return to the relationship you may have had once before.'

Cynthia pauses with her cup halfway to her lips and I wonder if I've gone too far with my unsolicited advice. She turns to me and I meet her gaze.

'That's good advice, Evelyn,' she says. 'Forgiveness is important, too, and also understanding when something is out of your hands and certainly not your fault.' She looks away from me, back towards the desk, where the phone doesn't stop ringing.

'The candle?' I say. 'I understood your intentions last night, but I've made my peace with Tony, or I'm certainly on my way to.'

'I'm not talking about Tony,' she says, and before I know it, she's slipped her hand inside mine.

Her fingers are warm, but they don't stop a spike of something icy piercing my insides. I know what's coming – of course Joy told her, and I'm not sure I can do it, not here, not now. I thought that after speaking to Joy, I might feel differently, but somehow it's much more difficult with Cynthia. I brace myself, but my defences are woefully inadequate against her words.

'I'm talking about your boy, Stephen.'

My boy.

'Can you tell me about him?' she asks, and it's the most unexpected question.

I thought Joy had done well to ask his name, but no one ever wants to continue a conversation about a dead child. Once they've offered up the expected condolences – *How terrible for you. I'm so sorry to hear that. Gosh, is that the time? I must be going* – it's conversation over. Can I tell her about him? Cynthia has her head turned slightly, her eyes still on the desk, and mine are on the wall in front. I can talk to a wall, surely. And it's as if she's not really listening, as she's not looking at me, but my hand is still tight around hers. I take a ragged breath and try.

'He had dark brown hair that curled up at the front, no matter how many times I flattened it down. His school photos were always terrible. He loved anything with wheels or wings; the bigger, the better. We have a small meadow behind our house and I used to make paper aeroplanes with him. He used to try to fly them there when the wind was right. He was never happy when they plummeted; even at five he'd try to make a better one, or get me to. He had a naughty hand,' I say, and an unexpected bubble of joy bursts from my lips.

Cynthia snorts beside me.

'Like his mother,' she says.

'I don't have a naughty hand,' I say to the wall.

'You broke into a house,' she says to the desk. 'Tell me what he did with it.'

'It was my sister's birthday. We were at her house and he swept the cards from the windowsill in one motion. They were on the floor in a pile. Carol was horrified. He said it was his naughty hand that had done it and I said his good hand would have to pick them up. And do you know, he did. He stood them all back, upright, one-handed, no mean feat for a young child.'

'God love him,' Cynthia says, her voice thick with emotion. 'Tell me about what happened to him, if you want to.'

My fingers find my locket, close around it and the first curl of Stephen's baby hair safely tucked inside.

'It was at school,' I say quietly and quickly. If I stop now, I doubt I'll continue. 'I was a parent helper before it was a thing, you were right. I wanted to be close to him, to make sure he was safe. I do know that's extreme, but that's how I felt. He was my world. It was playtime and I was in the dining room helping prepare the snacks...'

I pause and I'm right back there, cutting chunks of cheese and slicing apple for the children to have with a biscuit. Chatting with the two other mothers as we worked. Someone came in from the playground. A child had fallen from the climbing frame and hit their head. I remember thinking that some poor soul was going to have a headache or a nasty bruise. But it was neither of those things – it was a fractured skull and then it was an aneurism and it was Stephen. He died in hospital.

We're quiet for a while, although Cynthia's hand is still wrapped around mine.

'You obviously don't need me to tell you that it wasn't your fault,' she says.

'I was cutting an apple, a fucking apple.' And there it is, the anger, so acute still after all these years.

'It wasn't your fault, Evelyn. It was a terrible and tragic accident. So bloody unfair. Have you ever talked to anyone about it?'

'I just did,' I say and turn to look at her.

She's no longer staring at the desk and there's a moment of silence as one of the telephones stops ringing. It feels as if something significant happens. It's not something I can put into words, not properly, but there's a lightness suddenly in the air around me. Perhaps a first step, and maybe it won't be as difficult as I thought it would be.

'Thank you,' I say.

Our surroundings appear again at the edges of our conversation. The phone starts up and someone comes through the front door, letting it close slowly behind them. A blast of cold air hits us a second later. We go back to sipping our drinks.

It's only ten minutes later, when Joy appears in front of us, her solicitor disappearing quickly out of the door.

'Let's get out of here,' Joy says, her expression unreadable.

We leave the station and walk further into the high street. The snow has completely disappeared now and the pavements offer up a thin layer of winter mud. We find a pub and decide on an early lunch.

Joy is staring at the menu and we're staring at her. The sun has made a brief appearance and is shining through the window directly on her. It highlights the smile she has on her lips, the one she's trying to suppress.

'I'm starving,' she says. 'I'm going to have the steak and chips, lots of chips.'

Cynthia laughs, but I don't. I want to know what happened at the police station. Surely she's going to tell us. I order the fish pie and a glass of water, and Cynthia orders a steak, too. I don't have much of an appetite after what's just passed and my impending meeting with Sarah is beginning to sit heavily in my stomach. Hopefully, the fish will be easy to swallow.

'Should we be ordering champagne?' Cynthia asks, but Joy shakes her head.

'Not for me, thank you. It doesn't seem right to be celebrating. I've only had confirmation of what I already know, and yes, I was concerned for a while that it may have gone another way, but there is still a funeral to get through, the stepchildren to deal with, the house. I have a long way to go.'

'So, have they let you off?' I ask, the words sounding childish even to my own ears.

'Evelyn, the police don't let murderers walk free from their premises,' Cynthia says with one brow raised.

'I'm not sure that's strictly true, but what I'm really asking is, what happened, if that's OK with you, Cynthia?'

'NFA,' says Joy, but I'm none the wiser. 'No further action, they said.'

'But what does that even mean?' I ask.

'Literally what it says. They can't take things further because they have no evidence of foul play. The post-mortem showed cardiac arrest was the cause of death and on top of his ill health wasn't a huge surprise. They were kind to me, businesslike. There was no good cop, bad cop routine, like there is on the telly. I think they just genuinely wanted to find out the truth, not to pin a crime on me.'

'What did you say about the phone?' I ask quietly.

'I told them I lost it at the service station and that perhaps it may have been stolen.'

Joy doesn't look up as she says this and I glance across at Cynthia, who had suggested this almost word for word.

'Stephanie eventually came to the house four days later because I wasn't answering. Her and Marcus phoned the police to suggest I might have had something to do with his death. I mean it didn't look good, what with me having left, I suppose, but the phone messages tally. It looks like I was expecting Stephanie to look after him because my last message to the carer was to say she was on her way.

And to be fair to me, he was dead – there wasn't anything I could do.'

I glance at Cynthia, because this really isn't true. Joy said she thought he was unconscious and she should have really phoned for an ambulance, just as Tony should have. Cynthia won't catch my eye.

Joy tucks into her steak as she talks to us. It's the first time I've seen her eat anything more than a few sparrow-sized bites.

'It was unfortunate that he'd been lying there for four days when Stephanie found him. That can't have been nice for her, I suppose.'

'Did your husband make you sell your restaurant?' Cynthia asks, to both our surprise.

It's the last thing I'm expecting her to ask and I imagine Joy will dodge the question, but I'm wrong.

'Yes, he did. Because I wasn't giving him enough attention. He wanted to keep me at home so he could control what I was doing. He told me to sell it or he'd burn it down. It was the first time I realised how dangerous he could be. Why I didn't leave him then I don't know. I suppose it felt as if I'd made my bed so I'd have to lie in it or die in it.'

'Oh, Joy, how awful for you,' I say.

'I do realise I should have phoned for an ambulance, but in truth, I didn't think he deserved my attention, even in death.'

She tucks into another large piece of her bloodied steak and I try to swallow a lump of fish that seems stuck in my throat.

'I only have one question, Joy.' Cynthia jumps in. 'What on earth were you thinking?'

'About what?' she says, looking startled.

'You decide to leave your husband, you book a trip and luckily for everyone concerned, he drops down dead. No great loss there, by the sound of it. But, Joy, what possessed you, after years of incarceration in your unhappy marriage, when you're free to go anywhere you want to, to book a bloody coach trip to the Isle of Wight?'

There's a moment of silence as Joy decides how to respond, but before she can, Cynthia dissolves into childish giggling.

'Utter madness,' she says through tears that begin to spill down her cheeks.

She's clutching on to the table now, unable to control the hysterical hooting – that fine line between raucous laughter and wretched sobs. It's infectious, as that sort of humour usually is, and it's only another moment before my body reacts. It's an involuntary response but welcome.

'You could have gone to the Caribbean,' I say inelegantly as a shudder of laughter rips through me.

'Or San Francisco,' Cynthia says as she tries to wipe her tears with her napkin.

I don't think going to San Francisco is remotely funny, but my body does and my ribs are beginning to hurt.

'I hear the Great Wall of China is a wonderful experience and I know a lovely young man who could book it for you.'

Cynthia and I continue to hoot, although she can't possibly know what I'm referring to, but Joy is unmoved. In fact, she's beginning to look a little irritated.

'You do realise you both booked on the same trip as me, don't you?' she says. 'We're *all* on the Isle of Wight. You're buying a business here, too!'

Joy is at least smiling, even if she's late to the joke. I'm starting to regret joining in, though. There's always a comedown, like after a sugar rush.

'I know, I'm just being silly,' Cynthia replies. 'Sorry, Joy, I didn't mean to offend you. It's just an unlikely destination for an escape, that's all.'

As fast as it started, the laughter dies and I look to Cynthia to rescue the situation.

'How about a round of cocktails? In fact, there's no "how" about it. Waiter?' she calls and snaps her fingers in the air – she actually does that.

It's embarrassing but effective; he's rushing over. We order drinks with ridiculous names, which elicits more mirth, but it's subdued.

'Well,' I say, steering the conversation for once, 'you both know how bad I am with words. So please help me to decide what to say to Sarah.'

Chapter Twenty-six

An Unexpected Inheritance

Joy disappears with a book when we get back to the hotel after lunch and Cynthia is sketching out her vision for the much talked about conservatory. I'm getting ready to walk down to meet Sarah for coffee, but Cynthia catches my eye as I prepare to leave.

'You've surprised me, Evelyn,' she says, looking up from her plans.

'Oh?'

She glances at the door to the bedroom and lowers her voice.

'I thought you'd have something to say about Joy. Have a strong opinion about what she did, or perhaps what she should have done.'

I don't pretend to misunderstand her. Of course, we both know exactly what she's talking about.

'Joy is my friend,' I say simply. 'It was brave of her to admit the truth to us and...'

I trail off, because I can't put into words what I truly

think about it. I just know that Joy was there for me when I needed her and I'll miss her. I look at Cynthia now, her pen poised, her smile soft and gentle. I don't even want to think about how much I shall miss *her*.

I set off to walk at a pace, because I want to have the conversation I've practised in my head before I lose my nerve. The fish pie had been delicious, the cocktail perhaps a mistake. I don't know what was in it, but it's made my head fluttery. I'm first to the café – an Italian place with the most beautiful-looking cakes, pastries and desserts under a glass counter. I find a table close to the window so I can watch people passing as I wait. Hardly anybody is around apart from a few dog walkers along the seafront. There are only two other customers inside – an elderly couple sitting at a table in the corner, heads together, bent over a newspaper, doing the crossword. The sight of them fills me with warmth, and also the most abject loneliness.

'I'll wait until my friend comes,' I tell the owner when he approaches.

He's wearing smart grey trousers and a crisp white shirt, his dark hair slicked back from his face, handsome.

'Happy New Year to you,' I add as an afterthought.

'A very happy New Year to you, too,' he says with a broad smile and an Italian accent that I'm not convinced is authentic, but it doesn't matter.

I look away from the couple and out of the window at the sea. It's calm today and the sunlight that shimmers on the surface of the water belies the truth of the temperature out there. Nothing is ever really as it seems. But I'm not going to get maudlin, because the truth is, I'm in an Italian café, waiting for a friend, and I'm about to do something decent for someone who needs some help, if she'll let me, that is.

Sarah arrives a few minutes later, bringing a blast of cold through the door with her. She unwinds the thick wool scarf from around her neck and drops it over the back of the chair, her gloves with it. Her hair looks nice, pinned up at the side with a clip, and she's wearing lipstick that I haven't seen on her before.

'Hi, Evelyn,' she says, a little warily perhaps.

'Hello, Sarah. Happy New Year.'

It occurs to me that I didn't offer up that sentiment to anyone last year, not even Tony when he came home from the golf club New Year dinner. It feels nice to say it now, makes me feel hopeful.

The owner comes back over with a pen poised and I glance back to the display of cakes. They do look so appealing.

'A cappuccino, please, Matteo,' Sarah says, 'and one of those lovely apricot biscuits of yours, too.'

His smile is different for her. It has more warmth and definitely a hint of something else.

'A cappuccino, too,' I mimic when he turns his attention reluctantly to me.

'And to eat?'

I look back over, undecided.

'Surprise me,' I say, words that have never left my lips before today.

He grins before disappearing behind the counter and out the back.

'So, this is unexpected. I wasn't sure I'd see you before you went home. Isn't it tomorrow that you leave?'

'Yes, it is, but I had a couple of things I wanted to say.'

She looks at me cautiously, no doubt expecting some more dredging up of the past, and I suddenly want to lighten the mood. I lean across the table towards her and whisper.

'Is your man actually Italian?'

'Yes, Evelyn,' she laughs, her eyes sparkling. 'But he's not my man,' she whispers back. 'Shh.'

Matteo is walking back towards us, a laden tray in his hands.

'Two cappuccinos, ladies.'

He places the cups in front of each of us, a heart shaped in chocolate on top of the frothy milk. I raise an eyebrow at Sarah across the table and she stares me down, a smirk on her lips.

'Apricot biscuit for you, Sarah, and for your friend, a surprise.'

A lovely-looking slice of cake covered in almonds is presented to me with a luscious strawberry on the side.

'*Torte di Mandorle.*'

'Thank you, it looks lovely.'

'And this is for your boy, Sarah.' He hands her a small packet with another apricot biscuit inside. 'Please, enjoy.'

'Oh Gawd,' Sarah says when he's gone, turning the packet in her hands.

'Clever man, to remember your son like that. Is that the way to a woman's heart these days, through her children?' I sound playful and for a moment imagine what it would be like to be Cynthia, not to be reserved but to be able just to pluck the right thing to say and pop it into any situation. To be the sort of person people warmed to. 'You know each other, then?'

She turns to see if he's at the counter before leaning close to me.

'We had a date once; it was a disaster. He asked me out for dinner and we went to a lovely new place in Cowes. He told me he'd been plucking up the courage to ask me for ages.'

'Why a disaster? He's an attractive man, lovely meal out?'

'I think it was too soon after his wife died and he got upset in the restaurant. She had a brain tumour. It was such a tragedy, very sad, so young. Anyway, he was embarrassed, even though I told him it was completely understandable. He didn't phone for a while after that, but it was a long time ago now. I suppose we're friends.'

I point to the heart on the top of her drink and she laughs.

'You have one on yours, too.'

'Yours is bigger.'

'Eat your cake and shut your face,' she says, grinning.

This is what it's like to be Cynthia. Actually, this is what it's like to be me. I tuck into the almond cake, which is just as delicious as it looks, and we sip at our coffees. I'm putting off starting the conversation I came to have. Now we have this easiness between us, I don't want to spoil it.

'So, what did you want to talk about?' she asks between a mouthful of biscuit.

I put down my cup and plough in.

'First, I wanted to say it's been lovely to meet you, even though the circumstances haven't been ideal. Secondly, I want to apologise for raking up things from your past, and thirdly, I have a proposition for you.'

She places her cup back in her saucer and sighs. 'It's not all bad, Evelyn. You coming here has made me address things I thought I knew but was wrong about. And also vindicated me from years of wondering if I'd made a huge mistake. I've been thinking about it all over the last week and I've decided I need to let it all go.

'I reconnected with my mum before she died and she got to meet Liam. You know, she was so happy to see him. I did it for her and I was completely honest with him about who she was. I don't keep anything from my son. It felt like the right thing to do despite how I honestly felt about her. She made her choice to stay with Tony and I just decided to accept it.'

'You're amazing,' I say, and she laughs.

'Hardly.'

'You've learned forgiveness, acceptance and honesty far more quickly than I have. In fact, I'm still several steps behind you. Can I ask one thing?'

'Sure, why not? Honesty is my middle name,' she says with a smile.

'Did Tony ever meet Liam?'

'No,' she says quickly. 'I'm not that amazing, Evelyn!'

The relief I feel is instant, but I suppress the urge to let out a long, satisfying sigh.

'He didn't deserve to know my son. He had nothing to do with him. The moment he lied about that call, I knew I'd never speak to him again. I told my mum that if she wanted to see me in the hospital, he'd have to stay away. And he did until that last day, when I caught sight of him hanging around the café, but he didn't see me.

'He wasn't a genuine person. I mean, I do believe he loved my mum and he was nice to her – sorry if that's hard to hear. But there was something wrong with him fundamentally, though I hardly need to tell you that, do I? You know, Evelyn, you and me got a shitty deal.'

I nod in agreement, my throat too thick to speak. I swallow the last of my coffee.

'But that isn't why you're here, is it? What's your proposition?' she asks, perhaps happy to move the conversation on.

I know how important it is to frame this just right. I could blow it with the wrong words.

'Liam tells me he wants to go to college to study catering.'

'Yes, he does.'

She looks relieved and I wonder what she thought I was going to say. Liam is safe territory for her.

'He told me about a pipe dream, about going to Leith's School of Food and Wine in London.'

'Yeah, that place was on his search history for a while. He's looking at college here now. It's not that bad, you know, but I do worry for him. Island life can be so inhibiting. Sometimes it can be hard to get away.'

'Is it just the money for the fees that's stopping you, or do you not like the idea of him living in London?'

'Oh, well, it's everything, I suppose. The fees, the cost of accommodation... I have to do extra shifts at the hospital to cover the rent on the house. Dean isn't coming back and has only sent a couple of pathetic cheques in the last ten years. I'm on my own with it. And I know I'd miss him, but that certainly wouldn't stop me from letting him go. From experience, I'd want him to feel confident enough to leave home and know it's always here for him whenever he wants to come back.'

'What if you didn't have to worry about your rent every month and had fees for college?'

'What's this about, Evelyn? How much did you have to drink with your friends at lunch?'

She's still smiling at the moment. I haven't lost her yet, but I may be about to.

'Tony should have left you some money. He was your pretend father for years, someone you should have been able to rely on, but, actually someone who let you down in the most spectacular way. Think of the relationship you might have had with your mother if it hadn't been for him.' I watch her expression change from surprise to something darker. 'He owes you, Sarah.'

'I don't want anything from him.'

She crams the last of her biscuit into her mouth and wipes the crumbs with a napkin. Her face tells me the conversation is over and I'd dearly love to go back to where we were before, but this is too important.

'You said you wondered what would have happened if your mum hadn't met Tony, if he hadn't pretended to be your father. He lied to a lot of people, but I think when he finally tracked you down and bought that ticket for the ferry, he was on his way to make amends. He knew he owed you a lot more than you got from him; a half-baked father figure who was hardly ever there.'

I watch her face and I'm wondering if what I'm saying could be remotely true, or if Tony was purely visiting her to assuage his own guilt. He was getting older and his heart was obviously not good. Age brings out all sorts of old demons. Perhaps he was just a selfish being until the end.

'We had a little boy who died when he was seven,' I say and pause to catch my breath. It seems I'm telling everybody now.

'Oh, Evelyn,' Sarah says. 'I'm so sorry.'

'So, do you see how I have no one to leave any money to. I'd like this to be a legacy in Stephen's memory and surely it would be better now, rather than leaving it until after I die. Like I said, Tony owes you and as he's not in a position to do anything himself, I'd like to do it on his behalf. I'm quite determined.'

I watch as she shifts in her chair, perhaps weighing up the offer. Then I remember the ring. It found its way back into my handbag after the debacle at the hotel when Joy was arrested and I forgot to give it back when I visited her at home. I pull it out and with it a page from the back of my diary.

'Your mother's ring is certainly yours,' I say, passing it across the table.

She nods – a small and sad gesture – picking it up and sliding it on her finger.

'Look, I understand how you feel, but it could make all the difference to both you and Liam. Something good should come from all of his lies, surely.'

I scribble down my address and phone number and I put it down next to her empty coffee cup, but she doesn't take it. We both just stare at it and I assume I've blown it. She looks at me across the table, her expression beginning to brighten, and she licks her lips.

'How much money are we talking about?' she asks with a shy smile.

Chapter Twenty-seven

Then Three Arrive at Once…

It doesn't take us long to pack our suitcases and when we're done, they sit by the main door to the hotel like a sad reminder of how little time we have left here. Every moment now seems precious, the seconds ticking down to departure. We have an hour until the taxi comes to take us to Fishbourne and Cynthia suggests one last drink. Of course she does.

Cynthia, other than being a pusher of all things alcoholic, is a brilliantly organised woman and not only has she booked our ferry tickets, but she's also arranged a taxi the other end to take us back to the service station. From there, we have three other taxis to take us all on our separate journeys. I'm trying not to think about that part yet, because I honestly don't know what I'll do without her. Of course, my sister might suggest that without Cynthia's influence, I might already be at home, but that's Carol for you.

We sit on the settee in the large bay window and I track the progress of an airliner thousands of feet up as it crosses the sky. It's the only thing visible. There are no clouds, the sun is out of shot and a vast expanse of blue stretches from one side of the window to the other. I imagine being on board, jetting off to somewhere far away, and a seedling of a thought appears in my mind. I tuck it to one side for now. We each have a gin and tonic and a bag of peanuts. Cynthia poured them and they're strong. After nine days with the woman, I'm not surprised by this fact.

'I'm in,' says Joy, suddenly standing up. She leans her back against the window ledge and takes a large swig of her drink. 'I'd love to be your chef.'

'Oh my God!' Cynthia slams her glass onto a side table and gets up, begins waving her arms around like an excitable child, her multicoloured plastic bangles slapping against each other. 'Do you really mean it?'

She grabs Joy in a hefty hug, probably near crushing the poor woman, although Joy doesn't look unhappy about it.

'Yes, I mean it.' Joy's muffled voice comes from the region of Cynthia's armpit.

'That's wonderful news,' I say, but really I feel like the child at school who hasn't been picked for the team.

It's a natural response, I suppose, feeling left out, and I try hard to shake it off.

The women unwrap themselves and Cynthia sits back down. Her smile is enormous and I wonder for a moment if she needs Joy more than just for her skills as a chef. Maybe it's her friendship she needs as she embarks on this great adventure.

'It's a big thing, though,' Cynthia continues. 'What about family and friends at home, your house?'

'Are you trying to put me off?' Joy laughs.

'No, of course not. I just want you to be sure, that's all.'

'Cynthia, I have no friends, really. Patrick saw to that.

No family now, and I won't have anything further to do with Marcus and Stephanie. The house and everything in it will go to them. I don't want any of it, not that he left any of it to me. I couldn't possibly live there now anyway. As soon as I've put my things in a suitcase, I'm all yours.'

'You were talking about the funeral yesterday, sorting out the house,' I say, confused at her about-turn.

'I've changed my mind. I don't want to put myself through it. Patrick didn't leave me anything, so I'll let them get on with it.'

It seems that sometimes it's easy to walk away from your life.

'You can come and stay with me in the meantime,' Cynthia says. 'I've got a lot of packing to do myself.'

'No, I wasn't trying to impose. I meant I'm ready whenever you are. I can easily rent a flat or stay in a hotel until things are finalised.'

'Nonsense! I'd love you to come and stay with me, unless you'd rather do something else.'

'I'd really like that, Cynthia,' she says with, I think, a grateful smile. She gets up from the settee and steps forwards with her glass, offers it up to the two of us. 'To us all,' she says, and we all tip forwards and the sound of the crystal rings out as our glasses collide.

I'm happy for Joy and Cynthia, of course I am, but I can feel myself slipping away, back home, to what I was doing before. I try to remember what that was, what it was that I did before Tony died and blew my life apart. There was certainly a lot of washing, some food shopping and obviously the cooking of the food once I'd bought it. There was some cleaning, too, and a bit of gardening. It's a big house and I can easily fill a day with my jobs. A bit of telly in the evenings, either on my own or with Tony, mostly in silence until I'd say, 'I'm off to bed now.' And he'd look up and say, 'Righto.'

Occasionally, there would be an outing to a garden centre at the weekends with Tony or sometimes with Carol. Never on my own, though. I'd never have phoned someone and said, 'Come for a coffee.' Or go to the theatre with strangers. I wouldn't have dreamed of getting involved in cooking Christmas lunch for thirty-eight people or making a pot of tea for a friend who had been arrested. But now, I want something more. I want a project of my own. Not a hotel, obviously, but the school is calling to me. Maybe it's time to give that another go.

I take a long sip of my gin and rest my head back, listen to the sound of the sea.

There's a long blast from the horn of the taxi as it pulls up at the front of the hotel. Immediately I feel myself bristle at the lack of manners. Not having the common courtesy to get out and at the very least poke a head round the door. Cynthia grins at me and pats my arm patronisingly.

'It's OK. I asked them to toot,' she says, and I raise an eyebrow at her.

Of course she did.

'So, we'll just sort our own cases, then, shall we?' I ask.

'Yes, we will. Three independent women can do anything we want.'

I turn away so she can't see me smiling. I enjoy how this is between us. I'll miss it so much. I get a hold of the handle of my wheelie case, try to push down the emotion that's threatening to spill over. I was at home ten days ago, forcing myself to put one foot in front of the other to get out of the door. I remember how much I'd have loved for something or someone to stop me, for an intervention. It's exactly the same now. Perhaps another storm will pick up and we'll be forced to spend a few more days here in Cynthia's annexe, but no. Glancing out of the window, I can see that it's not going to happen. The sky remains cloudless. There isn't a breath of wind and the lawn has lost its crystal carpet, the line of icicles that hang from the eaves of the shed dripping to nothing. We're going home.

'You three had a good time?' the driver asks as he piles our cases into the boot.

'The best time ever,' Cynthia replies.

'Brilliant,' agrees Joy.

'We've been quite the holiday club,' I add.

We all turn back to look at the hotel as the taxi sails down the driveway. I can't wait to see it brought back to its former glory under Cynthia's enthusiasm.

'You should come and visit, Evelyn,' she says, reading my mind.

'I'd really like that.'

It's an automatic response, but one based entirely in truth. I'd love to come back. Part of me would love to stay.

As the ferry docks in Portsmouth, I realise a timer was set in motion when I woke earlier this morning. It occurs to me now that it's ticking down to its final moments. Cynthia is on the phone to the taxi driver, letting them know we're disembarking and only a matter of minutes away, but they're running late.

'I wished I'd thought to book it later, so we could go for a drink.'

'What do you think we've been doing all week?' I say.

'God, I'm about ready to book myself into rehab,' says Joy.

'Lightweights!' Cynthia hangs on to Joy's arm and laughs as we make our way off the ferry. 'Our lift is supposed to be waiting for us in the car park over the road. Oh! and before I forget,' she says, pressing slips of paper into mine and Joy's hands, 'the numbers for your taxis from Winchester. After that, you're on your own,' she laughs.

I push mine into my handbag, along with the lump in my throat.

But it's not the taxi that's waiting for us in the car park. It's Cynthia's daughter.

'Helen! What on earth are you doing here?'

If Helen had been in a line-up of a thousand potential Cynthia lookalikes, I'd have put her in last place. She is, I'd guess, average height, very slim and very neat. No make-up, her hair scraped into a perfect ponytail, and she's wearing a smart pair of jeans with a grey wool coat tied around the waist like a mac. I glance at Joy, who stares, wide eyed and open-mouthed. I imagine I look much the same.

'You're looking very well,' she says, her eyes not leaving her mother's.

Cynthia raises her hands in a gesture of surrender and lets out the biggest sigh.

'Helen, I'm sorry, I just couldn't face it.'

'Couldn't face me, you mean.'

'No, not you, darling. *It*. I couldn't face *it*. How did you find me?'

'Barbara, your neighbour. I drove over on Christmas Eve to see if you'd changed your mind and she admitted to booking your trip when I knocked on her door. We've been in touch ever since and she told me you'd messaged her about the change of your return date. I've been worried about you, Mum.'

Helen walks towards Cynthia and after a moment's hesitation, she wraps her arms around her mother in a gesture so tender that I have to swallow another blockage in my throat. Joy and I turn away and admire the back end of the Wightlink ferry getting ready for its next hop across the Solent.

'I want to introduce my friends, Evelyn and Joy. We've had the most amazing adventure.'

'Hello,' Helen says, walking over to us.

I lift my hand to shake hers, but she ignores it and pulls me into an embrace, kissing me lightly on the cheek. She steps away and envelops Joy, too. I marvel at the ease with which some people operate. It certainly proves that Cynthia is her mother if proof were needed. They share the same natural and uplifting personality.

'I've come to take you home, Mum. I thought we should talk.'

Cynthia turns to look at us, apologetic, and I experience a moment of panic. I don't want Helen to take her away. I thought we had another couple of hours together. I feel the flutterings of anxiety, the first for a while, but I try to squash it down. I will not be that person again. My mind has been so engaged since I've been away that the darkest side hasn't shown its ugly face. I obviously just need to keep busy and

I can't rely on Cynthia for that. In no time at all she'll be back on that ferry and away to her hotel. She certainly has got a lot to tell Helen.

'Joy and I can get the taxi. You two go and catch up. It's lovely to meet you, Helen. Cynthia told us lots about you.'

'I bet she did,' Helen replies with a grin.

There's another moment of silence. No one really knows how to say goodbye.

'You have my address and number, Cynthia. Keep in touch,' I say a little brusquely.

'Of course I will,' she says. 'You need to know when the hotel is finished, so you can book your extended trip.' She reaches out her hand and takes mine, squeezes it in hers. 'It's been an absolute pleasure, my lovely friend.'

'What hotel?' Helen asks as I blink away tears.

'Ah, we have some things to discuss in the car. I'll be in touch very soon, Joy,' she says as she turns away.

Lifting a hand above her head in farewell, she follows Helen to the car. And then after a toot of the horn as they pull out of the car park, Joy and I are alone.

'Right,' she says. 'That was unexpected, but actually kind of lovely. I guess they have a lot of catching up to do. So, it's just you and me, then.' She pulls up the sleeve of her coat and looks down at her watch. 'Taxi should be here by now. Cynthia gave me the phone number, so let's give it five more minutes and then I'll find out where they are.'

'So, you're going to move in with Cynthia, then?' I say to fill the silence. 'You know she's having a knee replacement soon, don't you? She'll have you running around after her,' I laugh.

'Do you think I'm making a mistake?' she says, her face clouding momentarily.

'No,' I say. 'Not at all. I'm just kidding. I think it'll be good for you not to be on your own for the moment. You've been through a lot, and one thing I will say about Cynthia is that she's a great person for taking your mind off things.'

Joy begins to laugh, too. 'Yeah, well, I'm good at rolling up my sleeves and getting stuck in, that's for sure.'

'I'm honestly thrilled for you both, really I am.'

'Thrilled isn't a word I'd have imagined you using a few days ago.'

'That's true. I'm not sure I'd have been capable of mustering up that level of emotion.'

'Oh, Evelyn, I'm not trying to be unkind. You've been through a lot, too. Do you think that maybe talking about it might have helped, even a little?'

'Yes, yes it has. I think it's helped me a lot more than even I realise yet. You and Cynthia have been amazing, you really have.'

Joy pulls me into a hug that takes me by surprise. The intensity of her hold is unexpected.

'Don't look back, Evelyn, look forwards,' she says and then releases me.

The space that opens up between us feels like a loss.

'I won't forget this trip for as long as I live,' she continues.

'You'll be back there soon enough reliving it,' I say. 'Well, the good bits.'

'Would you consider coming, too? I'll bet Cynthia would have a perfect role for you.'

'That's actually a more appealing thought than I'd have imagined a week ago, but no. I have some things here that need my attention.'

'It won't be the same without you,' she says. 'But then

it won't really be the same anyway. I assume Cynthia will crack her whip; it's not like we'll be drinking all the time.'

'I wouldn't put it past her,' I say, and Joy laughs.

'Joy, Evelyn, hello there.'

A car pulls up alongside us and the window slides down. Our coach driver, Alan, pokes his head out, a big, silly smile on his face that's all him.

'Do you need a lift?'

'Alan, what a surprise!' I say, although I can only imagine that Joy has been in contact with him, and by the look of delight on her face, I know I'm spot on.

'Alan, what are you doing here?' she says.

'Well, after you messaged me with your ferry crossing time, I thought I'd surprise you.'

He turns pink, suddenly looking anxious. 'Have I done the wrong thing?'

'We have a taxi coming,' I say, watching as his shoulders slump.

'You could cancel it?' he says, looking hopeful.

'I can't do that; it's too last-minute. It would be rude,' I say.

'Evelyn's right,' Joy says, but the disappointment on her face is too much.

'You go with Alan, Joy. I can get the taxi. I'm probably going to fall asleep anyway – I'm exhausted.'

This is a lie – I slept beautifully last night – but I really don't want to spoil an opportunity for them. Joy has a long way to go but deserves something nice after the week she's just been through.

'Are you sure?'

'Of course.' I inject as much enthusiasm into my voice as I can.

'We can wait until the taxi comes? I don't want to leave you on your own.'

'Don't be silly; I'm old enough to be in charge of myself. Just give me the number so I can phone them. And don't forget to cancel your taxi from Winchester, too.'

She hands over a slip of paper with the name of the company and their number, and I hand her my address.

'Evelyn, it's been such a pleasure, and I really hope you'll come out to see us. In fact, I'll keep phoning you until you do.'

'I will, I promise. And in the meantime, please do look after yourself.'

She throws her arms around me and hugs me tightly again. And then they're gone.

I feel a bit hollowed out, empty, and yet at the same time I know there's something different about me. Before I met these women, the thought of standing in a car park alone, waiting, would have been terrifying. Now, though, as I watch people coming and going, some smiling at me, others offering me a good afternoon, something stirs. Maybe I'm hollow because I've offloaded some of the hurt I've been carrying around with me. Not all of it, of course – that would be impossible – but some of it. What if I've made room for something else, something hopeful?

I'm not waiting long, when the car pulls up. A woman gets out and apologises for being late, complains about the traffic. She picks up my suitcase and pushes it into the boot.

'I thought it was supposed to be three of you?' she says.

'No,' I say, sliding onto the back seat, 'just me.'

And I surprise myself with being OK about that.

Chapter Twenty-eight

Flight

I find that my house hasn't been turned over when I arrive home and I tuck the insurance documents back in the drawer. The place looks as immaculate, as it did when I left it ten days ago. The afternoon light is fading and the curtains half pulled over the windows are making the house seem very dark. I throw them open in the living room and the dining room and lift the blind in the kitchen.

'What a big fuss about nothing, Evelyn Pringle.'

My voice seems very loud now that it's the only one, and I reach over and turn on the radio, find a station playing some music. Very unlike me, but I sway around the room as I make a cup of tea and empty the contents of my suitcase into the washing machine. I've been making a list in my head over the last few days, things I want to do, people and places I need to see. I suddenly have a pressing need to tick as many items off that list as possible.

When I've finished my drink and the last two biscuits in a packet from the cupboard, I go to Tony's study, open the bottom drawer and take out the toy aeroplane. It's been made from a kit and painted so perfectly that Tony must have spent ages on it. Something he didn't get to do with Stephen. I wonder when he built it. Was it years ago or more recently? There's no way of telling. Was his mind drawn back to his son after Margaret died? Because that's something that's been bothering me.

It occurred to me while I was in the back of the taxi coming home that Margaret died eight years ago and I hadn't noticed any particular difference in his behaviour. Maybe a few more nights at home, which I put down to his age, and lack of motivation and, frankly, the physical ability to fish and play golf like he had before. I assumed he was slowing up, and he probably was. Did he shut himself in his study and think about his son? Did he build this aeroplane wishing he'd done more with Stephen and Sarah; both of the children he'd lost? Was that the point where he decided to try to find his stepdaughter?

I'll never know the answers to any of the questions I have and that's something else I'll have to learn to live with. Don't look back, look forwards.

I take the aeroplane with me, the gift he never got to give to his son, the gift I knew nothing about. I climb the stairs, walk along the landing to Stephen's room and open the door wide, so wide that it touches the wall and will go no further. I walk to the window and glance briefly out to the meadow, still beautiful in the twilight, in the bleakness of this midwinter, and then place it on the windowsill. I don't hover, just turn and leave the room, but for the first time in many years, I don't close the door.

Back downstairs, with Tony's letter in one hand,

I rummage for the box of matches in the kitchen drawer and set fire to the paper in the sink. It no longer holds any power to hurt. The truth has been told to the one person who very much needed to hear it. When the last fragments are blackened and curling around themselves in an ashy pile, I turn on the tap and watch it all disappear down the plughole.

I'm on a roll now and walk into the hallway, pick up the frame with Tony's photo. I stare at him for a moment, this man who had been my husband, this complete stranger, this man who loved his son enough to buy him a gift but was never able to share that with his wife, because she wouldn't have wanted to hear about it. I take him into the study and place him on the desk between his paperweight and lamp, adjust it until he can see out of the window. It's a view onto a rose border that Tony planted a few years ago at the side of the house. He had incredibly green fingers when it came to his roses. Not in flower now, of course, but in June, it has the most beautiful display. I'll let him have that. In fact, that is where I'll scatter his ashes, I decide.

'You let me down, Tony, and I can't say I forgive you, because it's more than you deserve. I don't know if you set out to hurt people, but you did, and then when you could have accepted responsibility, you chose, instead, to drive a wedge between a mother and her daughter. However, because I need to move on, I'll say goodbye. I actually hope you find Margaret wherever you are now and I hope you're happy together.'

My words feel wooden but necessary and perhaps that's because I'm talking to a photograph. I certainly have no intention of repeating the gesture. I can't see his face from across the room; I've turned it round too far. Goodbye does indeed mean goodbye.

I close the door behind me.

It's as I'm about to lift my empty suitcase up and back on top of the wardrobe that I remember it tucked into the front zip pocket, wrapped in tissue paper and bubble wrap to keep it safe. The picture I bought in the gift shop in Godshill. In the kitchen on the wall above the table where I have most of my meals and where I read the newspaper and do the crossword, is an old painting of Cardigan Bay. I don't even know why I have it or where it came from, but I step up onto a chair and take it down now. Tony will have bought it at some point in the past; it's been up there for years. I make a note to find out if it's worth anything. I plan to sell most of Tony's artwork and give the money to a local children's charity, one that helps families when children are ill. Then I shall fill the house with things that I like. Things that I've chosen.

The picture made of seashells I bought at the Needles on the Isle of Wight fits perfectly in place of the painting and now I'll see it every morning when I come down. Making new memories is painful but important, Cynthia said, but this doesn't feel painful at all – it feels liberating.

'Hello, Carol, I'm home,' I say, the phone balanced on my shoulder as I negotiate a glass of wine. It's become a bit of a habit over the last ten days.

'Eve, lovely to hear from you. How was your journey?'

'Good, thank you. Look, Carol...' I don't want to make pointless small talk with her. I've been doing that for years.

'Can I see you tomorrow? Can you come over if you're free? I thought I might go to St Mary's.'

There's a silence on her end of the line, but I know we haven't been cut off. She knows what I want to do.

'Of course I can. I'll come in the morning and bring something nice we can have for lunch when we get back to yours. Does that sound OK?'

'That sounds wonderful,' I say.

The word wonderful hangs in the air as I replace the receiver.

'Do you think John might like Tony's Jag?' I ask Carol as we make our way to the church.

'Yes, he'd love it. Gosh, what made you think of that?'

'It's just hanging around. So many things are hanging around and I want to get rid of them; not everything, perhaps, but a lot. John has been very good to me and I'd really like him to have it.'

'Thank you; he'll be thrilled.'

She takes her hand from the steering wheel and for a moment I wonder if she's going to touch me, but she seems to change her mind and places it back again. I'm glad. I need to keep it together for now.

There's a layer of dew on the grass in the churchyard. A spider's web is strung between the fir tree and an ancient headstone, and it is studded with droplets that glisten like jewels. The church is a large, austere building, much larger than you'd expect in such a small village, but the grounds are sheltered by huge trees, their boughs scooping low, and the stones feel protected. I haven't been here for years.

I used to come in the beginning, on some sort of manic autopilot, but when the grief truly set in, when I stopped functioning in any human way, I couldn't. I could barely breathe most days, or leave my bed. I certainly wouldn't have managed a trip to my son's grave. Months and months later when I got help and medication, I tried again but I found it unbearable, and eventually stopped coming.

'What's in the bag?' Carol had asked me when she arrived to pick me up.

I'd been rummaging in the shed and gathered a collection of small gardening tools and cleaning equipment. I was expecting a bit of a mess to clear.

'Oh, Eve, you won't really need those tools,' she'd said quietly as I got into her car.

I can see now what she was hinting at. The gravestone gleams like it's only just been erected and the ground in front is a carpet of lovely pink cyclamen with dark green heart-shaped leaves. The sight of it hits me hard, my breath leaving me instantly. It's not only been tended in my absence, but it's also been cherished.

I reach out for the low stone wall that surrounds this tucked-away part of the graveyard and try to catch my breath. Carol looks worried and takes a step towards me. I raise my hand up to stop her.

'Give me a minute,' I manage.

Is this what my sister does while I glower at her behind her back? While I've been thinking about how smug she is with her perfect family, how self-satisfied she is, all this time she's been here with gloves on weeding my son's grave... Shame and grief sweep through me, leaving me winded.

'Have you done this, Carol?' I say, forcing myself to get the words out.

'Sometimes me,' she says, 'but mostly Tony. I'd often see him down here. He didn't talk much, just sat and thought, cleared and planted.'

I'm defeated by her words, at the sadness for everything I've missed.

There's a bench near the grave and Carol takes my arm, leads me over, and we sit, her arm still linked with mine.

'I've been a fool,' I say eventually. 'How differently this could have played out. If Stephen had lived, Tony and I may have found a way through this life together. And what if I'd behaved differently? Could we have made our way without him, too?'

'Stop blaming yourself for everything, Evelyn. Sometimes we're offered the opportunity to make choices and Tony made some terrible ones. But other times those choices are made for us. It's not always easy to accept what we've been left with. You lost your son, Evelyn. You do realise that you won't ever get over it, don't you? How could you possibly? It might become easier to talk about, but above all, please try to be kind to yourself.'

We sit in silence. Carol doesn't push me for conversation and I just think about Stephen. About that lick of hair and his naughty hand, the way he rolled around in the summer grass in the meadow. Roly-polies, he called them, like a little woodlouse. I suddenly want very much to talk about him.

'I'm going to talk to a grief counsellor,' I say before I've even thought about it. 'I do want to talk about Stephen. I should have done it years ago and maybe if I had,

I wouldn't have pushed everyone away.' I turn to my sister and try to ignore the tears on her cheeks like I ignore the ones on mine. 'I want you to know that I'm grateful to you for all the times you looked after me, invited me over to spend time with you and the girls. I didn't appreciate it at the time, but please know that I do now. Even that awful trip to Whipsnade Zoo.'

'God, the rain that day!' she says, pulling a tissue from her pocket to dab her eyes.

She hands me one, but I decline. Let them fall.

'The monkeys! There wasn't much left of your windscreen wipers, if I remember correctly.'

'Or my rear number plate.'

Our soft smiles subside and we sit again in quiet contemplation. I think about what Joy said to me in the churchyard on the island, about Stephen's grave; *he's not really there*. I know that deep down, but this could be a good place to come and think about him, away from home. I think about what Carol has just said, and she's right. Of course I'll never get over it, but it's slightly freeing to allow myself to know that. I stand up, my legs shaky and my body becoming cold. For now, it's time to go.

I look back down at my son's headstone and the dates that are far too close together, then at that beautiful carpet of cyclamen. I experience a moment of calm and perhaps peace. Then we turn to leave.

My sister holds me up on the way back to the car. I know I wouldn't have made those steps without her.

'I've bought some fresh bread from my local baker and some of that cheese you like,' Carol says, opening my door for me and helping me inside.

'I've popped a bottle of wine in the fridge,' I say with a smile.

I sit back heavily in my seat, feel my body relax. It knows I've done something monumental today. I think I may have set Stephen free at last.

And even though my limbs are heavy, my heart is soaring.

Epilogue

Seven Months Later...

I step down from the bus at the building site outside town and spend a few minutes seeing how much they've progressed. The gardens are being sculpted now and sold boards are going up. It's the end of an era and even though I'll always think fondly on those days when my father ran the factory, it seems fitting that the site has moved on now.

July has hit with a fiery blast from the south, the temperature climbing every day, and after a prolonged and damp spring, everyone is enjoying the weather. The smell of cut grass fills the air and people are picnicking in the park by the river.

I see the step ladder outside the library as I turn the corner on the high street. A man I don't recognise is at the top, unscrewing Tony's plaque. Rosamund, Carol's friend, is holding the bottom of the ladder for support and she catches my eye. She smiles in my direction and gives me a little wink. I mouth *thank you* to her and keep walking, the day suddenly brightening further.

Rosamund had been surprised when I phoned her yesterday but listened when I explained how much of a mistake it was to have a plaque to Tony above the door of the library. She heard me out in silence as I told her all about my husband's double life, and then she said how undeserving he was and that she'd have it removed immediately. She also told me that her lips were sealed and if anybody asked, she'd blame the council for the removal.

The plaque has been bothering me for months. I could push most thoughts of Tony to the back of my mind, but seeing that accolade to him every time I walked into town was becoming too much. I certainly didn't want to drag his name through the mud – no one would benefit from that, least of all me – but I wanted to acknowledge, in some way, the poor man who had died at his hands; Sarah's father, Margaret's husband. Carol had said I could trust Rosamund implicitly and so we arranged for the plaque to be removed and a tree to be planted in the round bedding outside the front door of the library. The garden centre is delivering a cherry tree this afternoon.

Sarah was pleased with the news when I spoke to her this morning. She said it was fitting and that it was enough. Liam had had his place confirmed at the Leith's School in London and had promised to come and visit me when he was settled. It brings me so much joy to think of this young man on the next step in his life and the opportunities he'll have. He deserves them.

Cynthia and Joy are on the island and the renovations are happening at pace, apparently. I miss them both so much, but the thought of them at The Retreat is comforting. We've been back and forth with ideas for the name of the hotel for weeks, but Joy's suggestion was the only one we all agreed on. Frankly, anything is better than The Welcome Rest.

I've got a cat coming to me in a few weeks' time. One of Rosamund's friends has to move into a care home and I offered to take the woman's beloved pet for her. He's called Roger, which isn't my choice of name but I suppose is something I'll just have to get used to.

Everything finally feels as if it's falling into place. I haven't ever been this content, felt this steady, and I like it. The school were delighted when I offered up my time to them and once all the appropriate checks are done, they want me to join their reading programme and asked if I'd consider running their Wednesday lunchtime Lego club when they return in September. I'm raring to go once I get back. Because that's the other thing – I'm going away.

I push the door open and step inside the travel agents, and a welcome blast from the air conditioner hits me. Gavin is on the phone but glances up and waves, gestures he won't be a minute. I peruse the brochures while I wait, pick one up with a picture of the *Orient Express* on the front. The thought of a luxury train trip through Europe is appealing, but I'm not swayed, though – I already know where I want to go.

'Good morning,' Gavin says brightly, his manner much less trainee than the last time I was here. 'How may I help you?'

'You probably don't remember, but you kindly booked me a trip at Christmas.'

'I remember,' he interrupts. 'Turkey and tinsel,' he says with a smile, offering a seat with an extended hand.

'Yes, that's me,' I say, amazed he remembers.

I sit down in front of him and clasp my hands together on his desk.

'There was a mix up with the hotels and where we stayed was awful.'

'I'm so sorry to hear that,' he says, beginning to squirm in his seat.

'Apparently the fault of the coach company, not you, and actually, it was the best trip I've ever been on. I'm not here to complain, but I do expect better accommodation next time, naturally.'

'Of course, that's great,' he says, unable to hide his surprise. 'So, where are you thinking of next? Bognor? Cromer? Hayling Island is very nice.'

I take a deep breath, glancing at his computer, which hasn't changed since I was last here. The Great Wall of China shines up at me from the screen.

'I was thinking of somewhere further afield,' I say, watching his eyes widen as they follow to where I'm pointing. I settle back in my chair and drop my handbag on the floor beside me as Gavin begins to move his mouse with excited fingers. 'How long, exactly, would you recommend I'd need to get the most out of a trip to China?'

Acknowledgements

W hat a joy it is to be writing acknowledgements for my debut novel!

Firstly I'd like to thank my wonderful agent, Robbie Guillory. He recognised something in Evelyn Pringle at only twenty-thousand words and his support of the book has been phenomenal.

To Kate Nash at the Kate Nash Agency for a timely mentorship opportunity that was both enlightening and welcoming.

A huge thank you to my incredible editor, Rachel Faulkner-Willcocks, whose incisive edits and shrewd suggestions have helped make the book what I always hoped it could be. And, of course, to the whole team at Aria who have made the experience of being a debut novelist considerably more comfortable than I thought it might be. People often say that the publishing industry works at a snail's pace – not these guys!

To my early readers for their solid advice: Anita, Rebecca, Neema, Suzanne and in particular to Nikki Smith and Danielle Devlin – superb writers and lovely friends.

To the amazing Amanda Reynolds who is so generous

with her time and expertise to many aspiring novelists. I was hugely lucky to have her support.

To the mighty #VWG who are the best champions in the world. For the advice, inspiration and the daily dose of humour. Talented writers, the lot of them, and advocates for never giving up on this book lark!

To my family, especially my parents who instilled an importance of reading at a young age. They are wholly responsible for me having my nose in a book ever since.

To my children: Sophie, George and Edd – bless them for always being interested in what Mum is up to and for not being demanding, but allowing me the space and time to write.

To my husband Richard and his unflinching love and support.

And lastly, to lovely Annette Reading. This book would not exist if it hadn't been for her incredible Christmas coach trip. Thank you for sharing your story.

About the Author

KATE GALLEY is a debut author who writes uplit and bookclub fiction full of heart and humour. She lives with her family in Buckinghamshire and works as a mobile hairdresser in the surrounding Chiltern villages. The idea for this book came from one client's tale of an incredible Christmas coach trip.